El Zarco, The Blue-eyed Bandit

Episodes of Mexican Life between 1861-1863

Lumen, Inc.
SITES Books
40 Camino Cielo
Santa Fe, New Mexico 87506
lumenbooks.org

Lumen, Inc. is a non-profit, tax-exempt organization.
ISBN: 0-930829-61-1
ISBN-13: 978-0-930829-61-2
Printed in the USA

Distribution:
Consortium Book Sales
800 283-3572
www.cbsd.com

Cover Photograph: Catalina Sierra and Cristina Barros
Ignacio Manuel Altamirano, Iconografía
CONACULTA/Gobierno Constitucional de Guerrero
Fondo de Culturá Economica: 1995, 64.

El Zarco, The Blue-eyed Bandit

Episodes of Mexican Life between 1861-1863

Ignacio Manuel Altamirano

Translated by Ronald Christ

Introduction by Christopher Conway

Edited by Ronald Christ and Sheridan Phillips

Helen Lane Editions

Lumen Books

Helen Lane Editions

Helen Lane was one of the world's foremost and most beloved of translators. To her more than 100 works translated from Spanish, French, and Portuguese, she added a model dedication to translation as practice, art, and spiritual endeavor in bridging the Dharma divide. She also stimulated other translators, beginners and veterans, through her advice, editing, and example.

At her death, Helen left a bequest to Lumen Books for the publication of translations and related works so that we have established Helen Lane Editions in her honor and tradition. Helen had broached *El Zarco, The Blue-eyed Bandit*, this latest volume in the series, but commited nothing to paper.

We trust that this series will further Helen's life-long goals, and we invite you to join us in this project by contributing to the Helen Lane Translation Fund, Lumen Books, 40 Camino Cielo, Santa Fe, NM 87506. Lumen is a federally designated non-profit 501(c)(3) corporation, and all contributions to Lumen are tax deductible.

Publishers: Ronald Christ, Dennis Dollens
Translation Editor: Héctor Magaña
Advisory Board:
Peter Bush
Margaret Jull Costa
Juan Goytisolo
Carol Maier
Margaret Sayers Peden
Elena Poniatowska
Nelly Richard
Paul West

Native Republican:
Ignacio Manuel Altamirano and
El Zarco, The Blue-eyed Bandit
Christopher Conway

El Zarco, The Blue-eyed Bandit, **a Mexican Classic**

In a 1912 study of bandits in nineteenth- and early twentieth-
century Mexico, Lamberto Popoca Palacios recounts a story that
may have provided the inspiration for Ignacio Manuel Altamirano's
classic novel, *El Zarco, The Blue-eyed Bandit*. According to
Popoca Palacios' history, a hacienda worker named Eufemio
Ávalos hired the notorious bandit leader Salomé Plasencia to
kidnap a sixteen-year-old girl named Homobona Merelo from the
village of Yautepec. Ávalos's plan was to stage a mock rescue in
order to gain favor with the beautiful girl, but Plasencia decided
that Homobona met his fancy and kept her. Surprisingly, he was
able to convince the girl's mother to bless the kidnapping by telling
her that her daughter would be safer with him than with Ávalos
or other brigands who might be commissioned to rescue the girl.
According to local lore, Homobona came to love her captor,
and became a *soldadera* (soldier-woman) in his gang of bandits,
tending his wounds and even fighting by his side.[1]

Altamirano's treatment of these events differs in
substantial ways from the particulars provided by Popoca Palacios,
either because Altamirano was working from a different version
of the same events or because he chose to take some liberties with
some of the true-life characters involved in the story. Instead of
having Plasencia play a central role, Altamirano relegated him
to a marginal cameo and in his place used a composite of two of
Plasencia's followers, Felipe *el Zarco* (Blue-eyes) and his brother
Severo *el Zarco*, as the titular antagonist of the novel. Moreover,
Manuela, the character modeled after Homobona, is not kidnapped
but falls in love with the bandit and elopes with him. Most
importantly, however, Altamirano introduces a hero to the story:
the brave Indian Nicolás, who embodies the dignity of his race and
the righteous courage and actions of a man of honor stirred into
action against those who would deprive his community of liberty,
justice, and progress. The result of Altamirano's re-imagining
of the story of Homobona Merelo, Eufemio Ávalos, and Salomé
Plasencia is a dramatic tale of adventure, love, and political

corruption set on the eve of the French occupation of Mexico in 1863.

Whatever the historical origins of its basic plot, *El Zarco*, as Doris Sommer established, is a foundational novel for readers interested in Mexican political and cultural history.[2] The novel captures the lawlessness and impunity that fostered the unchecked spread of banditry in the countryside during the nineteenth century, provoking more than one political administration to suspend constitutional protections in the name of military pacification. In this regard, the rural violence against which Altamirano and his generation had to fight foreshadowed the violence of the Mexican Revolution (1910), when a large number of regional *caudillos* struggled for control of the countryside with disastrous effects on the daily lives of peasants and townspeople. El *Zarco* also illustrates Altamirano's drive to use Mexican themes for the purpose of promoting a nationalist subjectivity and reclaiming the image of Mexico from foreign authors. In 1867, Altamirano wrote: "We run the risk of being viewed as they represent us if we do not pick up the pen and tell the world: 'This is who we are in Mexico.'"[3]

The importance of *El Zarco* is also tied to the singularity of the historical personage of Ignacio Manuel Altamirano. In nineteenth-century Mexico, no other Indian, with the exception of President Benito Juárez (1803-1871), rose to such prominence in political and cultural circles. In an age when Indians were seen as mentally inferior to *mestizos* and Creoles (Spaniards born in the New World), and as such received little or no education, Altamirano and Juárez were exceptional embodiments of how Indians who received the same education as their non-Indian counterparts could rise to national and international prominence. But it was not only his Indian ancestry that made Altamirano one of the most celebrated and controversial men of his time. Rather, his accomplishments as a political militant, a soldier, and an orator enabled him to fill a series of high-profile, political and cultural positions: he was a three-term congressman, a magistrate of the supreme court, a teacher, a battle-tested soldier, a journalist, and a diplomat. His Indian features, radical politics, and uncompromising character made friends and foes alike represent him in writing and caricature as an Aztec Mephistopheles.[4] Later in life he became a paternal or grandfatherly icon, mentoring the new generation of poets and novelists who came of age at the turn of the century and who lovingly bestowed upon their mentor the nickname of *el Maestro* (Teacher).

Although it would be farfetched to call *El Zarco* an autobiographical novel, the heroic Indian Nicolás, clearly embodies the ideological profile and personal contradictions of his creator. Any discussion of the novel should therefore begin with an account of the life and times of Altamirano, as well as of his public image as an Indian and a patriot. All of Altamirano's experiences, from his humble beginnings to the political debates in which he participated as a congressman or a journalist, provide us with necessary frames for understanding the historical, political, and cultural contexts of *El Zarco*.

From Humble Indian to *el Maestro*

Ignacio Manuel Homobono Serapio Altamirano was born on November 13, 1834 in the village of Tixtla in what is today the state of Guerrero in the southwest of Mexico. The names Ignacio, Manuel, and Altamirano all derive from a Spaniard named Juan Altamirano who baptized Altamirano's great grandfather and raised him as a son, with the condition that the Indian's descendants be called Juan, Ignacio, or Manuel and carry on the Altamirano name.[5] The names Homobono and Serapio, respectively, correspond to Ignacio Altamirano's birthday and baptism dates according to the Catholic calendar, underscoring the traditional nature of the modest family into which he was born. Although little is known about his childhood, one of his autobiographical essays allows us to imagine the barefoot Nacho (short for Ignacio) wandering the forests surrounding Tixtla with other Indians to gather palms for the processionals of Holy Week, while his mother toiled away in their small home, preparing the foods of the season.[6] Like other Tixtleco children of his background, Altamirano's first language was Nahuatl, and little is known about his mastering of Spanish.

Indian children in this period were not considered capable of reasoning, and, if they received any education, it consisted primarily of the memorizing the catechism by rote. However, since Altamirano's father was an *Alcalde de Indios* (Mayor of Indians), Altamirano was allowed to receive the same schooling as non-Indian children, who were called *niños de razón* (children with reason). Although the transition was a painful one—legend has it that his non-Indian classmates protested the arrival of the intruder into their class—Altamirano was a talented student who quickly distinguished himself among his peers.[7] When in 1849 the governor of the state of Mexico decreed that all the state's municipalities were to select a child and provide a scholarship to the Instituto Literario y Científico de Toluca, one of the country's finest schools, the fourteen-year-old Altamirano earned his municipality's scholarship and departed with his father on a six-day overland journey to the town of Toluca.

Altamirano's entry into the school was not without its difficulties as well as painful, awkward moments. First, upon their arrival at the office of Felipe Sánchez Solís, the school's director, the secretary told them that the director was not in but that they could wait for his return. When Altamirano's father sat down on a chair, with his son at his feet, the secretary curtly told them to move into the hallway, because "Indians are not allowed to sit here."[8] The return of the school's director did not improve an already awkward situation since Sánchez Solís demanded additional funds from Tixtla, in violation of the governor's decree, which stated that each municipality was responsible only for paying a modest sum in support of their chosen student. Altamirano was allowed to stay at the school until this imposition was ironed out in favor of Tixtla, but the affair surely left a deep mark on the impressionable boy, who found himself far away from his friends, family, and familiar surroundings for the first time in his life.

At the institute, where Altamirano studied for three formative years, the curriculum provided him with a large array of academic subjects: languages (Latin, French, and English), logic, metaphysics, arithmetic, algebra, geometry, physics, geography, gymnastics, music, and art. The school's library, where Altamirano worked for some time in 1851 (to help pay for his education when his funding was suspended), was well stocked with the most important authors of antiquity, the Enlightenment, and the nineteenth century, including Bentham, Chauteaubriand, Diderot, Homer, Humboldt, Rousseau and Voltaire.[9] One of the highlights of his life at Toluca was the return to the institute's faculty of a Liberal firebrand, Ignacio Ramírez, also known as *El Nigromante* (The Necromancer).[10] Ramírez was arguably one of the most uncompromising Liberal militants of his time, as well as one of the most learned and charismatic. In his writings, Ramírez attacked Church corruption and unflinchingly condemned the oppression of Indian peasants by the *hacendados* (large landowners).[11] Altamirano stood in awe of his teacher, who undoubtedly magnified and consolidated whatever forward-thinking, populist, and democratic tendencies that Altamirano may have entertained as an Indian and one of the poorest students in the institute.

Altamirano and a classmate, Juan A. Mateos, were expelled in 1852 because of their contributions to the student newspaper, *Los Papachos*, which was too liberal for the school's new director. At first, Altamirano supported himself by teaching French at a small school in Toluca, before moving to Cuautla in the state of Morelos (100 kilometers northeast of Mexico City, not far from the village of Yautepec where *El Zarco* is set). There he was befriended by the generous and progressive Spanish landowner, Luis Rovalo, who provided him with funds to study law in Mexico City, at the Colegio San Juan Letrán. Although very little is known about Altamirano's sojourn in Morelos between 1853 and 1856, it is worth noting that the character Nicolás may have been modeled on Altamirano in this chapter of his youth, when he resided at Rovalo's hacienda on the outskirts of Cuautla. As several biographers have noted, the statistics that Altamirano cites in *El Zarco* to describe Yautepec correspond to these years and not to the 1860s, when the novel explicitly takes place.[12]

Altamirano, like all Mexicans, was deeply affected by the Revolution of Ayutla (1855), which brought modern liberalism to the helm of Mexican politics for the first time. The bloody push and pull between Liberals and Conservatives could be traced back to the Wars of Independence of 1808-1821, when insurgents led armies against Royalists who were backed by high-ranking members of the colonial, Catholic establishment.[13] The 1821 Plan of Iguala attempted to reconcile insurgent and absolutist interests by making Mexico an independent, constitutional monarchy, by defending the influence of the Church, and by declaring the equality of Creoles and *Peninsulares*, Spaniards sent to the New World to hold office.[14] Plans for an independent monarchy, however, were disrupted in 1822 when civil war broke out between Liberals, who espoused a federalist system of government, and Conservatives, who favored political centralism. Although some measure of stability and continuity was achieved by the

Conservative dictator Antonio López de Santa Anna, who remained in power until 1855, it was also on his watch that Mexico fought a disastrous war with the United States, losing a vast swath of its territory.[15]

The Liberal movement that overthrew Santa Anna in 1856 in the Revolution of Ayutla represented ideological positions ranging from the radical to the centrist, but it was generally characterized by a drive to introduce European notions of political democracy and economic development into Mexico, and to limit military and Church privilege, which placed both corporations and their representatives outside the jurisdiction of the civil courts.[16] Apart from abolishing such privileges, the Liberals confiscated and redistributed Church lands and the Indians' communal properties in an effort to free up property for more efficient agricultural production and capitalist exchange. These two reforms, called the Juárez Law and the Lerdo Law respectively, were incorporated into the Constitution of 1857, which also decreed freedom of expression, the right to bear arms, habeas corpus, and the abolition of slavery and titles of nobility. In 1858, Benito Juárez (1803-1871), a Zapotec Indian, rose to the presidency, where he would remain until his death by natural causes in 1871, weathering two Conservative counter-revolutions: the Wars of Reform of 1857-1861 and the Conservative-backed French Intervention of 1863-1867.

Altamirano interrupted his law studies to aid the Liberal movement in the state of Morelos during the Revolution of Ayutla, although it does not appear that he fought as a soldier in any Liberal army or guerilla force.[17] In 1855, his stature as an orator and militant was well enough known to justify the city of Morelos in commissioning his speech in honor of Mexican independence, a speech later printed and distributed in Mexico City as a pamphlet. "If I spoke senselessly," Altamirano said in his vehement address, "I would advise 'unity with the conservatives,' fraternity with the executioners. But no! Never fusion, because the Conservative stretches out his hand to betray; when he embraces, it is to murder."[18]

Altamirano continued his studies at San Juan Letrán during the ferment surrounding the creation of the Liberal Constitution of 1857, attending the congress to hear the speeches of preeminent Liberal representatives, such as Ignacio Ramírez and Melchor Ocampo. When the Wars of Reform were unleashed and the Conservatives took control of the government, Altamirano was still at Letrán, desperately trying to finish his degree so that he could support his poor extended family and join the Liberals in their fight against the Conservative reaction. In 1859, the loss of two friends at the Massacre of Tacubaya, in which the Conservative General Leonardo Márquez (1821-1913) summarily executed over fifty Liberal captives, gave new urgency to his desire to serve the Liberal cause in the field.[19]

At the beginning of the summer of 1859, Altamirano married Margarita Pérez Gavilán and joined the Liberal revolution in the state of Guerrero, where in all likelihood he served as a volunteer and propagandist in Tixtla.[20] After the restoration of the Liberal regime, Altamirano was elected to the national congress and became one of its most celebrated and controversial representatives, particularly for his inflexible criticism of the Juárez regime, whose exercise of power he considered hesitant, weak, and inept. In the radical wing of the Liberal movement, no man was more fiery and unyielding than Altamirano in the quest to realize the Liberal revolution without compromise. For example, in his famous 1861 speech against amnesty for Conservative foes of the Liberal revolution, Altamirano declared: "I have many Reactionary acquaintances: with some I have cultivated friendly relations in other times, but I protest that the day they fall into my hands, I will have their heads cut off, because the love of homeland takes precedence over friendship, justice takes precedence over compassion."[21] This 1861 speech cemented his reputation as the Mexican Marat even though several months later, when Mexico was threatened by foreign invasion, Altamirano closed ranks with Juárez and supported an amnesty law.[22]

Internecine debates between Liberal factions were brought to a halt by a military crisis in 1862 and 1863: the French invasion of Mexico and the placement of an Austrian royal, Archduke Maximilian of Hapsburg, on the newly invented throne of Mexico. Mexico's failure to pay its foreign debts had precipitated the crisis, but the situation quickly devolved into a transparent imperial design by Napoleon the III on the American continent.[23] In 1863, Juárez and his government, including the congress, were forced to flee Mexico City as war between Liberal nationalists and the invaders with their Conservative supporters spread across the country, until 1867, when the Liberal *caudillos* and guerillas prevailed. It was during this war against the occupation that Altamirano, already one of the most recognized and celebrated leaders of his time, added the laurels of war-hero to his public profile as a patriot. Altamirano's heroic service had gotten off to a slow start, however, because his supervising officer, Don Diego Álvarez, the governor of the state of Guerrero, timidly refused to engage the enemy for two years. Altamirano finally broke with Álvarez and received his own military command, the First Brigade of the Southern Division, which routed the supporters of Emperor Maximilian in several skirmishes and battles in December of 1866. In 1867, at the decisive siege of Querétaro, where Maximilian himself was captured, Altamirano distinguished himself for his heroism, whose near recklessness did not endear him to the soldiers under his command.[24]

The period that followed the French Intervention was one of reconstruction and modernization in Mexico. After the war, Altamirano supported the presidential ambitions of General Porfirio Díaz, who had led the Liberals to victory at the Battle of Puebla in 1862 and successfully took Mexico City at the end of the war. By temperament, Altamirano had been wary of Juárez's approach to pacification and national reconstruction after the Wars of Reform, and now, after tasting the glories of war, he was drawn to the imposing, military figure of Díaz. To this end, and with Díaz's financial backing, Altamirano founded a newspaper, the *Correo de México*, to promote Díaz's candidacy against Juárez's. The paper blamed the Mexican president for a litany of errors during the insurgency and for circumventing the constitution in order to maintain his hold on the presidency.[25] But Altamirano's own political ambitions were dashed when his candidate lost to Juárez, and when he lost his own bid for a third term in the congress. Instead, Altamirano was named chief justice of the supreme court, where his exercise of judicial independence cooled his relationship with the followers of Díaz.[26]

If Altamirano's political aspirations were stymied after the defeat of the French, his leadership in cultural circles had begun to be felt in ways that would prove decisive for the development of modern Mexican literary history. Beginning in 1867, Altamirano became the central figure in a series of *veladas literarias* or literary salons in which partisan politics gave way to the concord of a shared love of literature. The younger literary bohemians became attached to the man they called *el Maestro* and went regularly to his home to read their compositions and to be mentored by Altamirano.[27] Inspired by this atmosphere of literary exchange, Altamirano published a lengthy and seminal essay analyzing Mexican literary history called "Revistas literarias de México" (Mexican Literary Magazines, 1868) in which he promoted nationalism in literature as a way of promoting citizenship and social progress. "Perhaps the novel is nothing less than the initiation of the people into the mysteries of modern civilization," he wrote, "and the gradual instruction that is given them for the priesthood of the future."[28] Whatever political disenchantments he may have felt, Altamirano believed that Mexico was experiencing a cultural rebirth after the defeat of Maximilian: he titled his short-lived but influential literary magazine *El Renacimiento* (The Renaissance). In its 1869 prospectus, he called for former foes to put down their arms and unite in the name of the patriotic pursuit of literature.

Aside from another stint in the Mexican congress in 1880 and his final, diplomatic assignment in 1889 as consular general in Spain, Altamirano would spend the last twenty-five years of his life as a teacher and a writer. Not only did he teach history and philosophy at the Escuela Nacional Preparatoria (1876), debate at the Escuela de Jurisprudencia (1881), and military history at Mexico City's military college (1882), he also was commissioned by the government of President Manuel González in 1882 to draft plans for a national school to train elementary school teachers. Altamirano's thorough report and proposal was ratified in 1887 and resulted in the establishment of the first school of this kind in Mexico.[29] But Altamirano taught not only by carrying out the concrete pedagogical duties of a teacher, but also by self-consciously seeking to educate through his literary production and cultural commentary. In addition to romantic poetry and the novel *Clemencia* (1869), a well-received melodrama set during the French intervention, Altamirano also published scores of articles on Mexican theater, literature, history, and life, including a seminal study of the Virgin of Guadalupe and her cult.[30] All these writings, no matter their genre or specific focus, are subtended by a passionate commitment to understanding Mexico and promoting its modernization through education, the arts, and sociological study. In one chronicle, he unflinchingly looked at urban poverty, traced its historical origins, and diagnosed its effects on the body politic of modern Mexico.[31] In another, he complained of the incestuousness of elite society, and called for journalists to find new, more edifying and transcendental subjects for their readers.[32] And despite Altamirano's anti-clericalism, which led him to bitterly denounce the corruption of the Church, in some writings he was not above celebrating the contributions of certain clergymen to the improvement of life in rural Mexico, a theme that he fictionalized in 1872 in the short novel *Navidad en las montañas* (*Christmas in the Mountains*).[33] In short, all facets of Mexican political and cultural life were filtered into eloquent, vivid expression through his pen. In Altamirano's conception, the intellectual did not stand on the margins of the social experiment, but at its center, like a pulsing heart. In this regard, no Mexican writer of his time better illustrated Victor Hugo's famous maxim, from the preface to his play *Cromwell* (1827), that romanticism was the literary expression of liberalism.

With the death of Juárez, and the 1876 coup that brought General Porfirio Díaz to power (where he remained until the Mexican Revolution of 1910), Altamirano began to fall out of step with the increasing political and cultural influence of Auguste Comte's adherents; these Positivists believed in the evolution of societies toward perfection and celebrated the role of science and reason in facilitating social improvement. Altamirano chafed at some of the more conservative Positivists' suggestion that the influence of the older generation of Liberals—to which he belonged—had passed and was anachronistic.[34] Nor did he agree, for obvious personal reasons, with these younger intellectuals' deterministic and fatalistic view of the Indian.[35] Although Altamirano's circle of young, literary acolytes remained strong, the ideological gap between the new generation of sociologically-oriented intellectuals and Altamirano was widening. On the political front, Altamirano was circumspect in airing any criticism of the president, but it appears that Díaz might have distrusted Altamirano enough to remove him from the country by appointing him Mexico's consul general in Spain in 1889. Although little is known about the motives behind this appointment, the historian Nicole Girón demonstrates that Altamirano himself felt that he was being punished.[36] Tragically, Altamirano's European journey was difficult from start to finish. His health was in decline and his relationship with other consular officials was not harmonious. For reasons of health, he was permitted to exchange consular posts with fellow novelist Manuel Payno, the Mexican consul in Paris, but his health continued its decline. Altamirano died of tuberculosis on December 13, 1893, in San Remo, Italy, where he and his wife Margarita had traveled in a desperate bid to find a healthful climate.

Historicity and Autobiography in *El Zarco, The Blue-eyed Bandit*
In *El Zarco*, Altamirano recreates the lawlessness that plagued southern Mexico at the hands of the Plateado band led by Salomé Plasencia, and to which the Zarco brothers belonged. The problem of rural crime, however, cannot be separated from the political conflicts of the middle of the nineteenth century. Between the Wars of Reform, which brought the Liberals to the helm of Mexico in 1861 and the French intervention that deposed them from power in 1863, much of the country continued to be ravaged by guerilla warfare between Conservative forces, led most notably by the fearsome Leonardo Márquez, also known as the Tiger of Tacubaya, and Liberal armies led by General Jesús González Ortega (1822-1881). One of the consequences of the conflict was that volunteers on both sides—peasants, townspeople, priests and ne'er-do-wells like the fictional young el Zarco from Altamirano's novel—turned to a life of crime, forming large bands of brigands that terrorized overland travelers, landowners, and town officials. The most famous and colorful of the bandit gangs spawned by the civil wars between Conservatives and Liberals were the Plateados, whose large, wide-brimmed hats, silver-ornamented clothing and tack made their appearance particularly extravagant. As Paul Vanderwood explains, the Plateados were much more than a simple band of rural outlaws: they were a social phenomenon that spread across different regions of Mexico.[37] In a rural landscape ravaged by factional violence as well as devoid of police or military protection, collaboration with the Plateados was more often than not a necessity for survival, not a choice. Citizens who did otherwise risked kidnapping, torture, and murder.

Altamirano and other Liberals complained of the Juárez administration's inefficacy in dealing with rural crime after the Wars of Reform. Congress had given Juárez extraordinary

powers in December 1861 to protect the security of Mexico
and its inhabitants, yet the crimes of the Plateados went largely
unchecked, including the murder of town officials in Yautepec,
kidnappings for ransom that ended in torture and murder, and
violent hold-ups of overland carriages and transports.[38] In 1861,
Altamirano was well aware of the damaging consequences of this
state of affairs. On the floor of the congress, he indignantly noted
that the Plateados were ruining Mexico's reputation as a civilized
nation, as well as its economy and the livelihood of working
families: "Isn't it true that the rich sugar haciendas that produce so
very much in these districts, are all in ruins, causing incalculable
damage to Mexican agriculture and industry, and propelling
thousands of working families into lives of misery?"[39]

These historical considerations explain the presence in *El
Zarco* of personages such as a composite of the Zarco brothers, of
Salomé Plasencia, Benito Juárez, and Martín Sánchez, nicknamed
Chagollán because of his silver smithing of *chagollos* (fake coins
and religious artifacts).[40] Sánchez was a private citizen who
formed a vigilante posse that pursued the Plateados and killed
many of them. The adulatory description of Sánchez in the novel
underscores Altamirano's belief that terrible times call for terrible
measures, as well as for men honest and strong enough to carry
them out for the public good. Similarly, Altamirano's treatment
of Juárez in the novel expresses his admiration for the president's
suspension of habeas corpus before the French Intervention.
Although Altamirano criticizes the Juárez of later years, in
the novel's historical setting he celebrates him by making him
Sánchez's double. The closing description of the two men standing
face to face, reflecting one another in their willingness to kill in the
name of justice, is one of the most chilling in the novel:

> Seeing those two short men stand, one facing the other,
> one in a black frock coat, as Juárez often wore then,
> and the other in a jacket, also black; one dark and with
> the appearance of a pure Indian, the other a sallow
> mixture of *campesino* and *mestizo* features; both serious,
> both grave, anyone who could read a little into the future
> would have shuddered.

Although set in the years between 1861 and 1863, the

novel should be read through the lens of a larger period. *El Zarco* was first published in 1901, but Altamirano began writing it in 1874 and completed it in 1888.[41] He wrote in stops and starts, even forgetting the name of his protagonist, Nicolás, after leaving the manuscript aside for some time.[42] His positive view of Juárez in the novel may have been a result of Altamirano's growing disenchantment with Porfirio Díaz in the 1880s and a reassessment of Juárez's legacy. Moreover, the validation of vigilantism was not a historical or anachronistic issue; it was contemporaneous with a journalistic debate over crime and punishment in which Altamirano participated in 1880. In an issue of the *Correo de México*, Altamirano complained about a popular jury that had released some bandits in spite of their admission of guilt.[43] He argued that Mexico was not ready for a popular jury system and called for its suspension, a measure that was later ratified by the government in order to fight banditry. Altamirano defended his position by recurring to the lessons of 1861, when congress had suspended certain individual rights in order to assist Juárez in pacifying the nation. In times of great crisis, he argued, certain rights can and should be set aside in the name of the public good.[44]

Another way that *El Zarco* is more than the sum of the historical realities of 1861-1863 shows in its representation of the noble blacksmith, Nicolás. The inclusion of an Indian hero in a nineteenth-century novel of this type is in itself worthy of note because Mexican and Latin American readers of literature had been raised on European, white, or *mestizo* heroic figures. The issue of whether or not Indians could be educated and included in the national experience had not been settled definitively in Mexico or in Latin America when Altamirano was writing his novel. For example, the turn of the century would see the publication of several influential, "scientific" racist tracts that associated Indians with barbarism and Latin American underdevelopment. While these views represented only those of one sector of the intelligentsia, the idea that a courageous, honorable, and educated Indian, such as Nicolás, might have more self-worth than a light-skinned, blue-eyed man, such as el Zarco, makes *El Zarco* a significant and controversial intervention in the nineteenth-century debate over the Indian.[45] The fact that Altamirano himself was an Indian only reinforces the sense that this novel should be read, at least in part, as the author's repository of idealized, autobiographical fragments.

While Altamirano was living in Barcelona in 1890, he gave a telling interview to José Rivas, correspondent for the Mexican newspaper *El Universal*. Altamirano revealed that as a child he had most wanted to be a blacksmith, but one year of apprenticeship revealed that he was not strong enough for the profession.[46] Rivas writes that Altamirano remained fascinated by blacksmithing into adult life, stopping on the street to wistfully observe blacksmiths at work in their shops.[47] The resonance between Altamirano and his protagonist, Nicolás, does not end here, however. Like Altamirano, who was sponsored by Luis Rovalo, Nicolás is employed at the hacienda of a progressive landowner who assists him in his education.

Most importantly, however, Manuela's pejorative description of Nicolás as an "ugly Indian" echoes the same image that Altamirano associated with himself and that others associated with him, sometimes maliciously. In 1873, the Spanish journalist José Triay traveled to Mexico from Cuba and visited with Altamirano. In his account of their meeting, which was published in the Cuban newspaper *Voz de Cuba* and reprinted in the Mexican paper, *La Iberia*, Triay writes that Altamirano told him in conversation that he was proud of possessing the "splendid" ugliness of the Aztec race.[48] One of Altamirano's disciples remembered a similar statement many years after the author's death: "He himself told us in a moment of good humor: 'I am ugly and I don't need to do much to prove it.'"[49] Although Altamirano was publicly proud of his Indian heritage—saying as much in a congressional debate in 1881—there are indications that the prejudice he had faced throughout his life had indeed left a mark on him. Another disciple recalled that at a newspaper office Altamirano once received a well-dressed Indian man who inquired after one of the writers employed there. Coincidentally, this gentleman was the same man who had insulted and humiliated Altamirano and his exhausted father in Toluca, telling them that they were not allowed to sit on certain chairs because they were Indians. Now, decades later, to the shock of all present in the room, Altamirano told this man to wait in the hall because "Indians are not allowed to sit in these chairs."[50]

Finally, the similarities between Altamirano's first novel, *Clemencia*, and *El Zarco* lend credence to the notion that

Altamirano was confronting personal experiences in both works. *Clemencia* is set during the French Intervention in the city of Guadalajara and tells the tragic story of two patriots, one of whom is honorable and dark skinned, the other, traitorous, handsome, and pale skinned. As in the case of Nicolás and el Zarco at the beginning of the later novel, both men vie for the love of a woman, and the "uglier" man of honor loses the contest to the more attractive, immoral man.

Ignacio Manuel Altamirano and the Literary Imagination

> But we desire morality before all else because outside it we do not see anything useful, nothing that can be called truly pleasurable; and since the sentiments of the heart can be led so easily to the individual good and to public happiness when they are formed beginning in adolescence, we want there to be a foundation of virtue in everything that is read in this age. To do the contrary perpetuates evil, corrupts a generation, and brings it bad fortune, or at least pushes it to make mistakes that are difficult to amend.
>
> Ignacio Manuel Altamirano
> "Mexican Literary Reviews" (1868)

The temptation to read Altamirano's novel in a biographical register should not distract us from its merits and importance as a work of literature. To begin with, *El Zarco* belongs to European and Latin American literary history as a particular kind of Romantic novel. Unlike late eighteenth- and early nineteenth-century German and English Romanticism, which developed themes of universalism, supernaturalism, and nature as a reflection of human subjectivity, Latin American Romanticism was more self-consciously political and closer to French Romanticism, which had been shaped by the Revolution of 1789. Similarly, Latin American Romanticism emerged after its own revolutions, the Wars of Independence, and was shaped by the ideology of liberalism: nationalism, secularism, and the ideal of freedom. As exemplified by works such as the novel *Amalia* (1851) by the Argentine José Mármol, and the epic poem *Tabaré* (1886) by the Uruguayan Juan Zorilla de San Martín, the Romantic canon of

Latin America sought to promote political stability and progress through the preservation of national culture and history, and through the celebration of heroic characters that embodied civic virtue.

In *El Zarco* these two characteristic strands of Latin American Romanticism—local themes and republican heroism—are evident. Rather than set a novel in a distant land, or in Mexico City, among Europeanized elites, Altamirano takes a modest rural setting and its distinctly Mexican characters to anchor his story. His description of the Plateado bandits, whose flamboyant dress and speech are distinctly Mexican, should be read within the frame of *costumbrismo*, a popular nineteenth-century genre of prose writing in Spain and Latin America that affirmed the originality of national culture by describing local scenes, speech, and characters. Altamirano's investment in Mexicanness is also expressed in the way that he introduces botanical, geographical, and historical knowledge into the novel through his contrasting descriptions of Yautepec and Xochimancas, both real places, one a symbol of fertility and promise, the other of degradation and ruin. Although such narrative choices affirmed Mexican culture by making it worthy of literary treatment, a nationalist novel is made out of more than landscapes and cultural types; it must contain an exciting plot, heroes, villains, and a socially relevant message. The blacksmith Nicolás, the vigilante Martín Sánchez, and, to a lesser degree, President Benito Juárez, embody the morality and civic virtue that Altamirano prized so much and wanted to disseminate among his readers. By the aesthetic and psychological standards of realism these are not complex characters with conflicted inner lives but, rather, models of nationalist manhood. In comparison, the villain el Zarco is a much more vivid character because Altamirano's description of his humble beginnings, life experience, and class envy provide a rich background story for his cruel and vain character, and for his feelings toward Manuela.

The novel's female characters speak to Altamirano's interest in defining the role that women could have in stabilizing Mexican society and promoting its modernization. Pilar represents a female type common to Western culture in the nineteenth century, the *angel del hogar*, literally the "angel of the house" or "household nun" as she was called in England. The *angel del hogar* embodies the domestic virtues of chastity, submission, sacrifice, and service to husband and children. In Pilar's case, these submissive attributes are qualified by her decisive actions in defense of Nicolás against the corrupt army officer who imprisons him. Manuela, in contrast, represents the woman whose vanity and rebellion against the domestic ideal result in her corruption. Such women, whose sexuality was not symbolically constrained by the role of virgin or self-sacrificing wife and mother, were commonly represented in nineteenth-century Western culture as seductive temptresses or as vampiric figures who threatened masculine power.[51] These misogynist tropes are invoked in Chapter VII, "The Oleander," when Altamirano re-imagines a scene from Goethe's *Faust* (1805) in which Mephistopheles helps Faust conquer Marguerite with the gift of jewels. In this powerful, gothic passage, Manuela chooses to wear the bloodstained earrings that el Zarco has given her although she realizes that they are the fruit of murder and robbery. Her choice casts her from the garden of domesticity into an infernal and grotesque landscape of desire, transforming the angelic virtue of her sex into something demoniacal and monstrous. Moreover, the two serpent-shaped, diamond-studded bracelets that Manuela is wearing as she stares at herself in the dark pool underscore the biblical overtones of the scene. El Zarco may be a snake because he tempts Manuela in the orchard with the promise of riches and love but, in her corruption, the village girl becomes a snake as well.

The root cause of Manuela's corruption brings us back to the themes of nationalism, literature, and morality, which Altamirano wove together in his other prose writings. In his 1867, in-depth study of Mexican literature, "Mexican Literary Reviews," Altamirano complained that foreign fiction—particularly French novels—threatened to seduce and lead women astray from acceptable social roles and actions:

> In the love story, we confess, there can be great danger.
> The young take pleasure in it, seek it out with energy,
> and devour it without precaution. It is just the time when
> the heart, like a flower in the morning, opens itself,
> innocent and pure, to first impressions, welcoming them
> and tenderly holding them close. Woe be it if, instead of
> a pure and healthy breeze, its bosom is corroded by the
> infectious and desiccating exhalations of the swamp of

the world! The danger is all the greater when the mentors of youth, relatives or teachers who defend the young soul from contact with the world and vice, are not enough to prevent exposure to those small golden books, in which one learns too quickly what is bad, and in which, along with the sweet nectar of feeling, one drinks the corrosive poison of doubt, disdain for honor, and love of sensual pleasure. (37)

Literary nationalism, then, was not only a function of politics and national development, but also of the well being of families and the protection of women's virtue. "Immoral" literature posed a threat to society because it could contaminate women and ruin them for marriage and motherhood, contributing to the dissolution of the family unit that late nineteenth-century Mexican commentators saw as essential to the preservation of morality in society. Altamirano restages this argument through Manuela, demonstrating that her idealization of el Zarco as well as her ultimate downfall were a result of romantic notions that made her crave a life of adventure. For example, the ignorant girl imagines that el Zarco and her men are colorful, legendary figures rather than murderous thieves and kidnappers, and that their lair, Xochimancas, is one of "those marvelous fortresses in old stories." In this regard, Manuela is hardly an original character, and Altamirano's thesis about the dangers of women's' fantasies is not new; literary precedents of Manuela include Dorcasina Sheldon from the American novel *Female Quixotism: Exhibited in the Romantic Opinions and Extravagant Adventures of Dorcasina Sheldon* (1801) by Tabitha Gilman Tenney, Pomposa from the Mexican novel *La quijotita y su prima* (1819) by José Fernández de Lizardi and most famously, the titular protagonist of Gustave Flaubert's *Madame Bovary* (1856). The thinking was that women had an inherent and quixotic susceptibility to the seductions of literature or fantasy that rarely led to socially redemptive or well-intended acts of selflessness like those of Cervantes's Don Quixote, a man gone mad because of his predilection for literature. On the contrary, as illustrated by Manuela, the over stimulation of women's imagination easily led to tragedy.

Altamirano's analysis of Manuela's character is not limited to the problem of her romantic, misdirected imagination, but also extends to historical themes. The sheltered, ignorant girl accepts banditry as something normal because the Liberal state, distracted by its protracted battles with Conservative forces, was too weak to assert its authority over rural crime and punish men like el Zarco and his followers. Altamirano argues that in this environment of unchecked violence, Manuela lacked exposure to assertive and decisive models of state authority that could enforce the rule of law and order. Yet, the materialization of the fearless, avenging angel, Martín Sánchez Chagollán supplies that model after Manuela elopes with el Zarco. It was not only her frivolous imagination, then, that predisposed Manuela to corruption, but also the absence of strong leadership and action by the state and its citizenry. Altamirano hoped that national novels like *El Zarco* with their clear, moral vision, and attention to historical themes, would strengthen moral and civic values by educating its readers properly. In fact, if Manuela had read novels like Altamirano's, perhaps she would have feared the Plateados from the beginning and smiled upon the upstanding Indian blacksmith who sought her favors.

The parallel, sentimental pairings of Manuela-el Zarco and Nicolás-Pilar in the novel are also significant for Altamirano's political program and provide us with rich interpretive possibilities. In her influential *Foundational Fictions: The National Romance in Latin America* (1991), Doris Sommer argues that the nineteenth-century Latin American novel sought to transform European love tales into a foundation for the continent's emerging nation states. While authors such as Rousseau, Balzac, and Richardson highlighted the fissures of the bourgeois family, "Latin Americans tended to patch up those cracks with the sheer will to project ideal histories backward (as a legitimating ground) and forward (as a national goal), or with the euphoria of recent successes" (18). In the case of *El Zarco*, Sommer suggests that Manuela's aristocratic, though naïve, dreams, may be read as allegorizing the endorsement of the Hapsburg Maximilian as Emperor of Mexico by the Conservatives, who rejected their Indian leader (Juárez) in favor of a foreign prince (Maximilian). Such an allegory, notes Sommer, requires that Altamirano take liberties with the historical record:

> He never hints, for example, that Maximilian would horrify his Conservative supporters by courting the opposition and passing Liberal legislation, nor that the

popular legend of El Zarco identified him as Salomé Plasencia, a valiant and admirable Robin-Hood-like character, nor even that the most brilliant hero against Márquez was Porfirio Díaz, who would ultimately replace Juárez's democratic ideals with inglorious maneuvering. Altamirano was evidently more concerned with writing an uncomplicated, programmatic, national allegory (the kind that embarrassed later Mexican novelists including Azuela) than with offering narrative richness or even respecting historical data. (228)

Yet, if Altamirano's goals were "uncomplicated," Sommer notes how his novel is unexpectedly rich in its treatment of gender. The novel attempts to reconcile heroism with domesticity through the characters of Nicolás and Pilar, who are simultaneously heroic (masculine) and domestic (feminine). In the other sentimental pairing, Manuela's love of adventure gives her a masculine attribute, while el Zarco's cowardice (to say nothing of his vanity) makes him stereotypically feminine.

Rediscovering *El Zarco*

For decades, nineteenth-century Latin American literature languished in the shadow of the literature of the Boom and more contemporary postmodern fiction, accused of being derivative and simplistic. Beginning in the 1980s, after the publication of Benedict Anderson's influential study of nationalism, *Imagined Communities: Reflections on the Origins and Spread of Nationalism* (1983), North American literary and cultural critics were increasingly drawn to nineteenth-century literature as a means of understanding the rise of nationalism in Latin America. Other groundbreaking and widely read studies, such as Jean Franco's *Plotting Women: Gender and Representation in Mexico* (1989) and Doris Sommer's *Foundational Fictions: The National Romances of Latin America* (1991), intertwined the study of gender with nationalism and helped to rehabilitate nineteenth-century literature by putting it at the center of discussions about identity and ideology in Latin American cultural history. In this context, *El Zarco*, long considered to be a classic in Mexico, was rediscovered in the United States and recognized as an indispensable novel for understanding nineteenth-century Mexican culture.

With this first complete translation into English, a new generation of readers can discover this seminal novel for the first time and explore its revealing treatment of politics, gender, and ethnicity.[52] Part nationalist morality tale and part melodrama, *El Zarco* is essential for readers interested in Mexican history and identity, as well as an illuminating introduction to the political and literary imagination of one of Mexico's most important thinkers. As literature, it converses with a rich array of themes that extend beyond the borders of Mexico, such as the romantic figure of the noble savage, quixotic women, crime and punishment in the modern age, the historical novel as a genre, and even Gothic literature. Yet, no matter the value of what *El Zarco* might teach us, it is also important to underscore its entertaining accessibility. In its treatment of good versus evil in a lawless countryside populated by rough and corrupt men, Altamirano's classic novel is also an engaging and exotic adventure that keeps the reader turning the pages.

About this Edition of *El Zarco*

The present translation of El *Zarco* is based on Manuel Sol's outstanding 2000 edition of Altamirano's autograph manuscript, not on the first edition of 1901, which contains errors, editorial changes, and omissions that have been reproduced to some degree in all of the novel's subsequent editions. Ronald Christ's translation scrupulously follows Altamirano's original, accurately capturing its melodramatic intonations and earnest didacticism. To facilitate an appreciation of Altamirano's cultural and historical frames of reference, as well as his inspirations, we have glossed his references to Mexican historical personages and events as well as to European literature, drama, and opera. (Where we have used all or part of Manuel Sol's extensive annotation, the page number in his edition is indicated at the end of the our note.)

Acknowledgements/En agradecimiento

This edition of *El Zarco, The Blue-eyed Bandit* was born out of a collaborative effort with Helen Lane, who in 2003 translated sections of the novel and helped me write a book proposal. Unfortunately, Helen left us before the project could proceed further. However, thanks to the efforts of Ronald Christ, this project was brought to fruition and found its rightful home

among the Helen Lane Editions at Lumen Books. Several
other organizations, institutions, and individuals have provided
invaluable assistance in the preparation of this introduction. In
particular, I want to single out the contributions of our copy editor
Sheridan Phillips, who, in collaboration with Ronald Christ,
groomed this introduction and the translation of *El Zarco*. I also
express my gratitude to the staff of the Rare Books Division of
the Nettie Lee Benson Collection at the University of Texas at
Austin. I am indebted to the College of Liberal Arts, the Office
of the Provost and the Center for Mexican-American Studies at
the University of Texas at Arlington for supporting my research.
I also thank Lisa Dillman, Desiree Henderson, Rick Todhunter,
Juan Carlos González Espitia, A. Raymond Elliott, John Charles
Chasteen, Max Parra, Julio Ortega, Nicole Girón, and Jane Miles
and the Staff at the Amon Carter Museum in Fort Worth, Texas. I
am also grateful for the insights provided by several members of
the H-LATAM Latin American Studies listserv. I dedicate my work
here to the memory of Helen Lane and Louis Owens.

---

1. My discussion of these contexts is drawn from Manuel Sol's invaluable
"Introducción" to *El Zarco* by Ignacio Manuel Altamirano (Mexico:
Universidad Veracruzana, 2000), 60-61.

2. Doris Sommer, *Foundational Fiction, The National Romances of Latin
America.* (Berkeley and Los Angeles: University of California Press,
1993).

3. Ignacio Manuel Altamirano, *La literatura nacional*, ed. José Luis
Martínez (México: Porrúa, 1949), 15.

4. For a discussion of Altamirano's image in nineteenth-century
Mexico, see Christopher Conway's "Ignacio Manuel Altamirano and the
Contradictions of Autobiographical Indianism" in *Latin American Literary
Review*, 34.67 (2006), and Catalina Sierra and Cristina Barrios' *Ignacio
Manuel Altamirano: Iconografía* (Mexico: Conaculta/FCE, 1993).

5. Ignacio Manuel Altamirano, "Enrique Muñiz," in *Obras Completas:
Ignacio Altamirano XIX: Periodismo Político II*, ed. Carlos Román Célis
(Mexico: Conaculta/FCE, 1989), 69.

6. Ignacio Manuel Altamirano, "La semana santa en mi pueblo," in *Obras
Completas: Ignacio Manuel Altamirano V: Textos Costumbristas*, ed. José
Joaquín Blanco (Mexico: Conaculta/FCE, 1986), 45-46.

7. Angel Pola, "Ignacio Manuel Altamirano," *Velada literaria que en*

*honor del Sr. Lic. D. Ignacio M. Altamirano celebró el Liceo Mexicano
la noche del 5 de agosto de 1889* (Mexico: Oficina Tipográfica de la
Secretaría de Fomento, 1889) 119-130. Altamirano was present during
Angel Pola's speech about his childhood.

8. See Nicole Girón, *Altamirano en Toluca* (Mexico: Instituto Mexiquense
de Cultura, 1993), 57-58; also Vicente Fuentes Díaz, *Ignacio Manuel
Altamirano: triunfo y viacrucis de un escritor liberal* (Mexico: Gobierno
del Estado de Guerrero/Casa Altamirano, 1986), 39. Girón surmises
that the anecdote may be apocryphal, but one of Altamirano's disciples,
claimed that Altamirano told him the story in person. See Juan de Dios de
Peza, "Aquí no se sientan los indios," *La Patria* 1 septiembre 1913. Año
37, Num 11,477: 2+.

9. Fuentes Díaz, 28-29; Girón, 15.

10. *Nigromante* means master of the black arts or magician and was a
pseudonym that Ramírez used as a journalist.

11. See Giron's account of the controversy surrounding Ramírez's essay
"A los indios," 105-113. For background on the liberalism of Ramírez
and Altamirano, see D.A. Brading's *The First America: The Spanish
Monarchy, Creole Patriots and the Liberal State* (Cambridge: Cambridge
University Press, 1991) 658-674.

12. Nicole Girón, *Altamirano en Cuautla*, in *Homenaje a Ignacio
Manuel Altamirano (1834-1893),* ed. Manuel Sol and Alejandro Higashi
(Mexico: Instituto de Investigaciones Linguístico-Literarias Universidad
Veracruzana, 1997) 35.

13. Virginia Guedea, "The Old Colonialism Ends, the New Colonialism
Begins," *The Oxford History of Mexico*, ed. Michael C. Mayer & William
H. Beezley (Oxford: Oxford University Press, 2000), 289.

14. Although the Wars of Independence throughout Latin America have
been typically associated in nationalist historiography with the rivalry
between Creoles and Peninsulares, in reality the conflict was much more
multidimensional than such a binary distinction allows. While Mexican
Creoles were indeed resentful of the privilege of the Peninsulares, they
were also quite fearful of the peasant armies composed of Indians and
mestizos that threatened the social order.

15. Mexico lost the present-day states of California, Nevada, Utah,
Arizona, New Mexico, Texas, and parts of Colorado to the United States
after the Mexican-American War of 1846-1850.

16. Vanderwood, "Betterment for Whom?" The Reform Period: 1855-
1875," in *The Oxford History of Mexico*, 371.

17. Fuentes Díaz, 42-45.

18. Ignacio Manuel Altamirano, "Ensayo de una oración cívica que pronunció Ignacio María (sic] Altamirano, el día 16 de septiembre de 1855, en la heroica ciudad de Morelos por encargo de la Junta Patriótica," in *Obras Completas: Ignacio Manuel Altamirano XXIII: Varia*, ed. Nicole Girón (Mexico: Conaculta, 2001), 187.

19. For Leonardo Márquez's Massacre of Tacubaya and Altamirano's memories of it, see Fuentes Díaz, 62-64.

20. Fuentes Díaz, 61.

21. "Discurso contra la amnistía" by Ignacio Manuel Altamirano, in *Discursos de Ignacio Manuel Altamirano* (México: Ediciones Beneficiencia Pública, 1934), 36.

22. Jean-Paul Marat (May 24, 1743 – July 13, 1793) was a leading radical revolutionist in the French Revolution of 1789. His murder at the hands of his lover, Charlotte Corday, was immortalized in the famous painting "The Death of Marat" (1793) by Jacques-Louis David.

23. Vanderwood, "Betterment for Whom?" 380.

24. Fuentes Diaz, 138.

25. *Ibid.*, 151-154.

26. *Ibid.*, 153.

27. *Ibid.*, 204.

28. Ignacio Manuel Altamirano, *La literatura nacional*, 39.

29. Fuentes Díaz, 249-257.

30. Ignacio Manuel Altamirano, "La Fiesta de Guadalupe," in *Obras Completas: Ignacio Manuel Altamirano V: Textos Costumbristas*, ed. José Joaquín Blanco (México: Conaculta/SEP, 1986) 115-243.

31. Ignacio Manuel Altamirano, "Bosquejos," in *Obras Completas: Ignacio Manuel Altamirano IX: Crónicas III*, ed. Carlos Monsivais (México: Conaculta/SEP, 1986) 22-45.

32. "La vida de México" in Altamirano, *Obras Completas V: Textos Costumbristas,* 79-86.

33. Ignacio Manuel Altamirano, "Cartas a Tartufo," in *Obras Completas: Ignacio Manuel Altamirano XVIII: Periodismo Político I*, ed. Carlos Román Célis (Mexico: Conaculta, 1989) 214-237; *El Zarco y La navidad en las montañas* (México: Porrúa, 1966).

34. Fuentes Díaz, 260. Girón, "Altamirano Diplomático," *Mexican Studies/Estudios Mexicanos* vol. 9, no. 2 (Summer 1993), 161-185.

35. T.G. Powell, "Mexican Intellectuals and the Indian Question," *The Hispanic American Historical Review* 48.1, February 1968: 19-36; Martin Stabb, "Indigenism and Racism in Mexican Thought: 1857-1911, *Journal of Interamerican Studies* 1.4, October 1959: 405-423.

36. Giron, "Altamirano Diplomático," 172, 174.

37. Paul Vanderwood, *Disorder and Progress: Bandits, Police, and Mexican Development* (Delaware: SR Books, 1992) 8.

38. Sol, "Introducción" 47-60.

39. *Ibid.*, 55. Although some hacienda peons may have been dispossessed due to the Plateados, many also joined their ranks in pursuit of better lives than those they could find on the hacienda. See Vanderwood, *Disorder and Progress*, 9

40. *Ibid.*, 61.

41. *Ibid.*, 29.

42. *Ibid.*, 29.

43. Alejandro Rivas Velázquez, "Altamirano y su nueva visión de la novela en *El Zarco*," in *Reflexiones lingüísticas y literarias. Vol II. Literatura*, ed. Rafael Olea Franco and James Valender (Mexico: Colegio de Mexico) 176.

44. Ignacio Manuel Altamirano, "Correo," *Periodismo Político II*, 57.

45. For a discussion of the image of the Indian in the writing of Altamirano, see Edward N. Wright Ríos "Indian Saints and Nation States: Ignacio Manuel Altamirano's Landscapes and Legends," in *Mexican Studies/Estudios Mexicanos* vol. 20, no. 1 (Winter 2004), 47-68. Wright Ríos' study demonstrates how Altamirano wed nationalism with indigenous identity and prefigured twentieth-century writings on the Indian question.

46. José Rivas, "Una visita en Barcelona al Maestro Altamirano," *El Universal,* 4 junio 1890, 1.

47. *Ibid.*, 1.

48. José Triay, "Cartas Mexicanas," *La Iberia*, 18 February 1873, 1.

49. Gregorio Torres Quintero, "En Honor de Altamirano," *La Patria* 28 marzo 1903, 2.

50. Dios de Peza, 2.

51. For a discussion of such images, see Bram Dijkstra, *Idols of Perversity: Fantasies of Feminine Evil in Fin-de-siècle Culture* (New York: Oxford University Press, 1986), 331-351.

52. The present translation of *Zarco* is based on Altamirano's original, manuscript copy, which was published by Universidad Veracruzana in 2000 with an introduction by Manuel Sol.

Suggestions for Further Reading

The following list is not intended to be exhaustive and primarily contains works in English.

Altamirano and Mexican Literature and Culture

• Conway, Christopher. "Ignacio Manuel Altamirano and the Contradictions of Autobiographical Indianism." *Latin American Literary Review* 34, 67 (2006): 34-49.

Through a reading of one of his autobiographical essays, "La semana santa en mi pueblo," Conway explores Altamirano's ambivalence toward his own native identity. The article suggests that Altamirano subordinates his indigenous origins to his identity as a Europeanized man of letters.

• Cruz, Jacqueline. "La moral tradicional y la identidad mexicana vistas a través de los personajes femeninos de *El Zarco.*" *Explicacion de Textos Literarios* 22, 1 (1993-1994): 73-86.

Cruz suggests that *El Zarco* restages the conquest of Mexico by Cortés, with the Plateados playing the role of plundering conquistadores and Nicolás the role of leader of the indigenous resistance. In particular, her analysis examines Manuela in relation to the story of Adam and Eve, to the figure of La Malinche, the indigenous woman who was both translator and concubine to the conquistador Hernán Cortés.

• Foster, David William, ed., *Mexican Literature: A History*. Austin: University of Texas Press, 1994.

This anthology of essays charts Mexican literary history from the Colonial period to the present. It is particularly useful for understanding literary movements such as Romanticism and its representative authors and plots.

• Franco, Jean. *Plotting Women: Gender and Representation in Mexico*. New York: Columbia University Press, 1989.

Franco's study demonstrates how women writers, from the seventeenth century to the twentieth century, have resisted patriarchal authority and found a voice of their own in Mexican literary history. Franco's discussion of the nineteenth century provides a useful frame for understanding Altamirano and his generation's treatment of women in literature.

• Vicente Fuentes Díaz, *Ignacio Manuel Altamirano: triunfo y viacrucis de un escritor liberal.* Mexico: Gobierno del Estado de Guerrero/Casa Altamirano, 1986.

This biography is the most complete and substantial in Spanish and provides a straightforward introduction to Altamirano's life and nineteenth-century Mexican history.

• Girón, Nicole. *Altamirano en Toluca.* Mexico: Instituto Mexiquense de Cultura, 1993.

Girón provides a thorough discussion of the years Altamirano spent at the Institute of Toluca, describing the history, functioning, and day-to-day life at the school at mid-century.

• Lindstrom, Naomi. *Early Spanish American Narrative.* Austin: University of Texas Press, 2004.

Lindstrom's overview of Latin American literary history reflects contemporary critical trends in the field while offering concise introductions to key authors and works, Altamirano and *El Zarco* included. The discussion of nationalism in nineteenth-century literature is particularly useful and to the point.

• McKee Irwin, Robert. *Mexican Masculinities.* Minneapolis/London: University of Minneapolis Press, 2003.

McKee Irwin's study of homosocial bonding, homophobia, and homosexuality in modern Mexican literary history contains valuable discussions of the meanings of masculinity in nineteenth-century fictions, as well as their treatment of heroism, love and marriage. The discussion of *El Zarco* and other works by Altamirano centers on the concept of male beauty.

• Nacci, Chris. *Ignacio Manuel Altamirano.* New York: Twayne's Publishers, 1970.

Nacci's biographical introduction to Altamirano is the only • • English-language book on the subject and provides a general overview of the writer's life and writing.

• Sol, Manuel. "Introducción", in *El Zarco* by Ignacio Manuel Altamirano. Mexico: Universidad Veracruzana, 2000.

Sol's lengthy introduction is the most complete and informative contextualization of *El Zarco* to date. It contains a wealth of information on the writing of the novel and its relationship to banditry in Mexico, and is accompanied by an excellent bibliography and chronology.

• Segre, Erica. "An Italicised Ethnicity: Memory and Renascence in the Literary Writings of Ignacio Manuel Altamirano." *Forum for Modern Language Studies* 36, 3 (2000): 266-278.

  Segre's study explores the ways in which Altamirano's defense of photographic or empirical precision in writing functioned as a way of resisting the homogenizing impetus of Mexican nationalism, specifically with regard to indigenous culture. The article provides a wealth of contextual information on the questions of Altamirano's ethnicity and his articulation of his Indian self in relation to contemporaneous debates about Mexican identity.

• Sommer, Doris. *Foundational Fictions: The National Romances of Latin America*. Berkeley: University of California Press, 1991.

  Sommer's seminal book explores the intertwining of eros and politics in nineteenth-century Latin American novels and suggests that they should be read as allegories of the national condition. Specifically, Sommer argues that *El Zarco* is an allegory of race and identity in Mexico, with Zarco and Manuela representing the Emperor Maximilian and his wife, Carlota.

• Edward N. Wright-Ríos "Indian Saints and Nation States: Ignacio Manuel Altamirano's Landscapes and Legends," in *Mexican Studies/ Estudios Mexicanos* 20, 1 (2004): 47-68.

  In his study of Altamirano's collection of writings titled *Paisajes y leyendas* (Landscapes and Legends), Wright-Ríos explores the author's commitment to an Indian-centered nationalism as distinct from the cultural discourse of his time. Wright-Ríos argues that Altamirano is an important precursor to twentieth-century Mexican debates about Indians and national identity.

Mexican and Latin American History
• D.A. Brading. *The First America: The Spanish Monarchy, Creole Patriots and the Liberal State, 1492-1867*. New York: Cambridge University Press, 1991.

  Brading's discussion of nineteenth-century Mexico, and specifically Altamirano, frames the author within the history of Mexican liberal thought and his relationship to his mentor Ignacio "el Nigromante"

Ramírez. Brading's argument elegantly links Mexico to other national contexts, and clearly charts the continent's intellectual history from Discovery to the middle of the nineteenth century.

• Halperín Donghi, Tulio. *The Contemporary History of Latin America*. Durham: Duke University Press, 1993.

    Halperín Donghi's history is a classic of Latin American historiography as well as a usefully organized study in which each chapter combines general statements about Latin America with concise discussions of individual nations.

• Meyer, Michael C, Sherman, William L, Deeds, Susan M, eds*., The Course of Mexican History*. New York/Oxford: Oxford University Press, 2003.

    As a standard textbook for the teaching of Mexican history, *The Course of Mexican History* is complete, accessible, and richly illustrated. It also includes substantive discussions of Mexican culture and everyday life corresponding to each historical period under discussion.

• Martin Stabb, "Indigenism and Racism in Mexican Thought: 1857-1911, *Journal of Interamerican Studies* 1.4, October 1959: 405-423.

    Stabb details different currents of nineteenth-century thought in Mexico relative to the Indian question and demonstrates the differences between the Generation of Reform, of which Altamirano was a part, and the late nineteenth-century, Positivist thinkers called the "Científicos."

• Paul Vanderwood, *Disorder and Progress: Bandits, Police, and Mexican Development*. Delaware: SR Books, 1992.

    Vanderwood's book documents the rise of the bandit in Mexico and the state's efforts to counter rural crime. Its discussion of the Plateados, and the consequences of rural crime in the nineteenth century and early twentieth century will be useful to readers seeking context for Altamirano's novel.

Translator's Note
Ronald Christ

Ignacio Manuel Altamirano's *El Zarco* has appeared in English-speaking countries, more than once; but the edition you are holding is the first to present Altamirano's entire, definitive text in an English translation close to what the author wrote in Spanish.

Such belated justice to a major figure of Mexican literature, culture, and politics is made possible, first of all, owing to Manuel Sol's critical, variorum edition of *El Zarco*, published as volume 6 in the Universidad Veracruzana's series Clásicos Mexicanos, to which Sol contributed a transcription of the autograph manuscript, a preliminary study, and notes. Any detailed consideration of the book entails this generous edition; this translation has benefited from Sol's equally generous response to queries and his permission to translate his work.

Christopher Conway discovered Altamirano to Helen Lane. In fact, Helen began to translate the book, penciling characteristic notes on photocopies of its early pages, which now reside in the Lilly Library at the University of Indiana. Unfortunately and unknown to Helen, she was working from an edition of the novel that had been edited for use in language-and-literature classes in this country. While that edition's overall presentation is helpful, the novel's literary quality was compromised by simplification and abridgment. I have retained an occasional nugget from Helen's preliminary work—"with barely time to bolt down our food," for example: quintessential Helen Lane—; yet I have translated as she would not have, following my perception and plan that, in other circumstances, she and I had discussed over lengthy disagreements and laughs. Now recalling Helen's collaboration at that time, I have gone ahead, hearing her over my shoulder—"I have no theory, every book creates its own theory of translation"—and all the while encouraging me to proceed.

A more seductive, extensive betrayal of Altamirano's novel came from the Folio Society in 1957. Translated by Mary Alt with wood engravings by Zelma Blakely, this little book fulfills the traitor portion of that wearisome Italian saying, *traduttore, traditore*. Not that Mary Alt is dishonest, confessing as she does that her work is a "free rendering in which the aim has been to retain the flavour of the original as far as possible, while putting it into modern English. Altamirano's writing is often repetitive, and a considerable amount of such purely repetitious matter has been omitted. A number of the more extravagantly romantic passages have also been toned down as it was felt that if given literally, they would raise a smile with the reader of today, and so falsify the author's intention."

That's somewhat like preserving the flavor of egg custard by eliminating the eggs—censoring repetition repetitively, repetitiously in the same sentence as well as in the novel. What this editor, as much an inventive translator, does not report is how she has elided chapters as well as deleted description and narration in her stated interest of forestalling a reader's smile at the expense of the author's hard-won style and vision. John Ford would have done better; a less-involved David O. Selznick, with his duel in the sun expanded to a quartet of crossed lovers, might have knowingly translated this romance to film. Only an inferior Mexican movie exists, itself traitorous.

Understandably, then, but in different circumstances, when I took over the present version, I found myself near Gaston de Vere's experience when coming to Vasari's *Lives* two years after Mrs. Jonathan Foster's 1910 visit:

> Perhaps I have gone too far towards the other extreme [of "Mrs. Foster's familiar English paraphrase—for a paraphrase it is rather than a translation"] in taking no liberties with the text . . . My intention, indeed, has been to render my original word for word, and to err, if at all, in favour of literalness. The very structure of Vasari's sentences has usually been retained, though some freedom was necessary in the matter of the punctuation . . ..

In short, I have chosen to honor the author and to translate closely, with my eye on Altamirano's rhetoric—his manner of invention, arrangement, and exposition, his diction and figures, his ethos—; one might say of his *literature*, for I concur with Everett Fox's magisterial method, although I cannot match it, and acknowledge the "difference between translating what the text means and translating what it says." I hew to what the author said, wrote.

Rhetoric is means and matter of this novel. Like Dickens, Altamirano generates his progress of language with steadfast figures of speech, which really are engines of his prose, motors of his invention; although, unlike Dickens, Altamirano never lets his figures or diction take on a life of their own. Altamirano's rhetorical inevitability also orders his prose and his narrative with a regularity, predictability, and reliability directly contrapositive to the story and emotions he narrates: unsettled and unsettling events find their expression in resolved and resolving language. To sacrifice the sustained stability of this Spanish prose for the sake of not ruffling too-smoothed feathers of fiction as we know it best is a price I rejected, even at the cost of some opinion.

Which means that like Fox, in his radiating *The Five Books of Moses,* I mostly adhere to Altamirano's "small-scale repetitions." Although instances of this smaller form, as Kenneth Burke might have termed it, are often less substantial than those in the Pentateuch, resulting as they frequently do from Altamirano's imposed limitation on diction, they ultimately accumulate an integrity as well as intensity of expression that testifies to Altamirano's ethical as well as social and literary purposes. To reapply one of his own formula phrases, we might well say that Altamirano is *un artesano honrado*, an honest, honorable craftsman, even when he is not much more; that he works his basic forms and schemes over and over—tried and true. These forms, geometrically congruent with English, can be translated directly, which is what I have done.

For example, when the author's moon shrouds itself in threatening clouds, my translation's shrouded moon, following his original, leaves the land similarly shrouded in shadow, both in the same sentence: "Era la noche, y la luna envolviéndose en espesos nubarrorones dejaba envuelta la tierra en sombras." We repeat repetitively and repetitiously—for meaning as well as for effect, and to keep the machinery going.

When Altamirano has seized a word, spontaneously it would only seem, he holds on to it, rejecting variation against rules of so-called style and my third-grade teacher, Miss Gramstetter. These words and phrases, like his plenitude of commas, are castors on his verbal vehicle: qualifiers such as *honrado, resoluto*; and local terms, sometimes from Nahuatal, that he italicizes: *apantle*, and even explains: *tarecua*, as part of his program for redeeming the indigenous world that he is part conserving, part inventing—Mexico. The first grouping calls forth his invariable values, the second his historically focused locale and peoples, and a third manifests his grand theme of Mexico's unique origins, in dream and nightmare, of individuals and groups from several races: *en ese tiempo, el indio herrero, hacendados*. Sometimes a repetition is only a repetition, but nonetheless an indicator of Altamirano's constructive manner. Above all these instances rings out Altamirano's *lúgubre*, a word tolled again and again, first in the novel's second chapter, finally in the book's last sentence, and valued here as *doleful*: the mournful, regrettable state of 19th-century Mexico, the tonality of Altamirano's book.

This author's literary qualities are determined choices; he means them, and the observant reader will come to respect them, as the translator should, perhaps even grow fond of them, as I did. Precisely how the author arrived at these choices may not be decided, since Spanish was his second language, and he learned it only when he was twelve years old in uncertain circumstances, although *El Zarco's* opening chapter casts a removed shadow on that background: "The inhabitants all speak Spanish, comprised as they are of mixed races. Pureblooded Indians have disappeared from that place entirely." The author did not come from that place, Yautepec, but he was a full-bloodied Indian; and while granted preliminary schooling as an exception, he later sat attentively outside the door of a revered lecturer, acquiring the elements of his style, which is formal, rooted in 19th-century oratorical conventions. Certainly his purpose in *El Zarco* is as ancient as Horace's balanced formula: *lectorem delectando pariterque monendo*—in this case, story for delight; history, geography, biography, vocabulary, scholarship, statistics, morality for instruction; in short, to forge the conscience of his troubled, emerging country in a useful work of art.

More than repetitive, hallmark of the pedagogue, Altamirano's expression is formulaic; seldom compact, he writes with few words, insistently the same, as his syntax fulfills identical forms. The effect is earnest, frugal of means and disinvites a translator's happy variation. Similarly Altamirano has his syntax, which is interrupted, serial, dependent on parallelism and, most of all, *polysyndeton*, the oral narrator's ritual: "and . . . and . . . and." With his *polysyndeton* comes *anaphora*, the repetition of a word or phrase at the start of clauses; *anaphora*, that equally venerable scheme so mercilessly abused by our contemporary line slicers.

If he had been one of those foolish, fatuous young men

who always interpret their beloved's gestures and words
in the manner most favorable to themselves; *if he had
been one of those* vengeful, tenacious men who turn
suffering into a means of triumphing and avenging
themselves; in conclusion, *if he had been one of those*
old rakes for whom desire is a shield that makes them
invulnerable and for whom possession at any cost is now
the only object of their sensual love, Nicolás would have
remained firm of purpose, sustained by the señora's
support—a major support to a daughter, regardless of
how contrary she shows herself.

This example demonstrates the sure, almost stately and
certainly measured progress of Altamirano's basically periodic,
climactic constructions. Founded in repetition. Let the translator be
aware. (Also of the many sentence fragments, typical of Spanish,
especially forceful here.)

Altamirano's essential sentence begins with a simple
subject, often enough a character's name, intruded upon by a short
phrase, which in English would typically fill the slot of a sentence
opener, followed by the verb and/or a series of parallel phrases
or clauses. Did I say long? Notoriously, modern English letches
after short sentences and long paragraphs while Spanish famously
luxuriates in long sentences and short paragraphs. In this regard
Altamirano stays classic in character. As he does with ellipses, not
for any Puritanical eye-shift from a taboo subject, but for the oral
fact of purposeful, uncompleted statements, bridges suspended
toward powerful yet unrealized terminal piers.

All of which invokes the editorial blue pencil. (Does
anyone still use a *blue* pencil?) But the translator, who is always an
editor, need not heed that particular call, choosing instead to enrich
his native language with a dependently different voice, but not
one so far removed from English-language writers of Altamirano's
time; with an authorial persona that bespeaks his time, a human
and social condition, and a noble will.

The result, true enough, does not flash by like one of
Barnett Newman's zips, and a reader may indeed smile. (I suppose
there are readers who smile when reading Carlyle, Hardy.) The result, however, provides an author to fill the shoes of that oversized,
overstuffed judgment *authentic*.

And it justifies both Altamirano's method and the translator's trust. The quantity of a word or phrase's recurrence does not in itself designate the repeated term's significance, no more than it does with a Homeric epithet, so, while some are frequent—*honrado artisano* (honest/honorable artisan/craftsman)—, others much less so—*este rumbo* (out this way)—all justify Altamirano's method and confirm his thematics. *Catrín*, for example.

Catrín occurs in one or other of its forms just four times in the novel, applied negatively to Manuela and rejected by el Zarco as applying to himself and his cohort. The word had great currency in the 19th century at the time when José Joaquín Fernández de Lizardi (1776-1827) wrote his brief novel *Vida y hechos del famoso caballero don Catrín de la Fachenda* (Life and Deeds of the Famous Gentleman don Catrín de la Fachenda) around 1819, but that novella, like *El Zarco*, was not published until after its author's death; while the figure of the *catrín* achieved literally iconographic status with Posada's well-known wood blocks of the *calavera* or skeletal figures, *El Catrín* and, especially, *La Catrina*, becoming popular, nearly anonymous images, again, after their creator's death.

In general use, *el catrín* is someone who pays more attention to appearance than substance, to the façade (hence Lizardi's character's name, Fachenda), most particularly of dress—a vain, dandified, foppish creature, who wears formal, foreign clothes—a frock coat to walk the streets. Lizardi makes the vanity clear: "In the end, the *catrín* is an insoluble paradox, because he is gallant without honor, rich without income, poor without hunger, enamored without a lady love, brave without enemies, wise without books, Christian without religion, and a rascal at every chance." Superficially French, then, like the term's etymology, and nothing essentially Mexican. Thus, when Altamirano describes Manuela as a *catrína*, he categorizes her vanity as Old World in his system of values, where the heroic, struggling Mexico is the measure of new worth. This single word weighs heavily within the elegant coordinate system of his allusions, where foreign elements—Goethe's Marguerite; Fra Diavolo, Saint Aloysius Gonzaga, etc.—back light these characters' and situations' true nature. The stiff subtlety is not unambiguous: President Benito Juárez is the only character in the book who wears a frock coat, as he did in life.

Nor is the result wholly beautiful. Altamirano took pride

in referring to himself as ugly, an ugly Indian; but a glance at photographs of him shows an arms-folded, settled determination matched by an open seriousness, if not sternness. By "ugly" he meant "dedidedly," "resolutely"—a self-respecting Indian. His stylistic self brings to my mind Henry James's visit to George Eliot, after which he reported to his father that at the start he found her horse faced but ended by falling in love with her. Beginning with no individual interest in this book and anticipating no joy from its prose, I have come to admire Altamirano's *El Zarco* from the inside out, to love its author for his flaws as well as his determined successes. My loyalty is to the author's method as much as to his matter, and if you can spare swift, shining modernity for a while, you may come, as I have done, to respect and admire this book as well. My translation aims, tries, to be close, then, in a double sense; tries to conserve Altamirano's writing—when not faithfully, all the more loyally.

The lowland area of Mexico, south of the Tropic of Cancer and west of the continental divide, where *EL Zarco, The Blue-eyed Bandit* is set, bears the name *tierra caliente* (hot land) because of its lower altitude and tropical climate. In Yautepec, scene of the opening chapters, the average temperature is $21.7°C$ ($71.06°F$). *Tierras frías*, in contrast, are highland regions, where temperatures are lower but still temperate. Between the two lie the *tierras templadas*, regions without extremes of heat or cold.

•

Indian place names are spelled phonetically in Spanish and therefore pronounced like Spanish words. An initial *x*, as in Xochimancas, however, is prounounced like the Spanish *s*, while *x* before other consonants, as in the name of Altamirano's native village, Tixtla, is pronounced like English *sh* in *ship*.

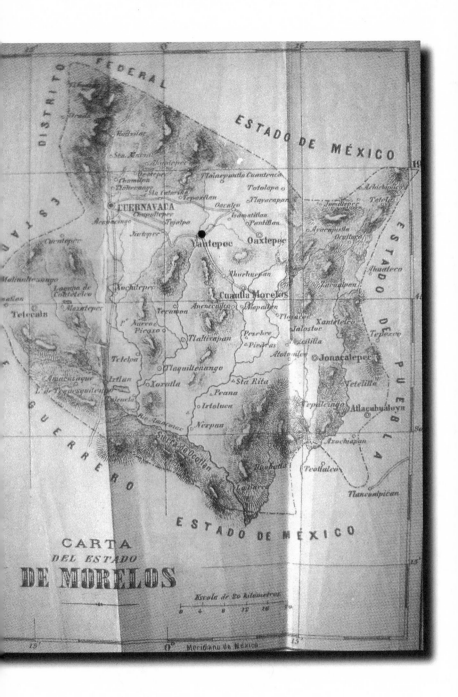

CARTA
DEL ESTADO
DE MORELOS

Escala de 20 kilómetros.

Meridiano de México

45

Yautepec

Yautepec, in the Tierra Caliente, is a town whose houses are concealed in a forest of greenery.

From a distance, whether one approaches from Cuernavaca by way of the rough road that meanders through Las Tetillas, two rocky hills whose shape has given the sierra its name; or whether one descends from the cold, steep Tepoztlán sierra, to the north; or catches sight of the town along the flat trail coming in from the east through Amilpas Valley, crossing the beautiful, fertile sugarcane haciendas of Cocoyoc, Calderón, Casasano, and San Carlos, Yautepec always comes into view as a vast forest, the low towers of its parish church barely peeking over the treetops.

From nearby, Yautepec has an original and picturesque air. The town is part eastern, part American.[1] Eastern because the orange and lemon trees we have mentioned are enormous, luxuriant, and always laden with fruit and blossoms that sweeten the air with their heady scents. Orange and lemon trees everywhere, an extraordinary cornucopia. It might be said that these trees are the spontaneous product of the earth, so exuberantly do they multiply, clustering together, crowding each other, creating dark, scraggy canopies in the large and small orchards tended by the inhabitants and grazing their luxuriant, shiny, deep-green branches laden with golden fruit across the tiled

---

(1) Altamirano's juxtaposing "East," "eastern" (*oriente, oriental*) and "American" may puzzle the reader, who should keep in mind, first, that lowland Yautepec lies west of the Sierra Madre Oriental (Eastern Sierra Madre) and, second, that the Italian context alluded to below comes from still farther east. Then, as Doris Sommer comments: "*Oriente* is, indeed, a strange word here, a clever way of making Europe seem pre-modern by means of a playful or pugnacious reference to a useful but superseded part of the world. Orange and lemon trees represent what comes from afar, a past grafted onto the present and future, which is modern Mexico. Mexicans did not forget Hegel's assumption that modernity was moving westward, and the underlying tension of the novel has to do with the need to overcome a taste for that European past."—*Eds*.

or thatched roofs of the dwellings. Mignon would feel right at home in Yautepec, where the orange and lemon trees bloom year-round.[2]

Of course, this oriental aggregate is partially tempered by the intermingling of various American flora, since banana trees are apt to display their slender trunks and broad leaves there, and mameys and other trees of the sapodilla family raise their towering crowns above the groves; but the orange and lemon trees dominate by virtue of their sheer abundance. In 1854, when Yautepec was still part of the State of Mexico, these citrus trees were counted, and it was learned that there were over five hundred thousand of them. Now, twenty years later, this number has naturally doubled or tripled. Yautepec's residents live almost exclusively off the produce of these precious fruit trees and, before the railroad between Veracruz and the capital was constructed, they were Mexico City's only source of oranges and lemons.

Aside from that, Yautepec looks like any other Tierra Caliente town in the republic: a few flat-roofed houses painted in screaming colors, others with dark roofs streaked by rust from the humidity, and more still with roofs of thatch or palm fronds from the Tierra Fría — all of them large homes, fenced in by adobe or stone or wooden walls, happy, abundantly supplied with water and awash in flowers, though lacking any modern refinements.

---

(2) *Mignon*: At the start of Book Three of Goethe's *Wilhelm Meister's Apprenticeship*, the Italian-born waif, Mignon, sings the German poet's most famous and influential lyric, sometimes known as "Mignon's Song" (1815): "Kennst du das Land wo die Zitronen blühn, . . ." (Do you know the country where the lemon trees bloom / Where golden oranges glow among the leaves?), which was set to music in Altamirano's lifetime by more than 100 composers in many languages, most famously in Ambroise Thomas's opera *Mignon* (1866; with a libretto by Michel Carré and Jules Barbier) as "Connais-tu le pays," but also quoted, twice, in Louisa May Alcott's *Little Women* (1869). Altamirano wrote about the novel in his "Week in Review," *La República*, 9 January 1881.—*Eds./Sol, 97*

A gently flowing river, whose calm, limpid waters rise impetuously only in the rainy season, separates the town from the forest, cutting through the plaza, lapping gently at the walled gardens, and allowing them to steal from it by means of numerous *apantles* that distribute the water in all directions. That river is truly the fecundating god of the region, the father of sweet fruits that cool us during hot summers and cheer popular Mexican celebrations year-round.

The people here are good, even-tempered, hard-working, peace loving, honest, simple, and hospitable. Yautepec trades actively with the magnificent sugarcane haciendas that surround it, as well as with Cuernavaca and Morelos; it is the center of numerous small, indigenous villages located in the southern foothills of the mountain range separating the Tierra Caliente from the Valley of Mexico, and so it also trades with the republic's capital, thanks to the produce of its immense orchards that we have already described.

Formerly part of the State of Mexico, Yautepec has risen from subordinate status as a dependency of Cuernavaca to become the political and administrative center of the Morelos district, the rank it holds to this day. The town took no active role in the civil wars and has more often been their victim, although it has also managed to recover from the wars' disasters, thanks to its inexhaustible resources and industriousness. The river and the fruit trees are its treasure house, which is why criminals, partisans, and bandits have often been able to make off with Yautepec's revenue but have never managed to diminish or destroy its capital. The inhabitants all speak Spanish, comprised as they are of mixed races. Pureblooded Indians have disappeared from that place entirely.

The Terror

The sun had scarcely set one day in August 1861 and
Yautepec already seemed to be enfolded by night's
shadows—such was the silence reigning over the town. In
these beautiful twilight hours, the residents, who by custom
always go outside to take a breath of fresh air on the streets
after concluding their day's business or to go for a swim in
the river's still pools and backwaters or to wander through
the plaza or the orchards in search of some relief, today did
not dare step from their doorways and, on the contrary, even
before the church bells had called people to prayer, they
hurriedly laid in their provisions and shut themselves up in
their houses, as if there were an epidemic, trembling in terror
at every sound they heard.

And at that time of day during that calamitous
period, towns without a strong garrison were beginning
to be in danger of attack by bandits, with the ensuing
horrors of massacre, kidnapping, and extermination. The
Tierra Caliente bandits were cruel above all else. However
horrendous and unnecessary an act of cruelty, they
committed it instinctively, brutally, and with the sole aim of
heightening the people's terror and taking delight in it.

The nature of the Plateados—or silvered ones,
as the bandits were called in those days—was something
extraordinary, aberrant, an outburst of viciousness, cruelty,
and baseness that had never been seen before in Mexico.

And so it was that the people of Yautepec, like
people in every Tierra Caliente town at this time, lived in
constant fear, always taking the precaution of stationing
lookouts in their church towers during the daylight hours to
give them timely warning of the approach of any party of
bandits, so that the people could defend themselves in the
plaza or on some promontory, or take shelter behind their

doors. But during the night such precautions were futile, as was stationing sentinels or scouts at the edge of town, since that would have required their employing numerous unarmed townsmen who, aside from the risk they ran of being taken by surprise, were too few to keep watch over the many roads and paths leading into town, all of which the bandits knew perfectly. Furthermore, it must be noted that the Plateados could always depend on many accomplices and spies within the towns and on the haciendas and that the pathetic authorities, turned cowardly from lacking the needed means of defense, found themselves obliged, whenever the occasion arose, to make deals with the bandits, settling for going into hiding or fleeing to save their own lives.

Emboldened by this situation and trusting that the government was too engaged in fighting the civil war to pursue them, the Plateados had organized themselves into large bands of one, two, and even five hundred men and so roamed the entire region with impunity, living off the country, extorting great sums of money from haciendas and townships, establishing tolls on roads on their own behalf, and making an everyday practice of *plagio*, that is to say, of abducting people whom they would release only after receiving a considerable ransom. This crime, which has sown terror in Mexico on more than one occasion, was introduced by the Spaniard Cobos, a clerical leader of fearsome renown who finally paid for his misdeeds by being tortured.[3]

---

(3) *Cobos*: Marcelino Cobos (c.1825-1861) was born in Spain and in 1845 arrived in Mexico where he fought with the guerrillas under the command of Father Jarauta during 1846-47 in the Mexican-American War. In the War of Reform, he fought with the Reactionaries and achieved the rank of general. After the republic's victory, he laid waste to the small towns of central Mexico. For example, *El Monitor Republicano* (No. 3902, p. 3) reports of him: "This champion of provincial charters most frequently descended upon the Nacapamilpa and Mazapa Haciendas. He seized a resident of Otumba who, after suffering a true martyrdom, then had to pay 6,000 pesos in order to save his life."

Or Altamirano might have in mind José María Cobos, who also was born in Spain and served with the Conservative Party. He was executed by order

Sometimes the Plateados set up a center of operations that they used as a sort of headquarters from which one or more leaders ordered the attacks and kidnappings and sent letters to wealthy *hacendados* and townspeople demanding money, letters those people had to heed under penalty of certain death. Here they had their hideouts where they locked up the kidnapped victims and subjected them to the cruelest of tortures.

At the time about which we are speaking, the bandits' headquarters was located in Xochimancas, an old, run-down hacienda not far from Yautepec and purposely situated so as to preclude any possible surprise approach.

Such proximity meant that the towns and haciendas in the region of Yautepec felt themselves under the pressure of a constant terror. Which explains the doleful silence reigning in Yautepec on that afternoon one day in August, when everything was an inducement to moving about and sociability, it not having rained as it so often did in that rainy season and the sky showing no menacing signs. On the contrary, the atmosphere was clear and calm: up there, on the peaks of the Tepoztlán sierra, some clustering clouds, still tinged with scattered purplish reflections; and to the east, out beyond the vast cane fields beginning to grow dark, shadowy masses of vegetation and stone marking the haciendas; and above the distant, rolling mountains, just coming into view, the tenuous, vague light of the moon at its fullest.

of Benito Juárez in Matamoros on November 17, 1862. It is difficult to determine which Cobos Altamirano had in mind; nevertheless, Marcelino Cobos is the one who earned his notoriety by the crime of plagio.—*Sol, 105-106*

Two Friends

In the inner patio of a poor but attractive-looking house, with its respective orange, lemon, and banana orchards, located at the edge of town and bordering the river, there happened to be a family, consisting of an elderly lady and two young women, both quite beautiful but of differing features, who were enjoying the coolness.

One, some twenty years of age, had the white, rather pale complexion found in the Tierra Caliente; along with her dark, sparkling eyes and crimson, pleasing mouth, she had something proud and haughty about her, surely the result of a faintly aquiline nose, the frequent frowning of her velvety eyebrows, the erectness of her sturdy, beautiful neck, or of a smile more mocking than kind. She was seated on a rustic bench, amusing herself by braiding a garland of white roses and red calendulas into her silken black hair. One might think her a disguised aristocrat in hiding within this Tierra Caliente back garden. A Martha or Nancy who fled from the palace for a secret meeting with her lover.[4]

The other young woman was probably about eighteen. She was dark-skinned with the Creole woman's soft, delicate complexion, at a remove from the Spanish cast without blending into that of the Indian and bespeaking a humble daughter of the people. But in her big eyes, likewise

---

(4) *Martha or Nancy*: Friedrich Von Flotow (1812-1883) wrote the comic opera *Martha, or the Fair at Richmond* (1847), in which Lady Harriet Durham, a lady-in-waiting to Queen Anne and weary of life at the court, withdraws to the country along with her confidante Lady Nancy, both disguised as maid servants. The young women attend Richmond Fair, where girls hire out as servants. Two farmers, Lyonel and Plumkett, hire them for a year, Lady Harriet giving her name as Martha. The disguised women escape their servitude and, through complicated reversals, Lady Harriet is eventually united with Lyonel, a banished nobleman, also in disguise. Here Altamirano romantically simplifies the plot of this popular opera, which nowhere presents a maiden fleeing a palace to meet her lover; but in his "Week in Review" for *El Siglo Diez y Nueve* (7 January 1868) he accurately summarized the plot.—*Eds./Sol, 110.*

dark, in her mouth, which depicted a sad smile whenever her friend uttered some scornful remark, in her bowed neck, her frail, sickly-looking body, in everything about her there was such sadness that of course it was understandable that her character was diametrically opposed to that of the other girl.

She, too, was slowly and listlessly weaving into her black braids a garland of blossoms, but only blossoms, that she had taken pleasure in clipping from the most beautiful of the orange and lemon trees, an activity that had scratched her hands and now brought down upon her the raillery of her friend.

"Look, mamá," said the pale young woman, addressing the older señora who sat sewing in a small straw chair, slightly apart from the rustic bench: "Look at this foolish girl, it will take her all afternoon to put in her flowers; she's already hurt her hands, determined to cut only the freshest and highest blossoms, and now she can't braid them in. And it's all because, no matter what, she wants to get married, and soon."

"Me?" asked the dark girl, timidly raising her eyes, as though embarrassed.

"Yes, you," replied the other girl. "Don't try to hide it. You dream of getting married, you do nothing but talk about it all day long, and that's why you choose only the choicest blossoms. Not me, I'm not thinking of getting married yet, and I'm happy with whatever flowers please me. Besides, with a crown of orange and lemon blossoms it looks as though a girl's dressing up like a dead person. That's how they bury virgins."

"Well, perhaps they'll bury me that way," said the dark-skinned girl, "and that's why I prefer these trimmings."

"Oh, girls! Don't talk about such things!" the señora admonished. "With times being the way they are and you two talking about mournful things, it's aggravating. You, Manuela," she said, addressing the haughty one, "let Pilar wear the flowers that suit her best, and you wear the ones you like. When it comes right down to it, you both look pretty with them . . . and as no one's going to see them," she added with a sigh.

"That's the pity of it!" cried Manuela, with feeling. "That's the pity," she repeated. "If we could only go to a dance or even peek out the window . . . then we'd see."

"Fine times these are" exclaimed the señora bitterly. "Charming, for going dancing or peeking out of windows. What do we want with more entertainment? God help us! We work hard enough just to live hidden away without the Plateados finding out we exist. I can't picture the time when my brother will come from Mexico City to take us away, even if only on foot. A person can't live in this place any longer. I'll die of fright one of these days. Lord, this isn't living any more. The life we're leading in Yautepec now is no life at all. In the morning, frightened if the bell tolls and running to hide at the neighbor's or at church. In the afternoon, with barely time to bolt down our food, frightened again if the bell rings or people go running by; in the nighttime, sleeping in fits and starts, trembling at every scurrying, at every sound, at every step you hear on the street and not shutting your eyes all night if shots or voices ring out. It's impossible to live this way! Nobody talks about anything but robberies and murders: 'They've taken don So-and-So up into the mountains''; 'his body's already been found in this gully or on that road'; 'there're vultures in such and such a place'; 'the priest's already gone to hear So-and-So's confession, he was so badly wounded'; 'tonight Salomé Plasencia's coming in'; 'hide your families: here comes el Zarco or Palo Seco.' And then, 'Here come the government troops, shooting and tying up the townsfolk.' You tell me if this is living. No, it's hell. I'm heartsick."

With those words and shedding thick tears, the señora concluded her horrific description of the life she led, which, unfortunately, was not only very accurate but even paled in comparison to the reality.

Manuela, who had flushed when she heard el Zarco mentioned, was moved on hearing the good woman complain of being sick at heart.

"Mamá, you never told me that you're sick at heart. Does it really hurt? Are you ill?" she asked affectionately, going over to her mother.

"No, child, I'm not ill. There's nothing wrong with me, but I mean that living like this grieves me, makes me feel sad, and it will end by making me truly ill. As illnesses go, thank God, I don't have any, and that's one piece of good fortune we still have, amid all the misfortunes that have befallen us since your father died. But with so many anxious moments, with so many daily frights, with the concern you cause me, I'm afraid of losing my health. Everyone tells me, 'Doña Antonia, hide Manuelita, or send her to Mexico City or Cuernavaca. Here she's at too great a risk, she's very pretty, and if the Plateados see her, or if any of their spies around here let them know, they're capable of descending on the town one night and kidnapping her.' Heaven help me! Everyone says so: the priest himself has advised me to do that; the prefect, our relatives, there's not one blessed soul who doesn't say the same thing to me every day, and I have no consolation, nowhere to turn . . . all alone . . . no other livelihood than this orchard, which is what keeps me here, and no help but my brother, who I pester by letter, but he turns a deaf ear. So you see, my child, what a cross I have always to bear and it doesn't give me a moment's rest. Were my brother not to come, we'd have only one means of saving ourselves from the misfortune threatening us."

"What is that, mamá?" Manuela asked, startled.

"For you to get married, my child," she replied with immeasurable tenderness.

"Get married! To whom?"

"What do you mean, to whom?" she responded, gently reproaching her daughter. "You know perfectly well that Nicolás loves you and would consider himself fortunate were you to say yes to him. The poor boy's been coming to visit us day after day for over two years now, never hindered by rain storms or the risk or your rebuffs, which are so frequent and so unjust, and all because he hopes that you'll be persuaded of his love, that your heart will soften, that you'll consent to be his wife . . ."

"Oh mamacita, did we have to end up on that subject again!" Manuela interrupted spiritedly, having stopped concealing her displeasure after her mother's last words. "I ought to have guessed from the start! You're always talking about Nicolás, you're always suggesting that I marry him, as the only solution for our bad situation, as if there weren't any other way . . ."

"But what other way is there, my girl?"

"There's going to Mexico City with my uncle, there's living here as we've been doing, hiding when there's danger."

"But don't you see that your uncle is not coming, that we can't go to Mexico City by ourselves, that trusting someone else is very risky these days, when the roads are full of Plateados who might have been alerted and surprise us? . . . Because people would know in advance about our journey."

"And, going with my uncle, wouldn't we run the same risk?" the young woman objected, considering.

"Perhaps. But he has our interests at heart, we're his family, and he'd enlist steadfast men to accompany us. Maybe he could take advantage of some government forces passing through or could bring them from Mexico City or Cuernavaca. He'd maintain the proper secrecy about our departure. He'd risk it at night, going by way of Totolopam or Tepoztlán. In any case, with him we'd travel more safely.

But, you already see: he doesn't come, he doesn't even answer my letters. He surely knows how things are in these parts, and my sister-in-law and her children won't let him take the risk. The fact is, we can't place our hopes in him."

"Well then, mamá, we'll carry on the way we have until now; these aren't the torments of hell, some day it will all be over, and better for me to stay and end up an old maid . . ."

"I wish that were the only risk you ran: staying and ending up an old maid!" the señora replied bitterly. "But we certainly cannot go on living like this in Yautepec. These are not really the torments of hell, and I even believe that they'll come to an end soon, but not favorably for us. Listen," she added, lowering her voice with a certain mystery, "I've heard that since the Plateados settled into Xochimancas, we're more overrun than ever with them out here; that some of them have been sighted, in disguise, prowling about our street at night, that they already know you're here, even though you don't leave the house, even for Mass; that people have overheard your name being mentioned by them; that their friends here have said more than once: 'Manuelita will end up with the Plateados. One of these days Manuela will be gone away to Xochimancas' —along with other similar words. My women friends, my relatives, as I already told you, the parish priest himself ran into me and told me: 'But doña Antonia, what can you be thinking, not yet to have sent Manuelita to Cuernavaca or Cuautla or to some large hacienda? She's at risk with these devils. Send her away, señora, send her away, or hide her underground; because if you don't, you will be filled with grief one of these days.' And with every piece of advice they give me, they stab a knife into my breast. Now, you consider if we can live here like this."

"But, mamá, that's gossip they're trying to frighten you with. I've never seen any shadowy shape on our street at night, on those rare occasions when I do peek out, and as

for the Plateados' coming to steal me away some time, you'll
see how difficult that is: we'd have to have had time to know
about it, to hear some scurrying, and we could escape from
them easily by running out through the orchard to the plaza
. . . Stop fooling yourself. Without their depending on me,
it seems impossible. Only if they were to surprise me on
the street, but since I don't go out, don't even go to Mass,
staying here instead under lock and key, where could they
see me?"

"Ay! No, Manuela! You're full of spirit because
you're still a girl, and you see things differently; but I'm old,
I have experience, I see what's happening now—something
I've never seen in all my years, and I believe these men are
capable of anything. If I knew there were government troops
here or that the villagers had the arms to defend themselves,
I'd rest easier, but you know full well that even the prefect
and the mayor run to the mountains when the Plateados
appear, that people in town don't know what to do, that if
these bandits haven't attacked the town yet, it's because
we've sent the money they demanded, and even I contributed
from what little savings I had; that the only refuge we have is
the church or the most secluded parts of the orchards. What
would you have us do if one day those bandits came to live
here in town, as they once lived in Xantetelco and as they
now live in Xochimancas? Don't you realize that even the
hacendados send them money in order to be able to work
their haciendas? Don't you know that they pay them tolls to
be able to take their shipments to Mexico City! Don't you
know that in big towns, such as Cuautla and Cuernavaca,
the townspeople with weapons are the only ones to defend
themselves? Maybe you think these marauders go around
in bands of ten and twelve? Well, no: they travel in bands
of three hundred, five hundred men! They even bring their
own musicians, their own cannons, and they can lay siege to
haciendas, to towns. The government is afraid of them, and

here we are, like lambs without a shepherd."

"Well," Manuela replied, not giving in, "and even supposing that's all true, mamá, what would we achieve by marrying me off to Nicolás?"

"Oh, dear child, we'd achieve your status as a married woman as well as putting you under the protection of an honorable man."

"But if this honorable man is no more than a blacksmith at the Hacienda de Atlihuayán, and if the owner of the hacienda himself, who's in Mexico City and who's an influential man, can do nothing against the Plateados, then what could the blacksmith, a poor artisan, do?" Manuela asked, protruding her beautiful lower lip scornfully.

"Although he's a poor artisan, that blacksmith is every inch a man. In the first place, by marrying him, you would come under his legal protection, and it's not the same, being a girl whose only protection is a weak old woman like me, who everybody can deceive, as being a married woman who can depend on a husband, who has the power to protect her, who has friends, many friends with weapons at the hacienda who would fight alongside him to the death. Nicolás is brave, they've never dared attack him on the roads; besides, his assistants at the forge and his worker friends on the property love him dearly. The Plateados would never dare touch him at Atlihuayán, I assure you of that. Those thieves, when all's said and done, attack only fearful townsfolk and defenseless travelers, but they don't take any chances with those who are strong hearted. In the second place, if you didn't want to stay here, Nicolás has earned a fair amount of money from his work, and he has his savings. The man who trained him, a foreigner who left him in charge of the hacienda's forge, is in Mexico City and loves him dearly, and we could go live there until these troubled times come to an end."[5]

"No! Never, mama," Manuela interrupted brusquely.

"I am determined, I shall never marry that horrible Indian, who I can't look at . . . He disgusts me dreadfully, I can't stand his presence . . . I prefer any thing to marrying that man . . . I prefer the Plateados," she added with arrogant tenacity.

"Yes?" said her mother, throwing down her knitting, incensed. "You prefer the Plateados? Well, be careful about what you say, because if you don't wish to honorably marry a boy who's honor's worth its weight in gold and who could make you happy and respected, then you'll be gnawing your knuckles in desperation when you find yourself in the arms of those bandits, who are demons vomited out of hell. My God, I shall never witness such a thing; no, I would die first of grief and shame," she added, shedding angry tears.

Manuela sat brooding as Pilar moved closer to the poor old woman to console her.

"Just look at that," the señora said to the humble dark-skinned maiden who had been listening silently to the conversation between mother and daughter. "You, my goddaughter and not so obligated to me as this ingrate, and you wouldn't cause me such pain, I am sure."

Then, after a moment's silence that was awkward for the three women, the señora said with marked irony and spitefulness: "Horrible Indian! You'd think this swelled head deserved nothing less than Saint Aloysius Gonzaga.[6] How do you come to put on such airs, a poor girl

---

(5) This description of Nicolás resonates with the author's relationship to a Spanish landholder, Luis Rovalo, owner of the Santa Inés estate in Cuautla, with whom Altamirano resided in 1853. Recalling his own rise from the Indian class, Altamirano singled out Rovalo in particular: "I, too, am an offspring of beneficence, I, too, born into the most humble and underprivileged of classes, into the Indian class, owe my primary instruction to the beneficence of a village, and my secondary education to the State of Mexico, and to a dignified and noble Spaniard whom I cannot recall without the most tender gratitude." *See* Ignacio Manuel Altamirano, *Obras Completas: Ignacio Manuel Altamirano IX: Crónicas III,* ed. Carlos Monsivais (México: Conaculta/SEP, 1986) 22-45.—*Eds.*

like you, even if you do have, thanks to the grace of God, that little white face and those eyes so talked about by all the shopkeepers in Yautepec? You're so puffed up anyone would think you were the mistress of a hacienda. Neither your father nor I put those ideas into your head. Your upbringing has been humble. We taught you to cherish honesty, not looks or wealth. Good looks come to an end with illness and age, and money disappears like wine; honor alone is a treasure that never dwindles. Horrible Indian! A poor artisan! But that poor Indian, that poor blacksmith is a principled boy who started out as a poor little orphan in Tepoztlán, who learned to read and write as a child, and then went into blacksmithing and, at an age when most people earn no more than a day's wages, he is already the master blacksmith at the forge and is held in high regard by the rich and has a good reputation and has earned what little he has by the sweat of his brow and his integrity. That would be good at any time, and all the more so now, especially in these parts; it's an honor few can claim. Perhaps there is no other boy around here to compare with him. Tell me, Pilar, am I right?"

"Yes, godmother," the modest young woman replied, "you are more than right. Nicolás is a very good man, a hard worker, a man who loves Manuela very much, who would make a husband like few others, who would please her in every way. I'm always telling that to my sister. Besides, I don't find him horrible at all . . . "

"How can he be horrible!" cried the señora. "Rather,

---

(6) *Gongaza*: Aloysius Gonzaga (1568-1591) was born in the castle of Castiglione. From the age of eight, he served in the Medici court for two years and then resided for a while with the Duke of Mantua. Still a boy, he adopted a chaste, ascetic mode of life in reaction to these courtly experiences. In Madrid, at thirteen, he and his brother Ridolfo were appointed pages to the king's son, don Diego, Prince of Asturias. In 1585, back in Italy, he renounced his inheritance in his brother's favor and was accepted into the Jesuit order. A brilliant scholar of philosophy and in his fourth year of theological studies, he devoted himself to the care of the sick during a famine and pestilence in 1591, dying that same year at the age of twenty-three.—*Eds.*

it's just that she's foolish, and, not loving him, dresses him in defects as if he were a scarecrow. But Nicolás is a boy like every other, and there's nothing in him to cause fright. He's not white, not Spanish, not glittering with gold and silver like the hacienda bosses and the Plateados, and he doesn't shine at dances and parties. He is quiet and shy, but that doesn't seem a fault to me."

"Nor to me," added Pilar.

"All right, Pilar," Manuela said, "since you like him so much, why don't you marry him?"

"Me?" she asked, first turning pale and then blushing to the point of tears. "Me, sister? But why would you say that to me? I'm not marrying him because it's you he loves, not me."

"So, if he courted you, you would return his love?" asked the relentless Manuela, smirking wickedly.

Pilar may have been going to respond, but at that moment there came a soft, timid knocking at the door.

"It's Nicolás," said the señora. "Pilar, go open the door for him."

The humble girl, still confused and flushed, swiftly removed the garland of blossoms from her hair and placed it on the bench.

"Why do you take off your blossoms?" Manuela asked, quickly throwing away the roses and calendulas that she had put on.

"I took them off because they are bridal flowers, and I am not the bride here," Pilar replied sadly, not a little cross. "And you? Why do you take off yours?"

"Me? Because I have no desire to look pretty for that Indian, an upstanding man who merits a shrine."

Pilar went to open the door, taking all the precautions that people took in Yautepec at that time.

Nicolás

Anyone hearing Manuela speak of the Atlihuayán blacksmith as contemptuously as she had might have imagined that he was a monster, a repulsive scarecrow who could inspire nothing but fear or revulsion.

Well: they would have been deceived. The man who, after crossing through the rooms of the house, made his way out to the patio where we heard the conversation between the older señora and the two girls, was a dark-skinned youth, markedly Indian in appearance, but tall and slender, herculean in build and well proportioned, whose intelligent, benevolent features certainly favored him. His sweet, black eyes, his aquiline nose, his wide mouth filled with gleaming, white teeth, his thick lips scarcely shadowed by a sparsely sprouting beard gave him something of a melancholy appearance, but strong and virile at the same time. Recognizably an Indian, but not a contemptible, servile Indian; rather, a cultured man ennobled by his work, and well aware of his strength and worth. Unlike laborers on the sugarcane haciendas, he was not dressed in a light-colored twill jacket but, like a sailor, in a kind of fine, blue flannel shirt, cinched at the waist with a wide leather belt stuffed with rifle cartridges, because at that time everyone had to be armed and prepared to defend themselves. He also wore *calzonera*, with dark buttons, sturdy boots, and a broad-brimmed, gray felt hat but without any silver ornaments. Obviously, in his way of dressing he made a determined attempt to distinguish himself from the bandits who flaunted silver ornaments on their clothing and, particularly, on their hats, earning them the name by which they were known throughout the republic.

On his daily visits to Manuela's family, Nicolás customarily left his horse and guns next door so as to depart, after night had fallen, for the Hacienda de Atlihuayán, less than a mile from Yautepec.

After the usual greetings, Nicolás went to sit beside the señora on another rustic bench and, noticing the roses that Manuela had torn from her hair and that now lay strewn haphazardly at her feet, he asked, "Manuelita, why have you thrown off all those flowers?"

"I was making a garland," she replied dryly, "but I got tired of it and flung them down."

"And they're so beautiful," said Nicolás, bending down to gather a few roses, which Manuelita observed with marked displeasure. "You're always so dissatisfied," he added sadly.

"My poor daughter! As long as we're in Yautepec and locked up," said the mother, "we can't have a moment's pleasure."

"You're right," Nicolás replied. "And your brother, has he written?"

"Nothing, not a single letter; we haven't had even an explanation from him. I'm losing hope . . . And what news do you bring us today, Nicolás?"

"You know already, señora," Nicolás said with a somber air, "the same as always . . . kidnappings, hold-ups, murders everywhere you turn, that's all there is . . . The day before yesterday the Plateados from Xochimancas took away the *purgador*[7] at the Hacienda de San Carlos. Yesterday morning, another gang carried off the field hand who had gone only as far as the hacienda gate; later they killed a group of muleteers who were on their way from Cocoyac to Mexico City.

"God have mercy!" cried the señora, "we really can't live in these parts any longer! I'm truly desperate", and I don't know how to get out of here . . ."

---

(7) *purgador*: worker in charge of the final stage of refining the sugar, purging it of the remaining molasses.—*Eds.*

"Speaking of that," Nicolás went on, "if you persist, señora, in wanting to go to Mexico City, and, given your rejection of my offer to accompany you, you'll soon have an opportunity."

"Really? How?" the señora asked eagerly.

"We've learned that government cavalry ought to have arrived here this morning, because yesterday evening they set out from Cuernavaca in this direction, and slept in Xiutepec; but at dawn they received orders to pursue a party of bandits who, that same night, held up a rich foreign family on their way to Acapulco, escorted by some armed men. It seems that the family, precisely to see if they could evade the thieves, set off from Cuernavaca once it was dark, and they were traveling hurriedly so as to reach Puente de Ixtla or San Gabriel early today. But near Alpuyeca a gang of Plateados was waiting for them. The other foreigners traveling with the family defended themselves, but the escorts turned traitor and took up with the bandits, so those poor foreigners were left dead there along with the family, who also perished."

"Dear Jesus! How awful!" the señora and Pilar exclaimed, while Manuela paled slightly and grew pensive.

"It seems it was something appalling," Nicolás continued. "At dawn the corpses were strewn about, but only the corpses, because the bandits naturally took the luggage, mules, horses, and everything else. The news reached Cuernavaca very early; later the residents of Apuyeca brought down the bodies, children among them, on stretchers. So there you have the reason why government troops, who were coming this way, received orders to go to join another troop that was leaving Cuernavaca in pursuit of the bandits."

"And they'll catch them? Do you think they'll catch them, Nicolás?" the señora asked.

"No," the honest young man responded, intensely bitter, "they won't catch anybody. They are few in number, compared to the Plateados, who must have taken refuge in Xochimancas. There alone they have more than five hundred men, well armed and mounted, without counting the many gangs roaming all the roads. Besides, we're accustomed now to these empty shows of strength. When there's a noteworthy robbery or distinguished people are held up, then they make a big fuss, the government in Mexico City sends intimidating orders to the local authorities, who then marshal their small forces, infiltrated by the bandits' many accomplices who give them early warning. There's a commotion for a week or two, and that's the end of it. Meanwhile, no one pays attention to the robberies, the holdups, the murders committed, day in and day out, all along the way here, because the victims are miserable wretches, without any titles or anything else to call attention to them."

"My God, Nicolás," the señora exclaimed with concern, "and you, risking your life every afternoon by coming from Atlihuayán just to see us! I beg you not to do it anymore . . ."

"Oh, no, señora," Nicolás replied, smiling calmly. "Don't you worry about me. I'm poor, I have nothing for them to steal from me . . . Besides, the distance from Atlihuayán to here is very short; truly, I risk nothing by coming."

"How can you not be risking anything?" the señora responded. "In the first place, although you're poor, everyone knows you're an honest, thrifty artisan, you're the master blacksmith at the Atlihuayán forge, and they must imagine you have something saved away; then too, if it were only because of the fine horses you ride and the fine arms you carry . . ."

"Oh, señora!" Nicolás exclaimed, laughing, "what I might have saved isn't worth these men's trouble in attacking me, because they only take risks for bigger gains. On the other hand, they know full well that I'd never let myself be kidnapped. That's not boasting, but the truth is, señora, I'd rather die once than endure the thousand deaths of the kidnapped. You must have heard what they do to them. All right then, the best way to escape those torments is to defend yourself to the death. At least that way, they're forced to pay dearly for their victory and a man saves his dignity," he added with manly pride.

"Oh! If only everyone thought that way," the señora said, "if everyone resolved to defend themselves, there would be no bandits, and we wouldn't need government forces, or to live here scared to death, trembling like scared birds."

"That's true, señora, that's how it ought to be, and all that's needed is a little cold blood. You see, in Atlihuayán, everyone was afraid when the bandits began to overrun the place, and they didn't know which side to take. But before they started stepping on our shadows, the machinists at the hacienda and we blacksmiths all got together and resolved to buy good horses and to arm ourselves well, deciding to always defend ourselves collectively, few as we might be. As soon as our decision was known, the administrator of the estate and all the hands also joined us, and since the great advantage the Plateados have in threatening haciendas and towns is their always having accomplices and spies among the people, we resolved to throw off the hacienda anyone suspected of conniving with the bandits. That way, all the workers at Atlihuayán are loyal and help us, the hacienda is well armed, and we only risk the bandits burning the cane fields. But by keeping close watch every night, we are able to avoid that danger as much as possible. They've already demanded money from the *hacendado*, they've already threatened him with burning down the hacienda, but he hasn't paid any heed to them. They've written letters to us as well, demanding money, too, but we haven't responded to them. As for me, in particular, I know that they hate me, that some have offered to kill me, and I don't know why, since I haven't harmed anyone, not even the bandits. Most likely it's because they know I'm determined to defend myself and my men are, too. But I don't worry, and go on as I have up to now, without anyone's attacking me on the roads."

"But you always ride alone, Nicolás," the señora said, "and that's foolhardy."

"When I can, I ride with others; for example, when I have to go to a hacienda at some distance . . . but coming here, I don't think there's any need for company. But in all this, what's important is the matter of your leaving here. As I was saying, the troops that were coming to Yautepec are engaged today in pursuing the attackers along the Alpuyeca road, who by now are probably in their hideout. As a result, the forces will return to Cuernavaca and come here afterward. Now's the time to take advantage of this turn of events, and you can be getting yourselves ready for the journey."

"It looks that way now," the señora said, "and we're certainly going to get ready. Thank you for the news, Nicolás, and I hope you'll come to see us, just as always, to tell us about anything new, and that you'll do me the favor of taking care of my things . . . I have no trustworthy man but you . . ."

"Señora, you already know that I'm at your disposal for anything, and you can rest easy about your things, since I'm staying here."

"I know, I know, and I'll expect you tomorrow, as always. Now it's time for you to go, it's already dark, and I tremble at what might happen to you on the little stretch between Yautepec and the hacienda, so short, but so perilous . . . Goodbye!" she said, taking Nicolás's hand. He went straight to bid farewell to Manuela, who held her hand out to him frostily, and to Pilar, who said goodbye with her usual, humble timidity.

When the horse could be heard trotting down the street, the señora, who had grown sad and silent, sighed painfully.

"My only regret in going away from this place," she said, "will be leaving behind that boy, who's our only guardian in life. How happy I'd be to have him as my son-in-law!"

"And stop about the son-in-law, mamá!" said Manuela, going over to the poor woman and embracing her lovingly. "Don't think about that! Now we're going to get out of here, and you'll have a different son-in-law who's better."

"This one offers you honorable love," said the señora.

"But not a love to my liking," the beautiful young woman retorted, knitting her brow and smiling.

"God willing, you'll never repent having refused him."

"No, mamá, of that you can be sure. I'll never regret it. The heart goes where it desires . . . not where it's commanded!" she added slowly, smiling gravely . . . helping her mother to rise from her stool.

Night in fact had closed in: the Tierra Caliente's plentiful drizzle had begun to fall, shadows from the trees in the orchard became darker in the light that began falling from the moon, and the family retired to their rooms.

El Zarco

At the same time that this was happening in Yautepec, to one side of the Hacienda de Atlihuayán, on a steep, rocky path leading down the mountain and lined with tall weeds and thick-crowned trees, a dapper horseman singing in a high-pitched, cheerful voice slowly picked his way, mounted on a spirited sorrel horse that seemed to be losing its patience with stepping tortuously along that trail on which its shoes clinked, throwing off sparks.

The rider held him back at every step and. with the calmest bearing, seemed to be giving himself over to delicious reverie, with one leg crossed over the saddle horn, like women riders, as he absentmindedly sang, over and over, one verse of an odd folk song composed by bandits and very well known in those parts:

> *Much as I like silver,*
> *I like glory more,*
> *That's why I carry a lasso*
> *For the woman I'll adore.*

Riding sidesaddle like that, the rider seemed in no hurry to get down to the flat land, and from time to time he stopped for a moment to give his horse a chance to breathe and to contemplate the moon through the clearings that cropped up among the mountain's trees. Gazing intently like that, he also observed the stars and seemed to check the time, as if he had some pending engagement.

Finally, upon his rounding a bend in the road, the trees began to grow more sparsely, the weeds smaller, the trail wider and less rough, the hill seemed to billow softly, and everything pointed to the nearness of the plain. After the horseman observed this region, tamer than what he had left behind him, he stopped for a moment, extended his crossed leg, stretched lazily, steadied himself in the stirrups, quickly examined the two pistols he wore at his waist as well as the musket hanging in its saddle case, then looked to the right and behind him, as was the custom in those days, and then carefully unwound the long strip of red wool wrapped around his neck and put it on again, but this time covering his face almost up to the eyes. Then he turned a little way off the path and rode toward a short flat stretch and set himself to studying the landscape.

By now the moon had appeared on the horizon and was rising majestically in the sky among clusters of clouds. In the distance, the mountains and hills created a thick, black frame for the gray scene in which stood out the dark masses of the haciendas, the enormous swathe of Yautepec, the knolls and groves, and, at the foot of the hill that provided the horseman with a look-out, the cane fields of Atlihuayán came into view distinctly, dotted with lightning bugs, and in their midst the hacienda's large buildings with their tall chimneys, arches, and light-filled windows. Noise from the machinery could even be heard, as well as the distant murmur of workers and the poor mulattos' melancholy song, like that of their grandparents, the slaves, allaying their weariness or bringing the day's work to an end.[8]

That calm, peaceful view of nature and that sacred sound of labor and movement, which seemed a hymn to virtue, did not appear to make any impression on the soul of that rider, whose only concern was the time, because, after having lingered in silent contemplation for some minutes, he dismounted and went walking his horse along the mesa for

---

(8) *slaves*: At the beginning of the 17th century in Mexico, Black slaves were introduced as replacements for indigenous workers, who were excluded from labor after the prohibitions of 1599. During the next two centuries, slaves constituted the nucleus of the haciendas' workforce in producing sugar. The total workforce at Xochimancas is unknown, but from 1660 to 1674, records show around 216 slaves.—*Eds./ Sol, 137.*

a while; then he tightened the saddle's cinch and surveying the moon and stars once more, he continued on his way cautiously and in silence. Shortly thereafter he was already down on the plain and entering upon a wide path that led to the hacienda's crossbeam gate, but on reaching a crossroads he took the road that leads to Yautepec, leaving the hacienda behind him.

He had scarcely started down that road, at a walking gait, when a short way off and riding in the opposite direction, he saw another rider, also moving at a walk and mounted on a magnificent dark horse.

"It's the blacksmith from Atlihuayán!" he muttered, pulling down the wide brim of his sombrero so as not to be seen, although his wool scarf covered his face to the eyes.

Afterward he murmured, turning his head slightly to watch the horseman slowly riding away: "What good horses that Indian's got! But he won't leave . . . We shall see!" he added threateningly.

And he kept on riding until he came close to the town of Yautepec. There he left the highway and took a little path that led to the basin of the river flowing through the town. Then he followed the southern bank all the way to a small bend where, after running between two high banks covered with weeds and cactus and wild trees, the river empties into a flat, sandy stretch before being channeled between the two rows of vast, dense orchards flanking it in the town. There the moon shone full upon the fields, shimmering on the river's clear waters, and by its light the mysterious horseman who had come down from the mountain could be seen clearly.

He was a young man of about thirty, tall, well proportioned, with herculean shoulders, and literally covered in silver. The horse he rode was a superb sorrel, of good height, muscular, with sturdy shoulders, small hooves, and powerful haunches like all mountain horses, a slender neck, and an erect, intelligent head—what ranchers call a *caballo de pelea*,[9] The rider was dressed like the bandits of that day and like our *charros*, like the most *charro* of today's *charros*. He wore a dark woolen jacket embroidered with silver and *calzoneras*, decorated down each side with a double row of silver *chapetones*,[10] linked by little chains, and lacings of the same metal. The broad, flat brim of his dark wool sombrero was trimmed, as much on the underside as on the upper, with a thick, wide band of silver braid embroidered with gold stars; encircling the low, rounded crown was a double silver hatband from which dangled, at either side, two thin disks, also in silver, in the shape of medals, topped by golden rings. In addition to the woolen scarf covering his face, he was wearing a woolen shirt under his jacket, and on his belt a pair of pistols with ivory hilts, in their silver-worked, patent leather holsters. Over his belt was tied a *canana*, a wide, double band of leather whose compartments were stuffed with rifle cartridges, and over the saddle a silver-handled machete in its sheath, worked with more of the same. The saddle he was mounted on was heavily worked in silver, the large saddle horn a mass of that metal, the same as the cantle and stirrups, while the bridle was laden with silver disks, stars, and whimsical figures. On top of the beautiful black goatskin saddlebag and slung from the saddle, hung

---

(9) *caballo de pelea*: a fighting horse; el Zarco rides an exceptionally fine and well-kept steed. Compare the Argentine Estanislao S. Zeballos's 1878 *La Conquista de Quince Mil Leguas*, in which the author categorizes military horses: 1. Marching and service horses, 2. Reserves for the same marching and service functions, 3. Fighting horses. The first are inferior, even frail, but serviceable; the second full-fleshed for sustaining wearisome marches and rapid deployments; the third "to be saddled only in extreme cases, usually selected, scrupulously cared for, and trained by the soldier. . . ." (Ediciones elaleph.com, 2000, 455)—*Eds.*

(10) *chapetones*: small, round-headed studs or flat metal plates, sometimes given decorative or figurative shapes, that run the length of the side opening or pleat in the *charro's* trousers, the opening being bridged by slim chains attached to the *chapetones.—Eds./Sol 39*

a musket in its case, also trimmed, and behind the cantle a large oilcloth cape was secured. And everywhere, silver: in the ornamenting of the saddle, on the leather stirrup straps, on the holster cover, on the tiger-skin chaps hanging from the saddle horn, on the spurs—on everything. All that made for a lot of silver and clearly showed the effort to lavish it everywhere. It was an insolent ostentation, cynical and tasteless. The moonlight caused the silvery ensemble to gleam, giving the horseman the appearance of a strange ghost in a sort of silver armor, something like a picador in the bullring or a mottled centurion during a Holy Week procession.

The rider sat examining the place for a few moments. All was peaceful and silent. The plains and sugarcane fields spread in the distance, blanketed in silvery moonlight, like transparent gauze. The orchard trees stood motionless. Yautepec seemed a cemetery. Not a light in the houses, not a sound on the streets. The night birds seemed asleep, and only the faint sibilance of insects could be heard in the banana trees while a cloud of fireflies fluttered in the shadowy masses of the dark groves.

The moon was at its zenith and it was eleven o'clock at night.

After this rapid survey, the Plateado withdrew to a bend in the river bed near a tree-lined bank and there, totally hidden in shadow, he dropped to his feet on the dry and sandy shore, unfastened his lariat, unbridled his horse and, holding it loosely by the lasso, allowed it to go a little way off to drink water. When the animal's needs had been satisfied, he bridled it once more, and mounted it nimbly, crossed the river, and turned into one of the narrow dark lanes formed between the orchards' walls of trees and leading out onto the river.

He kept to a walk for some minutes, as though exercising caution, until he came alongside the stonewalls of a vast, magnificent orchard. There he halted at the base of a colossal sapodilla tree whose leafy branches covered the entire width of the lane like an arch.

And with his eyes trying to pierce the pitch-dark shadow shrouding the enclosure, he settled for voicing, twice in a row, a sort of summoning sound: "Psst! . . . Psst!" he hissed.

To which another sound of the same sort responded from the wall, over which a white figure did not take long in appearing.

"Manuelita!" the Plateado murmured.

"My Zarco, here I am!" a woman's sweet voice responded.

That man was el Zarco, the notorious bandit whose renown had filled the whole region with terror.

The Tryst

The wall was not high, being built from large stones among which hundreds of creepers, nettles, and tall, slender cactus had sprouted, forming a thick barrier, covered with a curtain of greenery. Taking advantage of a clear spot on top of this wall and beneath the shading branches of the sapodilla whose knotty trunk offered a natural stairway from within the orchard, Manuelita had improvised a seat, from which to talk to el Zarco during their frequent meetings at night.

During these meetings, the outlaw did not dismount from his horse. Extremely distrustful, like all men of his kind, he always preferred to be prepared to fight or flee, even when speaking with his beloved in the late hours of the night, in the solitude of that deserted lane, while the townspeople slept by fits and starts, not one of them daring to show his face after the curfew.

What is more, being on horseback put him within reach of the young woman for speaking to her and embracing her comfortably, as the wall was no higher than his horse's saddle horn, and the animal, trained like all bandit horses, knew to keep still when his rider demanded it. On the other hand, a wide gap in the curtain of vegetation covering the stonewall allowed the lovers to speak to each other at close range, entwine their hands, and abandon themselves to the intimacies of a violent, impassioned love.

At different times some of the Yautepec neighbors, who were used to walking down that lane in the morning on their way to the fields, had noticed a horse's hoof prints after rainy nights, hoof prints coming from the river and going back toward it and indicating that someone had been halted there for a long time. But they supposed either that the tracks were those of a *campesino* who had come by there the previous afternoon or, at most, they suspected that Nicolás, the Atlihuayán blacksmith whose love for Manuela was well known, had met with her; although, everyone knew, on the other hand, that the girl showed a deep aversion for the blacksmith, something they attributed to a hypocritical deception belied by the accusing tracks.

As for doña Antonia, Manuelita's mother, she had absolutely no idea, as might be imagined, that her daughter met with anyone, and was totally ignorant even of the talk about hoof prints near her orchard wall.

So, cloaked by that deep secret, which no one would have dared to guess, Manuela went out to talk with her lover as often as his risky thieving and pillaging forays permitted. He seemed very much in love with the beautiful girl, since, no sooner could he spare a few hours than he took advantage of them, bartering rest and sleep, to come to talk for an hour with his lover, whom he regularly notified in advance by means of his messengers and accomplices in Yautepec.

This time she was waiting for him more impatiently than ever, alarmed by the dangers that the afternoon's decisions heralded for their love.

"I was afraid you wouldn't come tonight, and I was waiting for you so anxiously," Manuela said, quivering with passion and distress.

"Well, my love, I almost didn't come," el Zarco responded, drawing closer to the wall and taking her trembling hands in his. "We had a scuffle last night: a damned *gringo*[11] nearly killed me, and I scarcely had time to go by Xochimancas, change horses, have something to eat and a little coffee, and I've come twenty leagues to see you . . . But, what is it? Are you trembling? Why were you waiting for me so anxiously?"

---

11) *gringo: "A name for someone who speaks a foreign language. In South America the common people use gringo to refer to all foreigners, especially Italians.* Mexican usage designates all those foreigners not of Latin origin, and most especially the English and North Americans, as *gringos*." (Joaquín García Icazbalceta, *Vocabulario de mexicanismos*, Mexico: Academia de la Lengua, 1975).—*Sol, 145*

"Tell me: were you part of that Alpuyeca business?"

"Yes. I led the forces myself. Why do you ask me that? How did you find out so quickly?"

"Well, you'll soon find out: that tedious blacksmith came this evening, as always, and, with my mother telling him she couldn't wait to leave here for Mexico City but didn't see how, because my uncle isn't coming, he told her that a company of government cavalry had left Cuernavaca yesterday and was on the way to Yautepec, and that they'd stopped to sleep in Jiutepec, but that in the morning they'd received a frenzied order to chase a gang who'd killed some foreigners last night at Alpuyeca and that they'd left for there . . ."

"We knew that already . . . they say they're going to charge their troops at us . . . imagine: two hundred men at most! They'd better take care not to come close to Xochimancas. There, they'd lose their hides . . . And what else?"

"Well, then he went on to say that those government troops will never catch anyone, and that they'll turn back in the direction of Yautepec to continue their march; that then we could make the most of that opportunity to leave with the troops."

"You and your mother?"

"Yes, both us, and my mother said she thought it seemed a good idea to her, that we were going to get ready to leave, and she even asked the blacksmith to come tomorrow to bring her recent news and for her to charge him with her responsibilities."

"Ay, *caramba*! So it's true?"

"Really true, Zarco, really true. My mother is so frightened, have no doubt about it, that she'll make the most of this opportunity, and she's already told me that we're packing our trunks with the most necessary things, and that tomorrow she'll go to ask for her money from the person who has it in safekeeping, and . . . we're going away!"

"Impossible!" the bandit exclaimed violently. "Impossible! She can go, but not you. They'll have to kill me first."

"But, what do we do then?"

"Refuse."

"Oh! Zarco, it'll be useless, you don't know my mamá: when she says something, you do it; when she orders something, you can't answer her back. I have enough quarrels every day, because she wants to force me into marrying the Indian, and the more I show her my determination not to unite myself in marriage with that man, the more I slight him, and I've told him to his face many times that I don't love him, my mother persists in her stubbornness, and the blacksmith also keeps coming around, certainly because my mother doesn't clip his wings so that he'll give up his foolishness. But, when it comes down to it, I can disobey her about this, because I can plead my lack of love, but in the matter of our going away . . . you can see, it's impossible."

"Well, let me think," said el Zarco, beginning to ponder.

"Tell me," Manuela interrupted, "couldn't all of you attack the government troops at Las Tetillas or some other place and defeat them? There are a lot of you . . . "

"Yes, my love, that would be possible, and we'd win, but I'll tell you frankly: the boys take risks in these ventures only when they expect to seize loot or when they defend themselves, seeing no other way out . . . but here they'd have no inducement . . . they'll say that all they'd get in exchange for attacking these troops are bullets flying after them, and, at most, if they defeat them, a few underfed horses, old saddles, and uniforms in tatters. The government troops really look like beggars! Besides, they're a hundred men. We'd have to attack them with at least five hundred, and do you think we should gather forces just for that?"

"Well, fine," the vexed young woman replied. "I knew Plateados attacked only the defenseless . . . That's what my mother says."

"The defenseless?" asked el Zarco, piqued in his turn. "That's what your mother says? Well, the good woman is mistaken: we can attack troops too, and we're weary of doing it and winning . . . The defenseless! Well, she ought to have seen the skirmish last night. Those *gringos* were like devils . . . they defended themselves with their rifles, with their pistols, with their swords . . ."

"Oh, Zarco, they say women and children were killed!"

"Who says that?"

"The blacksmith."

"Lying Indian!"

"Isn't it true?"

"That they died? Yes, they died. But we didn't kill them, they died in the struggle. Anyway, let's not talk about that business, Manuelita, because you're wounding me."

"No, my love, no," she replied, her voice infinitely tender, her arms encircling the bandit's neck. "Me, offend you, who are everything I love."

"Yes, Manuelita," he said, breaking free of her arms, "everything you've been telling me is because you think I'm a coward."

"Me, think you're a coward, Zarco?" she asked, bursting into tears. "But, how could you think such a thing? When I believe you're the bravest man in the world, when I'm wild with passion for you, when I sometimes think my heart will burst from sorrow while you're gone, fearing all the risks you run . . . when I'm yours completely . . . and I do what you want."

"All right," the bandit said, sweetening his voice, kissing her ardently, "all right, now don't cry, I'm not resentful anymore . . . but don't say those things to me again."

"But really, I'm only telling you what people say. I get furious when I hear it, and my only consolation is telling you about it. Now, as for my wanting an attack on the troops, you have to see that it comes from the very love I feel for you, so they don't separate us. If you have another way . . . like getting married, for example . . ."

"Getting married?"

"Yes, why not?"

"But, haven't you considered that we can't get married?"

"Why? Tell me."

"For a thousand reasons. Leading the life I lead, being as notorious as I am, having so many cases pending in the courts, there being, naturally, orders to hang me wherever they catch me, where do you expect me to go to present myself so we can get married? You're crazy!"

"But, can't we go far away from these parts—to Puebla, the South, Morelia where nobody knows you—and get married there?"

"But to do that I'd have to take you away from here, I'd have to abduct you, you'd have to come with me to Xochimancas while . . . and later we'd travel somewhere else."

"All right," the young woman replied resolutely, after reflecting for a moment, "since that's the only way, take me away from here, I'll go with you wherever you want."

"But, can you reconcile yourself to the life I lead, even for these few days? We'll go to Xochimancas, you already know who my companions are; it's true they have their girls there, but they're not like you: they're used to working, they ride horses, go without food sometimes, stay up all night, aren't scandalized by what goes on, because sometimes quite nasty things happen . . . In short, they're like us men. You're a girl brought up differently . . . your

mother loves you very much . . . I'm afraid that you'll
be offended, you'll cry, thinking back on your mother
and Yautepec . . . you'll put the blame on me for your
wretchedness, you'll detest me."

"That will never happen, Zarco, never. I'll do
whatever work comes along, I too know how to ride a
horse, and I'll fast and stay up all night, and I'll observe
everything and won't be appalled, just as long as I'm by your
side. Look," Manuela added, her voice muffled, lost in her
frenzied passion, "I love my mamá very much, I really do,
although the last few days, for that matter, I seem to love
her less. I know that maybe I'm going to be the cause of her
death, but I promise you not to cry when I recall her, on the
condition that you're with me, that you'll always love me, as
I love you, that we soon go away from this place."

The bandit clasped her tightly in his arms and
devoured her with kisses, moved by this outburst of love,
so passionate, so excessive, so sincere, that it bordered on
frenzy; and he surrendered himself entirely to that young
woman, so beautiful, so longed for, so dreamed of during
his passionate, wishful hours. Because el Zarco also loved
Manuela; except that he loved her in the only way a man
mired in crime could love, a man to whom all notion of good
was alien, in whose dark, perverted soul there was room only
for the pleasures of a bestial sensuality and the despicable
emotions that robbery and murder can evoke. He loved her
because she was pretty, inexperienced, striking; because
of beauty's attractiveness and voluptuousness, her opulent
figure, her languorous, provocative walk, her fiery black
eyes, her pomegranate lips, her smooth, musical voice—all
this held a terrible sway over his senses, excited day after
day by sleeplessness and constant obsession with that vision.
This sensation was not love in the noble sense of the word;
it was desire, incited by impatience and coaxed by vanity,
because in fact the bandit ought to have considered himself

fortunate in winning the favor of the prettiest woman in the region.

Which is why as soon as el Zarco was sure that the young woman had resolved to face up to it all in order to take up with him, he felt happy, and all the blood in his veins flowed to his heart for that supreme instant.

"All right," he said, pulling himself out of Manuela's arms. "Then there's nothing more to talk about, you leave with me and we go away . . ."

"Now?" she asked, somewhat indecisive.

"No, not now," the bandit replied. "It's late now and you couldn't get ready. Tomorrow. I'll come for you at the same time, at eleven. Don't give your mother anything to be suspicious about. During the day, act as though it's a day like any other, make a show of it. Don't bring more clothing than what's absolutely necessary. You'll have everything you want up there, but take your jewelry and the money I've given you. You keep all that separate, don't you?"

"Yes, I have it in a small trunk, buried."

"All right then, dig it up and wait for me here tomorrow, without fail."

"And, if by chance, the government troops arrive?" Manuela asked uneasily.

"No, they won't, be sure of that. The government troops will have been riding around all day today, looking for us; and then, since the soldiers have such scraggy, miserable horses, they'll rest all day tomorrow and at best will return to Cuernavaca the day after tomorrow, so they won't be here for at least four days. So we have time. You get your trunks ready with your mother as if you were preparing for the trip to Mexico City, leaving out only the clothes you need to bring. If by misfortune some difficulty arises that prevents you from coming out to meet me, you'll let me know at once by way of the old lady, who must wait for me where she knows to warn me. But if nothing happens, don't say a word, even to her. Here," he added, pulling some small boxes out of his jacket pockets and handing them to the girl.

"What is this?" she asked, taking them.

"You'll see them tomorrow, and you'll like them . . . they're jewels! Keep them with the others," he said, embracing her and giving her one last kiss. "Now I must go because it's time. By dawn I'll just be getting to Xochimancas. Until tomorrow, my love."

"Until tomorrow," she replied. "Don't fail . . . "

"Tomorrow you'll be all mine."

"Yours forever," Manuela said, blowing him a kiss and waiting on the wall a moment to see him depart.

El Zarco rode off as he had arrived, at a cautious, walking gait, and soon he was lost in the twists and turns of the lane, scarcely lit by the moon.

The Oleander

As soon as the young woman lost sight of her lover, she
hastened down from the wall by way of the natural steps
formed by the sapodilla's roots, and quickly walked toward
a place in the orchard where a cluster of shrubs and bushes
formed a sort of small grove, dense and dark, at the edge of a
pool filled by the calm waters of the *apantle*.

Then she withdrew a dark lantern[12] from among
the plants and, making her way through the shrubbery,
went directly to the foot of a lush old oleander,[13] covered
in fragrant, poisonous blooms, dwarfing the grove's small
plants. Once there, she sat down on a little grass-covered
mound of earth and by the lantern's light, her hands
trembling, throbbing with impatience, she opened the three
little boxes the bandit had just given her.

"Oh, how pretty," she exclaimed in a low voice on
seeing a diamond ring whose brilliance dazzled her . . . "This
must be worth a mint," she added, taking out the ring and
trying it on the fingers of her left hand, one after the other,
watching it sparkle from every angle. "This really looks like
the sun!"

Then, keeping the ring on, she opened the second
box, and was left stupefied. There were two diamond-
encrusted bracelets, shaped like small serpents, whose gold
links, enameled in bright colors, gave them a fascinating
look. The serpents lay in several twisted coils within the

---

(12) dark lantern (*lanterna sorda* in Spanish, deaf lantern): a lantern whose light can
be blocked by means of a sliding or removable panel.—*Eds./Sol, 155*

(13) *oleander: Nerium oleander*, a tall, evergreen Mediterranean shrub, bears
clustering white, red, pink, or yellow flowers. The plant's leaves and stems, in addition to its flowers, are extremely poisonous—lethal for humans. Placing Manuela
beneath this shrub, Altamirano characteristically exploits his naturalistic setting in
order to evoke important qualities in his fiction; in this case, Manuela's Mediterranean beauty coupled with intrinsic corruption, poisoned as she is by vanity and
material greed.—*Eds./Sol, 155*

satin-lined box, and Manuela hesitated before untangling them but, once finished, she placed them on her wrist, very close to her hand, twining them carefully. And she began flashing them in every direction, holding her hand in various positions.

Then she closed her eyes for a moment, as though dreaming, and opened them again right away, crossing her wrists in the light and contemplating them for a long while.

"Two vipers!" she said, frowning. "The thought of it! They really are two vipers . . . the robbery! But, . . . bah . . ." she added, smiling and blinking her eyes, almost filled by her large, shining black pupils. "What do I care? El Zarco gave them to me, and where they've come from matters little to me . . .!"

Next she opened the third box. This one contained two earrings, also large diamonds.

"Oh, what beautiful earrings!" she said. "Like a queen's!" And once she had admired them in the box, which was scarcely visible in their glinting, sparkling beams, she took those out as well and put them in her ears, having already taken off her own modest gold hoops.

But as she was placing these hoops in the earring box, she noticed something she had not seen and that turned her white, as though paralyzed. She had just seen two drops of fresh blood that stained the box's white satin and must have splashed the earrings as well. Moreover, the box was broken: it did not shut properly, apparently having been wrenched away in a fight to the death.

Manuela remained solemn and somber for a few seconds; it might be said that a battle was being waged in her soul between an already perverted conscience's last pangs of remorse and the irresistible impulses of unbridled, overwhelming greed. The latter triumphed, as was to be expected, and the young woman, whose beautiful countenance then portrayed every sign of the vile passion holding possession of her spirit, shut the box quickly, arching her brows as she set it aside disdainfully and thought only of seeing how the two precious earrings looked in her ears.

Then she took the lantern and, standing up, adorned as she was with her ring, bracelets, and earrings, she walked over to the edge of the pool and bent down there, illuminating her face with the lantern, trying to smile, and yet exhibiting in all her features the sort of arrogant cruelty that is like the reflection of greed and vanity and is capable of disfiguring the perfect face of an angel.

If on that silent night, in the middle of that dark, solitary orchard, anyone practiced in reading character from faces had observed that pretty young woman contemplating herself in the pool's still black waters, illuminating her face with the dim light of a dark lantern and gesturing to give herself the airs of a grande dame, and then had seen that pale face, eyes glinting with ambition and greed, hair tousled, mouth half-open, displaying the close-spaced and whitest of teeth, swinging the earrings left and right, their glow bathing her in a bluish, reddish, or greenish light that blended with the similar glistening that came from the serpents wrapped around her left wrist, now held up to her chin, they surely would have found in that singular figure something frightfully sinister and repulsive, like a satanic ghoul.

This was not Goethe's Marguerite looking at herself in the mirror with natural coquetry, adorned with a stranger's jewels; but, rather, this was a thief of the worst sort, giving free rein to her despicable avarice, before the murky, black waters of a pool. It was not virtue about to succumb to largesse; rather, it was perversity contemplating itself in the mud.[14]

---

(14) *Marguerite*: Mephistopheles tries to help Faust seduce Marguerite by leaving a case of jewels in her clothes chest in order, he tells Faust, " To incline the sweet, tender girl toward the wish and will of your heart." After singing the famous lyric,

Giving way to herself at that hour and in that manner, Manuela allowed her face to show all the expressions of her vile passion, which did not stop at either shame or remorse, because she really knew full well that those jewels were the fruit of crime. That is why, above her head, radiant with flashes from the stolen earrings, could be seen in the shadows, not the mocking face of Mephistopheles, the demon of seduction, but the terrifying mask of the hangman, the demon of the gallows.[15]

Manuela remained there for a few moments, looking at herself in the pool and becoming guarded at the wind's every sound in the trees, and then she returned to the foot of the oleander, took off the jewelry, carefully replaced the pieces in their boxes, and, once finished, cast a look around her and, seeing that all was quiet, she retrieved from among the plants a small *tarecua*, a kind of sharp, wooden-handled, angular-bladed spade used in the Tierra Caliente for digging wells, and, removing the earth at a certain moss-covered spot, uncovered a small leather pouch that she hastily opened with a little key she safeguarded. Then she shone the lantern into the mouth of the pouch, making certain that her treasure was still there, touching it for a moment with peculiar relish.

"The King of Thule," Marguerite enters her room carrying a lantern and discovers the chest; but, though tempted, she soon recognizes that she could never wear the jewelry on the street or in church, and her mother, with a priest's help, demands that the wealth be donated to the Virgin Mary, thereby achieving a heavenly reward. Thus Marguerite shows naïve temptation in contrast to Manuela's poisoned corruption.

    In Gounod's opera (1859) based on Goethe's play, Marguerite's famous "Jewel Song" embodies that young woman's differing response to the Devil's temptation: putting on the earrings and looking into the mirror, she sings: "Is that you, Marguerite? / Answer, answer fast! / No, no—that's not you!" This and Altamirano's other allusions—literary as well as musical—create a contrary Old World frame of reference for the New World action.—*Eds./Sol, 158.*

(15) *Mephistopheles*: the Devil incarnate, who tempts the learned Faust with love, youth, and pleasure in exchange for his soul. Faust succumbs but, just as Marguerite was redeemed, he is finally saved, because his boundless striving permits the angels to rescue him. See note above.—*Eds./Sol, 159.*

It consisted of jewels wrapped in papers and strips of leather wadded with doubloons and silver pesos.

Afterward she carefully placed the boxes el Zarco had just given her in the pouch and reburied the treasure, covering it with moss so that every trace of the earth's being dug up disappeared.

Then, as though regretting the abandonment of those riches, she raised her dark lantern and headed back to the house, on tiptoe, entering through rooms where the poor señora, despite the day's worries, was sleeping the peaceful sleep of the righteous.

Who Was El Zarco?

Meanwhile, and even as Manuela was examining her new jewels, el Zarco, after having left behind the fringes of Yautepec and having crossed the river with the same caution as he had taken upon arriving, headed along the wide Hacienda de Atlihuayán road toward the mountainous one he had come down, which led to Xochimancas.

It was midnight, and the moon's shrouding itself in threatening clouds left the land shrouded in shadow. The Atlihuayán road was totally deserted, and the trees flanking it on both sides projected a sinister, doleful darkness that intensified the fleeting, pale arabesques sketched by glowworms and lightning bugs.

The outlaw, knowledgeable about those parts and practiced, like all men of his class, at partial vision in the dark, and, more than anything else, reliant on the exquisite sensitivity of his horse, which, at the slightest strange noise, pricked up its ears and halted to warn his master, made his way step by step, but wholly at ease, thinking about the coming happiness that the possession of Manuela offered him.

Finally, that most beautiful of young women, whose image had inflamed his sleepless nights for so many months, whose love had constantly absorbed him in the midst of his most risky and bloody adventures, and whose possession had seemed impossible to him when he saw her for the first time in Cuernavaca and fell in love, was going to be his, entirely his, was going to share his fate and lead him into savoring the sweetest delights of love—he, who truly had not known until then more than the poignant emotions of robbery and murder.

His crude, sensual makeup, accustomed to vice from an early age, did, it is true, know the pleasures of carnal love, purchased with gambling or stolen money or torn in the midst of their terror from the victims, on some night's attack upon defenseless villages; but el Zarco felt that he had never loved, never desired a woman with that feverish exaltation he had felt ever since he began seeing her, peeking from her window, ever since hearing her speak, and, even more, since exchanging the first words of love with her.

Since he had left his family's home while still a child, he had never felt the compelling necessity of uniting himself with another as he felt it now, of uniting himself with that woman, so pretty and so passionate, who embodied for him a world of unforeseen joys.

Thus, reviewing in his memory all the scenes of his childhood and youth, he found that his untamed, hardened character had always rejected all kindness, all fondness, whatever feeling it might be, having cultivated only those emotions from which he derived benefit. The son of honest parents—laborers in that region who had tried to make him into a hard-working, useful man—, he had soon grown tired of life at home, where he was made to do daily chores or obliged to go to school; and, taking advantage of the frequent trafficking among the towns out that way and with the sugarcane haciendas, he ran away, coming to settle into service as a groom at one of them.

There he stayed for some time, managing later, when he was sufficiently skilled at riding and the art of caring for horses, to find work on several haciendas, where he never lasted long, owing to his disorderly behavior, since he was an idler by inclination as well as taste and scarcely useful in that menial work, devoting his long stretches of spare time to gambling and idling.

Furthermore, from all that time he recalled feeling neither compassion nor allegiance toward anyone. Never staying long in any place, working a few days at each hacienda and striking up acquaintances only with stable hands or gamblers, which lasted but a moment and alternated with frequent squabbles that turned these relations into intense feuds, he truly had had no friends, only companions in pleasure and vice. Just the reverse: his character was fully formed in those days and there was no longer any room in his heart for anything but evil passions. In this way servility completed what idleness had initiated, and perverse instincts, unbalanced by any notion of good, finally filled that black soul like a swamp's foul algae.

He had loved no one; on the contrary, he hated everyone: the rich *hacendado* whose horses he saddled and adorned with magnificent trappings, the hand who each week earned good wages for his work, the well-off farmer who owned fertile land and a good house, the merchants from nearby towns who owned well-stocked stores, and even the servants who earned better salaries than he did. His was a greed complicated by a powerless, abject envy that led to this singular hatred and frenetic longing to snatch all such things at any cost.

Naturally, other men's loves irritated him, and those girls who, according to their station, loved the rich man, the salesman, or the day laborer inspired him with a senseless desire to snatch them away and sully them. There was not one among them who might have fixed an eye on him, because he had never attempted to approach any of them with amorous intentions. The women of his class were not to his liking, and higher-ranking women found him situated in too low a sphere—a stable hand!

He was young, his features not bad: dirty white complexion, light-blue eyes that the people call *zarco*, light blond hair; while his slim, vigorous build gave him a favorable look; but his sullen scowl, his aggressive, crude language, and his pinched, forced laugh had perhaps made him scarcely likeable to women. Besides, he had not met one beautiful enough to try charming her.

At last, tired of that life of servitude, vice, and

misery, el Zarco fled from the hacienda where he found himself, taking away a few horses to sell in the Tierra Fría. As was to be expected, he was chased, but already at that time, thanks to the civil war, a swarm of bandits had been let loose in the Tierra Fría near Mexico City, and they wasted little time before invading the rich Tierra Caliente regions.

El Zarco allied himself with the bandits immediately and as a matter of course; and, as if he had awaited only this opportunity to reveal himself in all the fullness of his perversity, he began to distinguish himself among those atrociously wicked men, for his fearlessness, his cruelty, and his insatiable thirst for plunder.

The year was 1861, and organized into large parties, pursued sometimes by government troops but, attracted, rather, by the wealth of the sugarcane districts south of Mexico City and in Puebla, the bandits made their way into those areas, sowing terror everywhere, as we have seen.

El Zarco was one of their most notorious leaders, and the news of his infamous exploits, his terrible vengeances against haciendas where he had worked, his cold-blooded cruelty, and his rash bravery had given him a fearsome fame.

Because of a lamentable, shameful error, the Liberal troops were obliged to accept the cooperation of these bandits in pursuing the Reactionary rebel Márquez [16] on his passage across the Tierra Caliente: some of those troops showed up comprised of numerous but irregular units, and one of them was headed by el Zarco. At that time, during the few days he spent in Cuernavaca, he met Manuela, who

---

(16) *Márquez*: Leonardo Márquez (1821-1913) was a Conservative general made famous during the Mexican Wars of Reform (1857-1860) and a military ally of the French during their occupation of Mexico (1863-1867). He was known as the Tiger of Tacubaya because of his 1859 massacre, not only of the leaders of the uprising and all official prisoners but also of medical students tending the Liberal army's wounded in the municipality of Tacubaya on the outskirts of Mexico City. Among

had taken refuge with her family in that city. The bandit then flaunted a military manner, despite his not having put aside the ostentatious horse tack that was almost an attribute of thieves in that epoch and gave them the name of Plateados, by which they were generally known.

The beautiful young woman—her character seemingly in accord with the bandit's and seeing the corps of high-spirited horsemen, showy and colorful, parading past her windows, with, at their head, riding a proud horse and freighted with silver to the point of excess, that terrible young bandit whose name had never sounded in her ear except in tones of terror—felt attracted to him by an emotion that blended sympathy with greed and vanity as in a piquant, delicious potion.

Thus was born a strange kind of love in those two souls made to understand each other.

And in the short time that he remained in Cuernavaca, el Zarco managed to communicate with Manuela and to strike up a romantic relation with her, which nevertheless, owing to the circumstances, did not reach the degree of intimacy we have seen in Yautepec.

General González Ortega,[17] recognizing the grave error he had committed in making a place among his

---

the executed was Altamirano's close friend and fellow novelist, Juan Díaz Covarrubias (1837-1859). See Altamirano's "Los mártires de Tacubaya," collected among his historical works.

In 1861, the year Altamirano refers to, Márquez defeated and then savagely executed, first, the Liberal Melchor Ocampo and then Santos Degollado. At that point, Benito Juárez sent troops against Márquez, who defeated them and executed their leader, Leandro Valle. Márquez later served Maxmilian as minister to Constantinople and head of one of the emperor's chief military divisions. After Maxmilian's execution, he fled to Veracruz and then to Cuba, where he remained in exile for twenty-five years. Granted amnesty in 1892, at the age of 78, Márquez returned to Mexico City, where for nine years he took up a pious, peaceful, tedious life. He finally returned to Havana, where he died, a bachelor, at the age of 93.—*Eds./Sol, 165-66.*

(17) *Ortega*: Jesús González Ortega (1822-1881), a Liberal general, fought during the Wars of Reform and led his troops to important military victories, such as the

forces for several bands of Plateados, who did nothing but devastate the towns they passed through, disgracing the army, wasted no time in setting out in pursuit of them, executing several of their leaders by firing squad. To save himself from a similar fate, el Zarco escaped one night from Cuernavaca with his bandits and headed to the southern part of Puebla, where he remained for a few months, leading horrific raids.

Finally, the Plateados set up their headquarters in Xochimancas, and el Zarco did not take long to learn that Manuela had returned to Yautepec, where she was living with her family. Naturally, he then tried to resume his scarcely interrupted relations with her and was able to make certain that Manuela still loved him

From that point began those frequent, nocturnal assignations with the young woman, assignations that posed no danger to him, given the terror his name instilled and the informers he cultivated in town, where the bandits depended on numerous go-betweens and spies.

Meanwhile, his crimes increased day by day; his vengeances upon his old enemies at the haciendas were atrocious, and his fear-inspiring name turned everyone into cowards. Those same *hacendados*, his former employers, had come trembling into his presence to beg for protection and numbered themselves among his humble, submissive servants, and on not a few occasions he, the old stirrup boy, had been seen holding out his horse's reins to the high-handed lord of the hacienda, whom he had once served, lowly and disdained.

Such vengeances and humiliations were inordinately frequent at that time, given the audacity and the number

---

battles of Querétaro (1859) and Calpulalpan (1860). After those wars, González Ortega was charged by President Juárez to hunt down Conservative guerillas, such as those led by Leonardo Márquez.—*Eds./Sol, 167.*

of bandits, whose power was unlimited in that unfortunate region and all the more so, given the powerlessness of the central government, which, occupied with fighting the civil war and confronting foreign occupation, could not divert its troops to suppress the bandits.

The Owl

El Zarco found himself, therefore, at the height of his arrogant complacency. He had partially realized his aspirations. He was feared; he had avenged himself; he had garnered plentiful spoils from his robberies; he had at his discretionary disposal the *hacendados'* pockets. When in need of a substantial amount of money, he seized a shipment of sugar or cane liquor or a rich employee and put them up for ransom; when he wanted to exact tribute from a hacienda, he burned a cane field; and, when he wanted to fill a town with terror, he murdered the first unlucky inhabitant he encountered on its outskirts.

Yet, even with his thirst for blood and plunder satisfied, he felt that something was still lacking: the pleasures of love, but not those venial pleasures that had been offered him by the passing indulgences of ruined women; rather, those pleasures that could be promised him by the passion of a beautiful, young woman, from a social class superior to his own, who loved him unreservedly and unconditionally.

Manuela would have been a woman beyond his reach when, half hidden in a wealthy *hacendado's* servile retinue, he crossed Yautepec's streets on Sundays. Back then he was certain that the pretty daughter of a well-to-do family—dressed in a certain rustic finery, smiling from her window to accept genteel compliments from rich *hacendados* and high-spirited workers who caracoled on spirited horses dripping with silver to show off before her— would never for a moment have noticed that sad, lackluster servant, badly seated on a sorry old saddle atop an inferior horse, who scurried silently after his masters.

At that time, had he dared approach her to speak, to offer her a flower, or to tell her that he loved her, he undoubtedly would have received nothing more than a disdainful gesture or a mocking laugh as his response.

And now that he was good looking, rode the best horses in those parts, went around wearing silver, was feared, beheld the rich *hacendados* at his feet; now that he could give away jewels worth a fortune; now that that girl, the most beautiful in Yautepec, wept over him, waited for him trembling with love every night, was going to forsake her family for him and give herself to him freely—now he was going to show her off to his partners, walk everywhere with her at his side, humiliate her former suitors.

Such importance did el Zarco give to this love that with Manuela he sensed a bitter, lewd taste of vengeance— upon the young woman herself and upon all the others— together with a note of insolent vanity.

So then, what stirred the bandit's heart was not truly love, in the noble sense of the word, was not the intimate, sacred sentiment that can sometimes make its way even into perverted souls and illuminate them, as a sunbeam illuminates the darkest, foulest of dens. No: it was a sensual, savage desire, aroused to the point of frenzy by the charms of physical beauty, as well as by the attractions of all-conquering pride and vulgar vanity.

If Manuela had been less beautiful or more in need, perhaps el Zarco would not have so forcefully desired to possess her, and it would not have mattered much to him that she had been virtuous. He was not looking to virtue for support in life's suffering but, rather, to coarse feelings of the senses to complement the good fortune of his present situation.

He was going to possess the pretty maiden to satisfy a need of his nature, avid for vainglorious sensations, now that he had savored the lesser pleasure of possessing magnificent horses and amassing doubloons and expensive jewelry.

But after satisfying that desire, the most cherished

of all, what would he do with her, he asked himself. Would he marry her? That was impossible and, besides, having a legitimate wife was not going to flatter his vanity. A sweetheart like her, indeed, that was a triumph among his fellow bandits. Could he give up that way of life and that career of taking risks to flee far away with her, to revel in some hole somewhere in an obscure, quiet life? But that, too, was impossible for that criminal who had already tasted the intoxicating pleasures of combat and robbery. To abandon that turbulent, restless life strewn with peril but also with fat rewards, was to resign himself to being poor, to being peaceable; it was to expose himself to some town's miserable mayor's tying him up one day and locking him up in jail to be judged for his previous misdeeds. He could convert his loot, which was significant, into farmland, a ranch, a store. But he did not know how to work and, more than anything, he was disgusted by an obscure, humble life of labor, so profoundly monotonous, unexciting, tedious, always exposed to the danger of an accusation, with eagerness for nothing except always concealing his criminal past, with no distraction except for taking care of the children, with no emotions except those of terror.

No: it was necessary to go on this way for now; later there would be time to make up his mind, according to what circumstances demanded of him.

El Zarco had reached this point in his deliberations when he stopped, startled by hearing an owl's slow, doleful hooting that came from the leafy branches of the huge *amate* tree by which he was riding.[18]

"Damned *tecolote*!"[19] he exclaimed under his breath,

---

(18) *amate: Ficus tecolutensis, obtusifolia,* etc. or wild fig derives its common Spanish name, *amate*, from the Nahuatl word *amatl*, paper, because bark paper, deriving from pre-Columbian civilization, is made from the boiled inner bark of several species in the genus *Ficus*, which yield fruit like the fig and abounds in the Tierras Calientes.—*Eds./Sol, 174*

feeling his blood run glacially cold. "It always decides to hoot when I pass by. What's that mean?" he added with the worry so common among coarse, superstitious souls. And for a moment he remained sunk in black thoughts.[20]

But he recovered somewhat and spurred his horse on, saying with a disdainful gesture, "Bah! Such things frighten only Indians, like the Atlihuayán blacksmith. I'm white and *huero* . . . it means nothing to me!"

And on he rode at a trot, climbing to the top of the mountain.

---

(19) *tecolote*: owl, a generic name from the Nahuatl *tecolotl.—Sol, 174*

(20) *black thoughts*: According to Friar Bernardino de Sahagún (1499-1590), who chronicled the beliefs and customs of the indigenous peoples of Mexico in his *General History of Things of New Spain* (composed1570s, published1829), the owl's hoot was considered a terrifying omen of impending death. See Juan Santamaría, *Diccionario de mejicanismos* (Mexico: Porrúa, 1974) 1018. This belief has been preserved through the proverb "Cuando canta el tecolote, muere el indio" (When the owl sings, the Indian dies.)—*Eds*.

Flight

The following day, Nicolás, the Atlihuayán blacksmith, came in the evening, as usual, to pay his visit to Manuela's mother, and he found her troubled, sad. Her daughter was sleeping, and he discovered the señora alone in the small patio where we found her yesterday evening.

"Is there any new word?" doña Antonia asked the young artisan.

"Yes, señora," he replied. "It seems the government cavalry will finally arrive, tomorrow. You both must be ready, because I know they won't stay for even a day, and they'll be going on to Cuautla, and from there to Mexico City."

"I'm all ready now," doña Antonia responded. "We spent the whole day packing our trunks and collecting my little bit of money. What's more, I've gone to see the magistrate about granting me a power of attorney, which I'm going to leave with you," she added, taking from her sewing basket a paper that she handed to Nicolás. "You'll take charge, if you'll do me the favor, of selling this orchard, as quickly as possible, or renting it, since the way things are, we won't be able to return soon, and I'm weary of so much suffering here. If you go to Mexico City, you'll find us there, as always, and perhaps then Manuela's willfulness may have changed."

"I doubt it, señora," Nicolás hastened to respond. "I've come to recognize that it's impossible for Manuelita to love me. I arouse repugnance in her, and that's beyond her control. So to me it seems useless to think about that now. As it has to be!" he added, sighing: "You can't tell your heart what to do. They say acquaintance breeds affection. Now, you can understand that isn't so, because if it depended on my acquaintance with her . . . I've done my best to please her, but my efforts have always been repaid with her

coldness, her remoteness, her hatred almost . . . because I'm
afraid she may even detest me."

"No, Nicolás, that's not so. Detest you! Why?
Haven't you been our protector since my husband died?
Haven't you heaped us with so many favors and kindnesses
that we'll never forget? How could such noble behavior lead
Manuela to detest you? No, what's going on is that the girl's
foolish, she's capricious. I don't know who she's gotten it
from, but her temperament seems strange to me, especially
these past few months. She doesn't want to speak to anyone,
when before she was such a chatterbox and so happy. She
doesn't want to say her prayers, when before she was so
pious; she doesn't want to sew, when before she spent the
days devising ways to alter her dresses or make new ones;
she doesn't want anything. For some time now I've noticed
something about her, I don't know what, something so
strange, that it makes me not know what to think. Some days
she's sad, pensive, wanting to cry, so pale she seems ill, such
a lazybones I have to scold her; other days she wakes up so
lively, but quick-tempered, she gets annoyed at nothing at
all, she grumbles, contradicts me, finds fault with everything
around the house, our humble meals displease her, our
being shut up as we are bores her; she'd like us to go out
for a walk, go horseback riding, go visit the haciendas; she
doesn't seem afraid of the thieves surrounding us on every
side, and seeing that I oppose these follies, she falls back
into her despondency and throws herself down to sleep . . .
Just today something strange happened: after I announced
that we had to get our trunks ready to go to Mexico City, as
soon as she saw that it was really true, that I came back with
my mite of money, and that I began putting all my things
in order, first she became joyful and hugged me, telling me
that she was lucky, that she was finally going to get to know
Mexico City, that it had been her dream, that she was going
to be happy there, since the only cause of her sadness is the

horrible situation we've been enduring these many months. Naturally, I had imagined the same thing, and that's why I hadn't worried much about the change in her temperament, since it was to be expected that a girl like her, who's at an age for enjoying herself, for showing herself out walking, ought to be upset by our being shut in. So I, too, became happy at seeing her pleased with thinking about the trip. But then her sadness returned, and when we sat down to eat, I saw that now she was in a bad humor, that she almost didn't want to taste a mouthful, and that she even felt she wanted to cry. Right then, I couldn't distract her, and after arranging her clothes in a trunk, when I went to look in on her, I found her asleep in her bed. Have you ever seen anything like it? Because, if it's on account of our leaving Yautepec, why has she been sad living here?"

"Señora," asked Nicolás, who had listened attentively and thoughtfully, "is it possible that she has some lover here? Possible that she'll be leaving behind someone she has loved or someone she loves still, without her having told you about it?"

"I've sometimes asked myself that from time to time, but I don't think there's anything to what you say. What sweetheart could she have had who I wouldn't even have suspected? It's true, some of those *gachupín* clerks from the store with the vaulted roof managed to tell her sweet nothings, to send her billet-doux and messages, but that was long before we left to live in Cuernavaca. After we returned, those fellows weren't here any longer, they'd gone to Mexico City, and Manuela hasn't thought about them again or even mentioned them.

"Some boys from town are in the habit of passing by here and they show some interest in her, but she exhibits great disdain for them, and shuts the window as soon as she's seen them approaching. They haven't come back recently. Manuela finds the few boys she knows tiresome. So I'm sure she isn't in love with anyone in town, and that's why, at the beginning of this year, when you began visiting us, I thought she was inclining toward you and that we'd easily arrange what we had planned."

"Well, now you see, señora," Nicolás answered bitterly, "you weren't right, and Manuelita has thought me more tiresome than the Yautepec boys. To such an extent that, holding her as dear to me as I do and having thought so seriously of marrying her, because I thought with our marriage to carve out her happiness as well as mine, I naturally was unable to remain untouched by her constant rebuffs, and I resolved to remove myself from this house for ever. But my considering that you bear me a fondness, which I'm certain of, and my mother's charge to watch over you, since nowadays a man's support is so necessary in these towns, have made me continue . . . plaguing you with my presence, which, otherwise, you would have been spared."

"Plaguing me?" asked doña Antonia, moved to tears.

"No, señora, not you. I see clearly that you harbor friendship for me, that you'd want my good fortune and my happiness, that if it were up to you, I'd be your daughter's husband. I'm not ungrateful, señora, and please know that for as long as I live I'll act toward you like a grateful, affectionate son, without any ulterior motives and always provided that I don't stand in the way of Manuelita's happiness. But I was telling you that for the sake of this girl. Fortunately for her, you are both going away from here now, so she won't be tortured by seeing me, and I'll have the satisfaction of being useful to you from a distance. I'll do everything you entrust to me, and I'll write to you often, giving you an account of the orchard and the state of things out this way. Tomorrow, when the government troops arrive, I'll come too, to see what they offer you, and I'll even accompany them when they leave for Morelos, or farther if it's necessary."

"Ay, Nicolás, how good you are and how noble!" the
señora said tenderly. "I accept everything you offer me and,
in turn, I assure you that in me you'll always have a second
mother. Whatever lot God may hold in store for me and my
daughter, know that I'll always remember your generosity
to us, and that I'll never forget you're the most noble,
honorable young man I've known. I'll expect you tomorrow,
and if you wish to accompany us, as you offer, I'll be very
glad to depend on your company, which I so need. But I'm
afraid something may happen to you on your way back."

"Don't be afraid about anything, señora," Nicolás
said, standing up. "I'll bring some of my men from the forge,
well mounted and well armed, and we won't run any risk."

"All right," said doña Antonia, pressing the
blacksmith's hand with both of hers, affectionately, as would
a tender mother with the apple of her eye.

Then, hearing him ride away, she exclaimed in tears,
"Oh! What a wretch I am not to have that man for my son-
in-law!"

Manuelita awoke when it was already growing dark,
and in the candlelight doña Antonia saw that her eyes were
red . . .

"Aren't you feeling well, child?" she asked
affectionately.

"My head aches terribly, mamá," the young woman
answered.

"It's because you're half asleep, and besides, you've
eaten so little!"

"No, I feel a little sick."

"Maybe you have a temperature?" her mother asked
uneasily.

"No," Manuela replied, calming her, "it's nothing,
I got up very early this morning and, in fact, I haven't had
much to eat. I'm going to have something and go back to
bed, because sleepy is what I feel. But I have an appetite,

and that's a good sign. You know this always happens when
I get up very early. Besides, we need to sleep now, while we
can, because who knows if on the journey we'll be able to
rest comfortably, and in the company of soldiers," she added,
smiling mischievously.

The poor mother, very much at ease now, prepared
dinner, which Manuela ate happily and heartily. Afterward
they both said their prayers and, following a long talk
about their travel arrangements and their new hopes, the
señora retired to her room, next to Manuela's and scarcely
partitioned from it by a thin wall.

At that hour there was a heavy downpour, one of
those Tierra Caliente downpours, mingled with thunder and
lightning, in which the floodgates of heaven seem to open
and inundate the world.

The rain made a frightful noise on the roof, and the
trees in the orchard, lashed by that torrent, seemed to be
uprooting. In the street, water rushed headlong, forming a
river, while the patio was flooded from the rising *apantles*
and the water pouring down from the roofs.

After telling Manuela to cover up well and to pray,
doña Antonia fell asleep, lulled by the monotonous noise of
the downpour.

Pointless to say that Manuela did not close her eyes.
This was the night arranged with el Zarco for her flight: he
must come without fail, and she had to wait for him, ready
with her clothes and her pouch that contained her treasure,
which she had to go to dig up at the foot of the oleander.
This sudden storm upset Manuela greatly. If it did not stop
before midnight, the storm was going to make traveling
very unpleasant, and even if it did stop by that time, she was
going to find the orchard transformed into a pond and to get
herself completely drenched under the trees. Still, what is a
woman in love not capable of bearing, as long as she carries
out her designs?

When she knew that it was close to the appointed hour, she got up, barefoot and on tiptoe, carefully wrapped up, her head and shoulders mantled in a woolen coat; and, lifting her muslin underskirts to her knees, she opened her bedroom door softly and plunged out into the patio, lighting her way with the dark lantern, which she covered carefully.

It was the last time that she was going out from her maternal home, and she spared scarcely a thought for the poor old woman, sleeping without a care and trusting in her beloved daughter's love.

Beyond that, Manuela, intent only on accomplishing her escape, aimed at nothing but hurrying, and if her heart beat violently, that was from fear of being heard and spoiling her scheme.

Fortunately for her, the downpour continued full force and no one would have suspected that she might leave her room in that storm. That is how she rushed across the patio, entered the orchard, passed over the *apantle* that encircled the oleander's grove, and there—hastily digging, without bothering about the rain that had drenched her completely, and taking care only that the lantern did not go out—she extracted her treasure pouch, wrapped it in her shawl, and made her way toward the wall, climbing up the sapodilla roots toward the spot where she usually waited for el Zarco.

She had scarcely gotten up there when she heard the sort of whistle by which her lover announced himself and, in a flash of lightning, she was able to make him out, wrapped in his black oilskin cape and pressed up against the wall.

But he had not come alone. Three other riders accompanied him, each of them wrapped, like him, in a cape and armed to the teeth.

"Damned night!" exclaimed el Zarco, addressing his beloved. "I was afraid you wouldn't be able to get out, my love, and that everything would be ruined today."

"Why of course not, Zarco!" she replied. "You've always seen that when I give my word, I keep it. This couldn't be put off for another time, since tomorrow the troops arrive, and maybe we would have had to leave immediately."

"All right, you're carrying everything?"

"Everything's right here."

"Then come, cover yourself with this cape," el Zarco said, holding out an oilskin cape to the young woman.

"That's useless, I'm already drenched, and really, I can just keep on getting wet."

"That won't do, put it on, and this sombrero . . . Good God!" he said, taking her in his arms. "Poor thing! You're soaked to the bone!"

"Let's go, let's go," she said quivering. "Who are those men?"

"My friends, who've come with me in case of whatever might happen . . . Let's get going, then; come on, boys, before that river rises," el Zarco said, spurring his horse, on whose cruppers, Tierra Caliente style, he'd seated the beautiful young woman.

And the group of riders pushed on hastily to the edge of town, crossed the river, which was already beginning to rise, and disappeared into the pitch-darkness.

Some superstitious *campesino* seeing that tight-knit band of horsemen passing by at such an hour and in such weather, illuminated by bolts of lightning, wrapped in black capes, slipping between storm-lashed trees, would surely have thought them a band of hellish ghouls or the lost souls of bandits, purging their sins on so ghastly a night.

Doña Antonia

Doña Antonia had slept badly. After her first slumber, which was peaceful and deep, the tempest's many noises finally awoke her. Restless after that on account of thoughts and concerns about her approaching journey, she began to toss and turn in her bed, a prisoner of insomnia and uneasiness.

She thought she had heard, amid distant claps of thunder and sounds of rain and wind in the trees, some strange sounds, but she attributed those to her own apprehensions. She really would have liked to get up so as to go to Manuela's room in order to talk or pray for a moment in her company, but she was afraid of interrupting the rest of her child, whom she thought deeply asleep and feverish since the previous day.

So, when having spent long hours in that most distressing situation, fighting off a thousand dismal, tormenting thoughts as well as the room's suffocating heat, which led to her troublesome insomnia, when she heard that the storm was letting up, that the trees seemed to be quieting down, and the roosters were starting to crow, announcing dawn and good weather, the poor woman at last fell asleep again, only awakening very late, when the sun's first rays entered through the room's cracks.

Then she quickly got up and ran to her daughter's room.

She did not find her but, seeing the unmade bed, she supposed that her daughter had arisen much earlier than she and was probably in the patio or the kitchen. She sought her there and, still not finding her, imagined that she must have gone walking in the orchard, examining her flowers and surveying the storm's ravages, and she even told herself that Manuela was wrong to expose herself that way to the morning's damp after having been indisposed the day before, that she was going to get soaked with water off the trees and get her feet terribly wet from the mud in the orchard, which was thickly wooded, threaded by *apantles*, and, with the slightest shower, filled with puddles.

In fact, the orange, sapodilla, mango, and banana trees let cascades of water fall at every scraping of their branches; sunlight was reflected as in thousands of diamonds in the drops of water hanging from the smallest leaves, and the grass on the ground stood submerged in an enormous swamp.

The girl was wrong to be out walking in the orchard that way. And doña Antonia then called to her, scolding.

But having waited in vain to see her appear and not hearing her answer, she began to be alarmed and ran to look for her in the places where she usually went. She was not in any of those either. Then doña Antonia went on searching, shouting to her in every direction and, a thought having come to her suddenly, she returned to the house to see if the door onto the street was open, but finding it shut and barred, she went back into the orchard, fearful, imagining that perhaps her daughter had been bitten by a snake and might have fainted or maybe died in some corner of that wood. The poor old woman, pale as death, shaken by terror and anguish, went into the deepest part of the orchard, not bothering about the mud or the weeds or the thorns, searching every place, calling everywhere to her daughter, by the most affectionate and the most despairing of pet names, her throat parched, her eyes bulging from their sockets, hardly able to breathe, her heart in her mouth . . . crazed by pain and fear.

But nothing, Manuela did not appear.

"But, my God, what's happened to my daughter?" doña Antonia exclaimed, stopping and leaning against a tree, since she felt her legs weakening.

No one answered her. Indifferent, Nature pursued its normal course. The sun shone brightly, fully illuminating the now cloudless sky on that beautiful summer morning, calmer and bluer after a stormy night; the birds chirped happily in the groves, insects buzzed among the flowers, and everything seemed to take on new life in that tropical, vigorous land.

Alone, the poor mother was growing weak, bracing herself against the trees and feeling death's chill freezing the blood in her veins.

After a moment of anguished paralysis, she made a desperate effort and dragged herself to the center of the orchard. Another idea came to her there and, crossing over the *apantle* encircling the oleander's grove, which was like a round bank of bushes in whose center arose the venerable shrub in full flower, she approached the oleander and, reaching it, halted in surprise. There, next to the trunk, was a hole that had filled with water and, on the grass, was thrown the *tarecua*, the little *tarecua* that Manuela usually used to dig in her garden's soil.

Then she noticed that despite the rain the weeds and bushes were still bent back, as though someone had opened a path through them.

She examined the ground carefully and, in the part not covered by grass, she detected footprints. With difficulty she followed their direction through the thick, uneven layer of vegetation covering the ground and was able to follow it up to the *apantle*. On its muddy rim and on the part its overflow had flooded during the night, the tracks were clearer: the trail of small, bare feet that had sunk deep into the mire. Who could have walked through here, this morning, if it was not Manuela? And who could have those tiny feet, if not the girl? But why had she gone barefoot, having caught cold the day before?

The wretched mother lost herself in conjecture. Then, taking a few steps beyond the strip of land flooded by the *apantle*, she again recognized footprints. They were identical to Manuela's; surely she had gone in the direction of the wall. In fact, the prints led up to the wall and stopped

alongside the ancient roots of the huge sapodilla. The old
woman crept up the roots laboriously, as though driven
by a terrible premonition. On top of the wall, there were
also signs of someone's having passed by there. The plants
appeared to have been trampled down, some of their stems
were broken. Doña Antonia peered down from the top of
the wall and carefully examined the lane. And then she
saw, right there, precisely at the foot of the place where she
found herself: clear-cut tracks of horses that seemed to have
been halted there for some time; and there must have been
several of them, because the mud was pitted and dug up by
numerous, recurring prints clustered together.

The sharp, cold blade of a knife that pierced her
heart could not have produced the feeling of intense pain and
faintness in the miserable mother as such a sight gave her.

She understood nothing, but she intuited that what
she saw signified something terrible. Her daughter crossing
the orchard during that night and making her way to the
wall! Those horses standing there as though waiting for
her! Because it was obvious that no man had gone with her
on foot. All this involved a mystery, incomprehensible but
terrifying for the poor woman. Had Manuela fled with some
man? Had she been kidnapped? Who could the kidnapper
be?

In the midst of her stupor and terror doña Antonia
was scarcely able in her confusion to ask herself such
questions, because she felt terrified, devastated—standing
there like a fool, her eyes fixed on the mud in the lane, her
hair standing on end, her heart pounding to the point of
strangling her—mute, tearless, powerless, the living image
of anguish and agony.

But one final hope seemed to bring her back to
herself. She thought it was all impossible, that everything
she was seeing was a dream, or that her daughter had nothing
to do with this complex of circumstances, that Manuela

must have gone back to her room, and that if she had fled, she would certainly have taken her clothes, her jewelry, something.

And doña Antonia, hastily climbing down from the wall, made her way, staggering like a drunkard but at a run, toward the house and Manuela's room. The room was just as before: desolate, the bed unmade, an open trunk. There could be no doubt, the girl had run away: her best dress was missing, her embroidered shirts, her jewelry, her new satin shoes, her shawls were missing as well. She had taken what she could fit into a small suitcase.

Then, the stricken old woman, now convinced of her misfortune, collapsed onto the floor and burst into tears, letting out shrieks that would have grieved the stones. This fit of supreme sorrow past, she left the house, as though lifeless, without taking care to lock up, and went to the home of her goddaughter Pilar, who lived nearby in the house of an aunt and uncle, because Pilar was an orphan. Doña Antonia could barely get out a few words to explain that Manuela had disappeared and to implore them to go back with her to her house to make certain of the fact.

As a result, they accompanied her, surprised and frightened as well, especially the beautiful, sweet young woman who, like her godmother, understood nothing about such a mystery.

The Letter

The inspection of the orchard and street made by Pilar's aunt and uncle, and by Pilar herself, only confirmed doña Antonia's suspicions. Manuela had fled in the arms of a lover.

Pilar's aunt and uncle found at the foot of the wall, half hidden among the weeds and mud, the dark lantern that the young woman had used to light her way and then had flung down there in escaping.

It now remained to determine what person or persons could have abducted the young woman, and no one dared venture a single word on that question, because not one of them had a basis for the slightest conjecture.

In her fit of anguish, the poor mother had made bold to mention the honorable Atlihuayán blacksmith's name, but the moment she did, she as well as Pilar and her aunt and uncle cried out in wonder and surprise: "Impossible!"

"Impossible, surely," doña Antonia was saying, "why would Nicolás need to carry off the girl when I'd have given her to him with all my heart. I'm such a fool! And only my distress can excuse that rash word. May God forgive me for it. Nicolás wouldn't forgive me for it."

"Besides, Godmother, Nicolás wasn't loved, and you know that very well. Manuela couldn't even bear his presence. For this to be possible, it would have been necessary, as much for him as for her, to pretend they loathed each other, but such deception, what for?"

"Of course that's right," doña Antonia replied. "No, there's no reason to think about that, but then who, for God's sake?"

"It will be necessary to inform the authorities," Pilar's uncle said.

At that moment a boy, a young worker from the outskirts of town, came into the house and said that some men traveling on horseback with a lady had seen him at day break and stopped him very near Atlihuayán, just where the slope of the mountain begins, and the lady, who was a girl, had told him to go to Yautepec to bring a letter to her mother, giving him directions to the house.

Doña Antonia hastily unfolded the sheet of paper, handwritten in pencil and containing only these brief words:

Mamá:
Forgive me, but I had to do what I've done. I'm going away with a man I love very much, even though I can't marry him right now. Don't weep for me, because I'm happy. And don't let them come after us, because it's useless.
Manuela

Hearing these words, they were all left amazed and struck dumb, their faces expressing the surprise and distress that such conduct in Manuela caused them, since until then she had been a good daughter.

The poor mother let the paper fall from her hands and stood for a moment with her head bowed, her eyes fixed on the floor, overwhelmed, wordless, gloomy, as though benumbed, until a moment later her grief burst forth in horrendous sobs. Pilar as well as her aunt and uncle turned to embrace and console her, not knowing, however, what to say to soothe her pain.

"And who can I protest to now?" she exclaimed. "Advise me," she said, "what shall I do?"

"We'll go to see the prefect," Pilar's uncle said. "It's essential that the authorities take their measures."

"But what measures!" the old woman retorted. "When you see that the authorities themselves don't dare leave town, have neither the troops nor any means of making themselves respected. Truly, God has forsaken us!" she added hopelessly.

"But, who can it be, then, the man who's carried her off?" asked Pilar. "Because I can't even hazard a guess, and we need to have at least some suspicion to point us in some direction . . ."

"And here am I alone, absolutely alone," doña Antonia cried, wringing her hands, in distress. "Oh, how they've wronged a miserable old widow—forsaken!"

"Not so alone, godmother, you're not so alone," Pilar said spiritedly. "Aren't you counting on Nicolás's friendship?"

"That's true, child, in my despair I'd forgotten about him. I do have that generous man, who just yesterday told me, without any regard to winning Manuela, who he was certain didn't love him, that I could depend on his total support. You're right; I'm going to write to him this minute."

"That's not necessary," Pilar's uncle said. "I'll go saddle up right now and ride to Atlihuayán to fetch Nicolás. We need him to help us at least inquire into this business."

The old man was getting up to comply with his offer, when the sound of a horse was heard on the street, and a man dismounted at the front door.

It was the Atlihuayán blacksmith.

Everyone stood up to run toward him. Doña Antonia outstripped the others and could scarcely stretch her arms out to him and sob, "Nicolás, Manuela has fled!"

The young man turned deathly pale and murmured sadly, with a gesture of bitter disdain: "Ah! Yes, my suspicions are confirmed."

"What suspicions?" they all asked.

The blacksmith led the señora back into the room and, still standing, said: "This morning, very early, a field guard came to tell us—the manager and me—that at daybreak, while scouring the fields at the foot of the mountain and after the downpour was over, he found at his cabin, where he hadn't slept, a group getting ready to leave on horseback who surely had taken shelter there from the storm. Suspecting that they were bad people, he didn't approach along the road but instead hid amid the sugar cane to watch them carefully. As it turned out, they were Plateados: four men and a woman, young, very beautiful, and wearing a narrow-brimmed sombrero, over-laden with silver, to which she was tying a white scarf before mounting. Because of that delay, he was able to recognize them clearly. Apparently he'd seen the girl in town on several occasions and the man, who appeared to be the others' leader—it was el Zarco!"

"El Zarco!" they all cried, terrified.

"That's right, the most fearsome and wicked of those bandits, who, according to what they say, is young and not bad looking! This was the man who clasped the girl so as to lift her into the saddle and who appeared to be taking her away. They all set out immediately, and in haste, on the mountain road without noticing the field guard, who didn't lose sight of them until they got high up and veered off into the scrubland. Then he came to report. I don't know what terrible premonition I had and, without knowing why I did it, I got on my horse and came to see if anything new had occurred here. So that's how," he added, intensely bitter, "you know now who Manuela ran away with."

"Ah! She's right to say it's useless to go after her!" cried doña Antonia angrily, showing Nicolás the sheet of paper, which he examined intently.

"Certainly," the young man replied, "it's perfectly useless. Who would go after that bandit at his headquarters where he has more than five hundred men to defend him? And most of all, what for? Didn't she go completely of her own free will? When a woman takes that step, it's because she's passionate for the man she goes away with. Pursuing her, that would mean killing her, too."

"I'd rather see her dead than know she's in the arms

of a thief and murderer like that man," Doña Antonia said resolutely. "Now it's not only pain I feel, it's shame, it's rage . . . I wish I were a man and strong, and I assure you I'd go in search of that wretch, even if they killed me. Better for me! A Plateado! A Plateado!" she muttered, shaking with anger.

"All right then, señora, I'm ready to do what you want, no matter how futile the pursuit seems to me, not so much on account of el Zarco's people as because of Manuelita's determined will to follow after him. In all truth, she wasn't abducted . . ."

"But, can I consent, however crazy in love my daughter might be, to her chasing after a bandit? And my rights as a mother?"

"Your rights as a mother can be represented only by the authorities, in this case, since you have no close kin," Pilar's uncle explained. "We'll help the authorities, but they must take charge. And do you think they'll presume with these outlaws, when they can scarcely make the people in town obey?"

"But if they wanted to . . . the government cavalry arrives today."

"Let's go see the prefect," the old man replied, "to ask him to speak to the troop commander, but don't forget that the day before yesterday these troops were unable to go on hunting for el Zarco, who committed the murders at Alpuyeca, . . . and in spite of the Mexico City government's having ordered his pursuit in all earnestness."

"It's useless," they all exclaimed, "it's impossible: neither the prefect nor those soldiers will want to."

At that moment they heard trumpets blaring in the plaza. The government cavalry was making its ceremonial entrance into town.

Crazed by rage and suffering, doña Antonia rushed from the house, intending to speak to the prefect.

The Major

The poor prefect happened to be in the town hall, dressed in his Sunday best to receive the troops with suitable honors; and, at the moment when Doña Antonia arrived, accompanied by Pilar's uncle and Nicolás, who had followed her out of deference, the prefect was engaged in watching those badly dressed and even worse-mounted forces lining up for roll call in the little plaza.

Giving orders to the troop was a nasty-looking major, dressed, in singular fashion, in a torn military uniform, his head covered by a dirty old *charro* sombrero

After he had finished mustering his men, this major came over to greet the prefect and to declare, which surely did not need saying at that point, that he needed rations for his soldiers and fodder for his horses, since they must resume their march that same afternoon.

The prefect gave the orders required to supply those provisions, imposing such burdens on the better-off citizens, who had been accustomed to bearing them for some time.

Afterward the troops were billeted, and the prefect invited the major and some of his officials to drink something and eat lunch at the prefecture.

Such were the duties imposed in those days by the towns' political authorities in regard to a military that neither defended the peaceful citizenry nor dared confront the bandits overrunning the region.

"How are things going, major?" the prefect asked. "Did you have a good day's work with the Plateados yesterday and the day before?"

"Hard, señor Prefect," the major replied, stroking his scraggy moustache, "Very hard: we haven't rested day or night."

"And did you have any success?"

"Oh! We gave those Plateados a *correteada*, a real

chase—something fierce. I'm sure they won't be showing up again. We taught them a lesson."

"So you caught some, then?"

"Yes, and we left them there, hanging from the trees, where they must be swinging like bells . . . right now."

"But, all of them were captured?"

"All, no. You know that's difficult. Those cowards attack only defenseless people, but then, when they see organized troops, like mine, they run away, they scatter . . ."

"But el Zarco . . . because they say it was el Zarco who was leading the gang."

"Yes, it was him, but he takes to his heels faster than any of the others. He didn't even wait for us, so, when we reached Alpuyeca, not even a hint of el Zarco. We tried in vain to overtake him. After his robbery, he paused scarcely long enough to pick up his wounded and then he packed off in haste, so as not to leave us even a scent. In not one town or ranch that we passed through in our pursuit could they give us information about him, either because he hadn't gone that way or because he has accomplices everywhere, which is more likely. The thing is, my cavalry couldn't go any farther in those rugged mountains."

"But then, major," the prefect asked maliciously, "in the end, who did you catch, because didn't you just finish telling me that you left some men hanging from the trees?"

"Oh, my friend," answered the military man, unabashed, "we rounded up some suspects who I'm certain were his accomplices. I know these rogues well, they can't hide their crime. They run away when they catch a glimpse of us, turn pale when we speak to them, and, at the slightest threat, fall to their knees, begging for mercy. Now, don't you see, these actions are proof, because if not, why would they do all that? Their crime indicts them: they're the accomplices who warn the bandits, who cover their tracks and share in the booty. It was several of these men—and, in my view, the most important of them—who I left twirling in the air. It'll set an example! Don't you think so?"

So the valiant major had executed a few miserable *campesinos* and villagers on mere suspicion so as not to appear before his superior in Cuernavaca with his hands unbloodied.

The prefect understood him that way, and for that reason responded insistently: "Yes, major, sir, that was good after all, but, in the end, what about el Zarco?"

"El Zarco, señor Prefect, must be far from here by now, maybe in the Matamoros district or near Puebla, dividing up the stolen goods in complete safety. Pretty good for him if he'd stayed around here!"

"But they say," the prefect objected, "that he has his den in Xochimancas, a few leagues from here, and that he reckons with more than five hundred men. At least that's what's they say around here and it's what we do know, because gangs often come from there to attack haciendas and towns. That den of thieves is where they keep their stolen goods, where they hold their kidnapped victims, their horses, their munitions; in short, according to the reports we receive daily, it seems that they live there as in a kind of fortress, with even their own artillery, their own musicians and brass bands, which they sometimes take along on their forays to entertain them at their dances."

"I know that already, I know," the major said, with some annoyance, "but you recognize how simple people exaggerate. Those are all just fairy tales, those men probably did seek refuge up there some time or other, probably stayed there two or three days, probably sounded two or three bugle calls, and people's fear invented the rest; because you won't contradict me, señor Prefect: you people live as though scared to death, and they don't seem like real men, the people who live in these districts."

"But with good reason, Major," said the prefect,

piqued to the core. "With all the reason in the world, in fact, if everything you call fairy tales seems reality to us: when we see parties of one and two hundred men, well-armed and well-mounted, traveling our roads; when every day they carry people from town and workers from haciendas off to the mountains; when they barge in anywhere at all, as though right at home, how are we not going to believe?"

"All right, then, and your people? Why don't you defend yourselves? Why don't you arm yourselves?"

"Because we don't have the wherewithal, all of us are without weapons."

"But why?"

"I'll tell you why: we had weapons to defend our towns, that is, weapons that belonged to the authorities and weapons the residents had bought for their own self-defense. Even the poorest people had their shotguns, their pistols, their machetes. But first, along came Márquez with the Reactionaries and stripped us of all the arms and horses he could find in town. Some weapons eluded him, though, and some horses too, but then along came General González Ortega with the Liberal troops, and he ordered the confiscation of all those remaining arms and all those horses, leaving us to sit on our hands. Then, the bandits scarcely learn that somebody has a middling horse when they immediately move in to seize it. Who would you want to buy either guns or horses now, knowing he'll have to forfeit them in any case? Besides, even when we still have machetes and knives left, do you think we're going to stand up to men who carry good muskets and rifles?"

"Well then, man," the major replied on reflection, "that's really awful, because, like this, anyone can take advantage of you. And then what do you do?"

"All we do is flee or hide. We have a lookout in the tower during the day. When he rings the bell, raising the alarm, families hide in the parish church or wherever they can, in the most secluded parts of their orchards; men run away, and the authorities . . . we cringe," the poor prefect added, shrugging his shoulders in shame and resignation.

"*Caramba*, man! That's appalling!" the major exclaimed, pouring himself a large cognac. "I wouldn't be an authority here for anything in the world."

"Well, I've resigned from the prefecture fifty times, but they don't accept my resignation, and it's all the same."

"All the same, how?"

"Well, it's obvious, it's all the same whether there's a prefect or whether there's not. They'd say as much happens if I'm here as if somebody else were, and in the meantime, here you find me, limiting myself to providing fodder and rations to troops passing through, unable to do more, unable to call upon a single guard, a single soldier, anyone at all . . . going into hiding myself at night, because at night we're exposed to everything, not being able to maintain the watch we have during the day—and by day always tending to our business apprehensively. So, they're not fairy tales, the things we report to you, they're not inventions caused by fear. They're truths, and everyone will repeat them to you."

At the moment the prefect finished speaking, doña Antonia, tired of waiting for the conversation to conclude, had the office secretary announce her, saying she had a matter of the utmost urgency to communicate to both the prefect and the major.

"Send her in," said the prefect.

Doña Antonia entered, weeping and despondent.

"What's happened to you, doña Antonia?" asked the prefect attentively.

"What's happened to me, señor Prefect, is a great misfortune: my daughter was abducted last night."

"Your daughter! Manuelita! The prettiest girl in Yautepec!" the prefect exclaimed, addressing the major, who turned to him, all ears.

"Yes, señor, Manuela. They've stolen her from me!"

"And who, go on, who do you say?"

"El Zarco," doña Antonia cried furiously, "that great thief and murderer!"

"Now do you see, major?" the prefect said, smiling wickedly. "He's hasn't gone so far off, the way you thought, he's still hereabouts, abducting girls, after having robbed and murdered in La Cañada."

"But, how did this happen? Tell us quickly, señora," said the officer, rising.

Doña Antonia recounted the events we already know. Nicolás was summoned to declare what he knew, and then there was no longer any doubt that, indeed, el Zarco had been the kidnapper.

"And so, what do you want us to do now?"

"Señor," the old woman responded with a pleading gesture, "order the pursuit of this outlaw, have them take my daughter back from him, and I'll give what little I have if they succeed. Let them bring her back dead or alive, but it must be soon, señor. They can find her very close to here, in Xochimancas, where el Zarco has his headquarters. I know, señor Prefect, that you have no troops or people to command for this, but now that this military gentleman is here with his troops, he can render a great service for justice and humanity . . . "

"What do you say, major?" the prefect asked sarcastically.

"Impossible, señor Prefect, impossible!" the major repeated resolutely. "I have orders to continue my march to Cuautla, it's a matter of escorting a man who's very close to the President, don Benito Juárez,[21] who must go to Mexico City. Now, you can imagine, if yesterday I was unable to continue my pursuit of that villain, and on account of theft

---

(21) *Benito Juárez:* Considered one of Mexico's greatest presidents, "the father of his country," Benito Juárez (1806-1872) was the son of Indian laborers in Gualetao.

and murder, much less can I dally to go searching for some
missy in those out of the way places. . . Bah! Bah! . . . Leave
us in peace, señora, the girl will make herself happy now
with that bandit . . . she has no choice! Government troops
can't waste time going around rescuing pretty girls! Besides,
I don't know this territory very well."

"But I do know it very well," Nicolás said, "and if
the señor prefect were to agree, some of my friends and I
could accompany the government troops to guide them and
help in their searching."

"Well, if this young man has some friends, armed I
suppose, to go with him, then why doesn't he undertake the
pursuit himself?" the major asked.

"Because that would be the same as sacrificing
ourselves futilely," Nicolás responded. "My friends and I,
to be precise there will be ten of us, and the bandits we may
find at Xochimancas are more than five hundred or, at the
very least, three hundred. What could we do, ten against
three hundred? We'd all die fruitlessly. But not so going
with the government troops, because you have more than
a hundred men, and besides, those of us going from here,
we're well armed and, backed by the cavalry, we'd count
for something. We know roads by which we'd manage to
surprise the Plateados."

"But, all this wrangling over one girl?" asked the
major, who remained unconvinced.

"No, señor," Nicolás replied indignantly, "it

Orphaned at the age of four and deprived of education, he later fled his guardian's
for Oaxaca, where he received good intellectual training and eventually became
governor, then rising to the positions of president of the Supreme Court of Justice
and vice president of the republic. He opposed the French Intervention, from which
he emerged victorious at the battle of Querétaro. Juárez assumed the presidency
in 1858, after Ignacio Comonfort's expatriation, and was elected to the office in
1861, 1867, and 1871. An adversary of clerical influence more than of religion, he
advocated the moral and material improvement of his race, always maintaining an
unimpeachable integrity. —Eds./Sol, 206.

wouldn't be only for the girl, because we'd accomplish other, more important objectives. We'd accomplish shutting down this den of thieves, which has been terrorizing the district; we'd accomplish, maybe, killing or seizing the murderers the good major pursued in vain yesterday and the day before; we'd retrieve the stolen goods and we'd retrieve the rest of the loot they have hidden up there all this while; we'd set free the men they kidnapped long ago; and the good major would fulfill his duty, restoring the whole region's security once again. I believe that even the Supreme Government would thank him for it."

"No one teaches me my duties as a soldier," the major replied, his eyes flashing in anger, realizing he could not answer the young man's arguments in any other way. "I know what I ought to do, and that's why I have superiors who give me orders as they see fit. Who are you, my friend, to come in here and lay down the law to me and speak to me in that tone?"

"Señor," replied Nicolás, facing the major with dignity, "I am an upright citizen of this district; I am foreman of the smithy at the Hacienda de Atlihuayán and the prefect knows that I have rendered more than a few services when the authorities have had need of me. What's more, I'm a citizen who knows perfectly well that you're an officer of the Civil Guard, that the troops you bring here are paid to protect the people, since they're not troops exclusively dedicated to federal military service but, rather, a government troop dispatched to pursue thieves, and at this very moment we're providing you the opportunity to carry out your commission."

"You, what would you know about that, señor Something-or-other? You have nothing to shout about at me here, nothing to read me the riot act about, and no one who has empowered you to speak to me in that tone. Who is this man, señor Prefect?" the major asked in a paroxysm of fury, his moustache standing on end as he reached for the butt of the Colt he wore at his waist.

"This young fellow," the prefect answered, turning pale because he feared some outrage from the arrogant officer, who, like all those of his kind, treated honorable, peaceful men with scorn, "this man is, indeed, a very honorable and very worthy citizen, who has rendered the people his very good services and is well respected by all."

"Well, all that amounts to nothing so far as preventing my shooting him goes," the commander said. "I'll teach him to disrespect the military!"

Nicolás folded his hands impassively and replied without arrogance, but colder and prouder in tone: "Do as you please, señor Major. You have your armed forces out there. I am alone, unarmed, and standing before the authority of my town. You can shoot me, I'm not afraid of that, and I was already expecting it. It's only natural: you have not been able or you have not been willing to pursue or shoot the bandits, who would require your having to take some risks in battle, and for you it's easier to murder an honest man who recalls you to your duties. It's clear . . . this won't bring you any glory . . . but it's the only thing you can and know how to do."

"So you think I'd make use of my power to punish your insolence?"

"That's what I think," Nicolás replied, his arms still crossed,[22] his voice cold and confident.

"Well, you're wrong, friend," the major shouted. "I don't need to call upon armed forces to punish those who insult me. I know how to punish them myself, man to man."

"That remains to be seen," Nicolás replied, with

---

(22) *arms still crossed:* Two paragraphs above, Altamirano wrote that Nicolás folded his hands (*manos*); here, without further indication, he writes that the blacksmith's arms (*brazos*) continue to be crossed.—*Eds.*

a fleeting smile of contempt. "And," he added, "here near Yautepec there are some quite secluded spots where you could prove that valor . . . Leave your troops here, let's the two of us go out together to choose a place with that in mind."

"Oh yes? You're challenging me?" the officer asked, livid with rage

"I'm accepting, major. You said you're quite capable of punishing those who insult you, man to man and without resorting to your power. I accept and I am ready, with similar weapons, and where nothing favors either man but his own valor."

"Fine," the commander agreed. "Now you'll see whether or not I'm capable." And, rushing out of the room, he shouted to several soldiers standing nearby: "You there! Sergeant, seize this scoundrel and hold him in the barracks with a guard on watch! If he makes a move, kill him!"

"A nice way of settling things man to man," murmured Nicolás, with a look of deepest disdain at the major.

"Now you'll see about bragging to me, insolent fool!"

"But, major," said the poor prefect, intervening beseechingly, "please forgive this boy, he's over-wrought, but he's a good man, incapable of the smallest crime."

"Quiet, you damned prefect!" the major retorted, furious, like one possessed: "Be quiet or I'll haul you away too! That's all you authorities around here are good for, taking these buffoons under your wing! You'll take notice if I make another example! Take him away, take him away!" he said to the soldiers seizing Nicolás, who put up no resistance, limiting himself to saying to the prefect, "Don't plead, señor Prefect. Let them do what they want, but don't debase your authority."

Nevertheless, the prefect was fully aware that the

blustering, cowardly officer was capable of carrying out his threats.

At that time and in those regions, such deeds were, regrettably, all too common. The bandits reigned in peace but, on the other hand, when it came to killing, the government troops killed honest men, which was quite easy for them and incurred no risk, the country being unsettled to such an extent and notions of order and morality turned so upside down that no one knew any longer whom to appeal to in such a situation.

The local town authorities were mock authorities, and any minor military man, no matter how low his rank, presumed to affront and humiliate them.

The unfortunate magistrate of Yautepec could do nothing but summon the town council, which gathered, in truth, with great fear and not knowing what to deliberate. In addition, the prefect immediately sent word to the Hacienda de Atlihuayán's manager, who at once got on his horse and galloped down to Yautepec, accompanied by the hacienda's chief workmen, with the aim of procuring the honorable blacksmith's freedom.

Pilar

As for doña Antonia: from the start of Nicolás's altercation with the major, seeing how the affair was turning out and finally realizing that she could expect nothing from the authorities and that, on the contrary, a great injustice was going to be committed and perhaps even a crime against her generous defender, she had fallen into such an extreme state of despair that for a moment she thought she had become ill. But no one heeded her, all eyes and ears focused on the outcome of that terrible dispute.

When the soldiers took Nicolás prisoner, the poor woman did not have even the strength to stand up and follow him, settling for moaning in neglect and astonishment on a bench in the prefecture.

Finally, when the prefect left, doña Antonia, accompanied by Pilar's uncle and several townspeople, went to her house, where young Pilar, her aunt, and some neighborhood men and women concerned about her misfortune were waiting for her.

In a few words, she told them what had just happened and, her strength drained by so much suffering, feeble, debilitated from not having eaten anything since that morning and having been soaked in the orchard during her earliest searching, she threw herself onto her bed, trembling feverishly. Her goddaughter and those faithful neighbors lavished simple attentions on her. But as soon as the beautiful and good young woman had administered the required remedies to her godmother, she began to busy herself with something else that had stirred her to the depths of her soul.

The news of Nicolás's imprisonment had struck Pilar like a bolt of lightning. She felt distraught but, concealing her anxiety and distress as best she could in the presence of her aunt and uncle and those strangers, she took her shawl and, on pretext of going to fetch some remedies, she rushed out onto the street.

Where was she going? Even she did not know, but she felt the need to see Nicolás, to speak to him, to meet with some people, to endeavor, in short, to save that generous young man who for so long had been the idol of her heart, the idol loved all the more since she had had to worship him in silence and in the presence of a rival he loved dearly and she loved dearly as well.

In other circumstances, Pilar, sweet and submissive by nature, timid and shy, would have died before revealing the secret that simultaneously made for her heart's delight and torment. But just then, when the young man's life was in danger and she imagined him forsaken by everyone else, in the clutches of those arbitrary, violent officers, the good, chaste young woman took into account neither her age nor her sex, did not consider that her sheltered upbringing had produced the isolation surrounding her, did not at all fear what people in her town would say, did not think of anything but Nicolás's salvation; and in order to achieve that salvation she left her godmother's house and went in haste to the barracks where she had been told that they had just placed the blacksmith in solitary confinement.

Nicolás did not find himself in any kind of prison, because those makeshift barracks in a house in town did not meet the required conditions. That is why Nicolás had been placed in an entryway facing the street, where two sentinels quartered there, along with the guard himself, kept watch over him, so that Pilar could see him clearly by mixing in with the group of people whose curiosity had gathered them around the house.

She stepped out of the group and, moving toward the prisoner, who took notice of her immediately and rose in a gesture of greeting, she could say no more than this one word among choked sobs: "Nicolás!"

And she fell to her knees upon the ground, speechless with pain and overcome by tears.

Nicolás was about to speak to her, but the sergeant of the guards intervened and, somewhat sympathetic toward the girl, told her: "Step back, señorita, because the prisoner is being held incommunicado and may not speak to you."

"But if he's my . . . but if he's my relative," Pilar said beseechingly.

"That makes no difference," the sergeant responded. "You may not speak to him. I'm very sorry, but that's the order . . ."

"Just one word! Take pity, let me say a single word to him!"

"That's not allowed, my child," the sergeant said. "Please withdraw. If the major comes, he's apt to treat you badly and it's best that you be gone."

"Let me be killed!" she cried, "but let him be saved!"

These words, reaching Nicolás's ears clearly and audibly, revealed to him the whole truth of what was transpiring in the beautiful girl's soul and to him were like a resplendent light that illuminated the dark clouds in which his spirit was sinking. Pilar loved him, and she indeed knew how to love. So then, he had been intoxicating himself for so long with the lethal scent of the poisonous flower and had indifferently left to one side the humble flower that could impart life to him.

What joy he took in learning this! But what grim misfortune, discovering it at that moment, perhaps the last of his life, because Nicolás did not doubt that the major would exact his revenge along the road that same afternoon! The humiliation of the officer had been so unmerciful, so shameless, that he could not pardon it, and with all the more confidence, since no qualm could restrain him, this kind of arbitrariness and murder being an every day occurrence at that time.

These thoughts and sensations swirled in Nicolás's head like a fit of vertigo, more powerful than his strength, even with that strength's being so great and with his possessing a character of bronze, forged in the fire of all his sufferings. He did not want to see any more: he covered his face with his hands, as if to conceal the two tears that flowed from his eyes. But that instant of dreadful crisis over, he raised his head again to look upon Pilar. The girl, gently pushed along by the sergeant, was slowly moving away from the group of guards, but she frequently turned back her head, looking for Nicolás. At one of her turns, Nicolás thanked her, placing one hand over his heart, and he signaled for her to go away. How he would have liked that gesture to express the joy he took in knowing that she loved him and to assure her that, at that moment, a deep and tender love had just then blossomed in his heart, upon the ashes of that noxious love of days gone by!

But those curious people, those soldiers obstructed such an effusion and, more than anything else, his surprise, his bewilderment, almost, it could be said, his happiness. And so, he collapsed ponderously onto the stone bench where they had allowed him to sit, and he gave himself over to deep, bitter reflections.

Meanwhile, Pilar did not rest for a moment. She went to see the prefect, whom she found at precisely that moment meeting with the council men and mayors as well as with the hacienda workers, who were deliberating about what ought to be done to prevent Nicolás's being held prisoner. The young woman appeared before them in tears; she begged them, no matter what, not to abandon Nicolás and, if possible, to accompany him on the march, because that perhaps would avoid a murder's being committed on the road; and she withdrew only when they had all assured her that if they could not procure his immediate freedom, they would accompany the troops.

Then Pilar went back to her home and prepared something to eat and carried it to the prisoner herself, taking care to entrust it to the sergeant who had spoken to her earlier and to slip a coin into his hand, begging him to tell the prisoner that *he had nothing to worry about, they were watching over him.*

Nicolás realized that the young woman had done a thousand things on his behalf; but what were those things and how and who were these people watching over him? That he did not know, nor did he need to know. From that moment, something like trust in a divine being arose in his soul. He had a guardian angel protecting him, and for all his recognition that Pilar was an unknown girl, frail and shy, with no influential relations, something inside told him that this girl, inspired by love, had changed into a strong, brave woman, teeming with resources.

And so, cheered by that inner peace, he no longer feared for his life and gave himself over to his fate, confident and calm.

Scarcely had he ended these soothing reflections and eaten something when the boots-and-saddles bugle call sounded at the barracks, and the cavalrymen prepared to march out.

A little while later, they brought Nicolás a scrawny, badly saddled horse and made him mount and ride between their lines. Then the cavalry formed ranks, and the major arrived, half-drunk, and, placing himself at the head of the troops, he left town, scowling at the numbers of people crowding the streets to show their support for the young blacksmith, who rode calmly in the midst of the dragoons.

Nicolás searched eagerly among those crowds for the beautiful girl and, not finding her, his face clouded. But when the troops reached the outskirts of town and took the road that leads to Cuautla by way of the haciendas, they came up against a large group of people on horseback, including the prefect, the councilmen, the Atlihuyán steward, his workmen, and other well-armed private citizens. Next to them, in the doorway of a hut at the far end of a large orchard, stood Pilar with her aunt and uncle. The beautiful young woman's eyes were red, but she showed herself calm and tried to smile when she caught sight of Nicolás, and, bidding him goodbye, she seemed to be saying, " *'Till soon.*"

At the sight of her, Nicolás thought no more about his situation; he felt only love's vertigo, the pounding of blood coursing to his heart, eclipsing his sight in a tender swoon. He turned crimson, waved to Pilar with impassioned affection, and turned several times to fix on her an adoring and grateful look. He loved her profoundly now: just blossomed in his soul, that love had already taken deep root in her. In three hours he had experienced three years of life and populated that ardent fantasy with all the dreams of a happiness missed in hindsight.

As for Pilar, she no longer concealed her emotions after the moment when they burst forth on account of the terrible danger to which Nicolás was exposed. Saving him was her whole objective, and the rest mattered very little to her.

The notorious major, in so far as he can be understood, was overly suspicious: he grew alarmed at the sight of the group on horseback, who appeared to be awaiting him with a threatening attitude, and, spurring his horse, he rode over to the prefect.

"Hello, señor Prefect! What are so many people doing here?"

"Waiting for you," the civil servant replied.

"For me? What for?"

"To accompany you, señor, to Cuautla."

"Accompany me? And for what purpose?"

"For the purpose of vouching for the conduct of that

boy you are taking as a prisoner, to the authorities you're going to turn him over to."

"And which authorities are those, señor Prefect?"

"You ought to know," dryly answered the prefect, who appeared more determined now, backed up as he was by numerous well-armed citizens. "I know only that I am the principal civil authority in this district and, in regard to my powers, I have no superior here. The state judge is also the principal authority in the judicial branch of this district. He's here because he's currently the mayor. That's why, on the supposition that you're taking prisoner a citizen who, one way or another, ought to be under our jurisdiction, it's evident that you are going to bring him before some authority higher than ours, and we are going to appear before that authority as well, in order to inform him fully and in case of whatever happens.

"But, are you aware that I have the authority to do what I'm doing?" the officer asked, trying to get out of the predicament in which the prefect's arguments had placed him.

"No, I am not aware of that," the prefect replied. "You have not had the courtesy of showing me the order stating that, nor has the federal government, which is my superior, communicated anything to me. If you have the order, . . . you may show it to me."

"I don't have to show any orders to you people," the major replied haughtily. "I take orders from no one but my commanders, and I don't have to give any account of my conduct to anyone but my commanders."

"That's why we're going to see those commanders of yours," declared the prefect decisively.

"In that case, it's pointless for you people to accompany me, because my commanders aren't in Cuautla, they're in Mexico City."

"Then we'll go to Mexico City," the prefect insisted,

seconded by the Atlihuayán steward, who repeated: "Yes, señor, we'll go to Mexico City!"

"And if I do not permit that?"

"You cannot prevent our following your troops. I'm the prefect of Yautepec; the town council and a number of peaceful, honorable citizens are traveling with me. By what right could you keep us from going where you go?"

"But, do you realize that by now this farce is wearing my patience thin and that I can bring it to an end?"

"You do as you wish, we'll then do as we ought."

The major was enraged. He ordered his cavalry to halt and conferred briefly with his captains. Perhaps he might have wanted to commit some arbitrary act, but it was not so simple for it to go unpunished. The prefect was there, accompanied by the town council, the Atlihuayán hacienda's employees, and numerous well-mounted and armed locals. At a moment's notice, they could enlist other locals, even though unarmed, and that could become serious.

The major therefore decided to endure that affront, but not to release Nicolás. He turned toward the group standing with the prefect and said to him: "So you've come to take the culprit, the man, from me?"

"No, señor," the prefect replied, "we've already told you that we aim to follow you to Cuautla or to Mexico City, and you won't be able to accuse us of any offense."

"It would be better if you'd display such resistance to the bandits as you display to government troops!"

"Yes, we'd display it," replied the prefect angrily, "if government troops didn't occupy themselves with pursuing, honest men instead of chasing bandits, that's what they're paid for. You've been offered the help of men from around here to pursue the Plateados, and you haven't wanted it, and that, precisely, is the offense for which you hold this honest individual liable."

"All right, all right" said the major, "we'll see now

who's in the right; follow me wherever you like, it's all the same to me."

And he ordered the troops to resume the march.

The prefect rode along beside the column of cavalry, but Nicolás could now be sure nothing would happen to him.

They rode that way all afternoon and, well after nightfall, finally reached Cuautla, where the prefect of Yautepec went to speak with his Morelos colleague and to make use of all his connections with the aim of achieving the blacksmith's freedom.

The major submitted a special report to Cuernavaca, accusing the young man of being a threat to public safety, presenting the occurrence in Yautepec as a rebellion, and assuming airs of being the vigorous deliverer. But Yautepec's prefect and town council, as well as the Cuautla authorities, turned to the state's governor and the federal government, and the Atlihuayán steward to the hacienda's owner and his friends in Mexico City, reporting what had happened. Memos, reports, and recommendations were exchanged, and ink and money were spent to clear up that matter. Nicolás remained prisoner in the barracks, while the troops awaited orders to escort the president's friend. But on the third day, orders arrived directly from the Ministry of War to set the young blacksmith free and for the major to appear before the authorities in Mexico City to answer for his conduct.

This whole imbroglio and disorder were frequent occurrences during that disturbed time of civil war.

And so, just the abduction committed by el Zarco had resulted in the poor mother's grave illness, the Atlihuayán blacksmith's imprisonment, the Yautepec authorities' commotion, many communications, many measures, many tears; but the crime went unpunished.

It is true that the happiness of two good hearts had been brought about, and this was the only sunbeam illuminating that scene of anarchy, corruption, and misery.

True Love

Scarcely set free, Nicolás returned to Yautepec. What had happened there during his short absence? He trembled to think of it! Strictly incommunicado from the time he gone out of Yautepec until he was set free, he had been unable to learn anything at all about the fate of doña Antonia or about Pilar, but he had hardly spoken a word with some of the neighbors, who'd come to talk to him, when he learned that Manuela's unhappy mother, too weak to withstand so many blows, had taken to her bed with a violent attack of brain fever. It was very possible that the poor woman had succumbed. And Pilar? Undoubtedly the beautiful, virtuous young woman would have lavished every kind of care on her godmother; certainly she would not for a moment have left the bedside of the sick woman, who, though abandoned so wretchedly by her daughter, nevertheless still found herself surrounded by kind, charitable people, but most especially that angel who, more than a goddaughter, seemed to be her true daughter, heir to her virtue, her good sense, and her noble character.

But in the bosom of that family improvised out of hardship, at the bedside of that dying old woman, a man was needed, a mainstay, a force breathing life into the others and providing those necessities always made greater by bereavement. And that man, who could it be but he, Nicolás, the man that good lady had chosen as her son-in-law, who, in turn, had been an orphan since infancy and had concentrated all his filial affection on her? How the sick woman must have searched for him in her delirium! How Pilar, too, must have invoked his name, silently, wishing to see him at her side during those moments of terrible anguish! In the midst of her worry, this last consideration was like a drop of nectar that fell upon her heart, overflowing with sorrow.

Since his departure from Yautepec, a prisoner and

placed under threat of death by that insolent, high-handed officer, Nicolás had done nothing but contemplate those two objects of his affection: doña Antonia and Pilar; and his troubled mind alternated unceasingly between the miserable old woman's misfortune and the beautiful young woman's love, a love all the more gratifying for having been revealed so unexpectedly and exactly at a time when all life's horizons had grown dark for him.

That is why, in the preceding days, the enamored youth had scarcely given a thought to the state in which he found himself, to the solitary confinement in which he was held, to the thousand discomforts of his prison, even to the danger of an unfavorable resolution to the intervention undertaken on his behalf—to everything.

Doña Antonia and Pilar were his sole concern, and not to see these two people, who meant everything in the world to him, provoked his impatience, an impatience that led to desperation.

As for Manuela . . . she had entirely vanished from his memory. Like all men of strong character, the blacksmith was proud, and if in those last days he had still shown some feeling for the disdainful young woman, if in his heart the fire of another time still seemed unextinguished, that was only because the gust of doña Antonia's hopes had relentlessly kindled that fire, nearly turned to ashes.

But Nicolás had finally realized, many months ago, that he was an unacceptable man for Manuela's affections. Beyond that, with his native insight, with that perceptive faculty possessed by humble lovers, he had guessed, upon returning from Yautepec night after night and analyzing, detail by detail, his fruitless, increasingly icy meetings with the girl, that she not only felt indifferent toward him, but repulsed as well. Now of course, the expression of this attitude, which is harsh and disagreeable, even on a beautiful face, is unendurable for a lofty spirit such as Nicolás's. If he had been one of those foolish, fatuous young men who always interpret their beloved's gestures and words in the manner most favorable to themselves; if he had been one of those vengeful, tenacious men who turn suffering into a means of triumphing and avenging themselves; in conclusion, if he had been one of those old rakes for whom desire is a shield that makes them invulnerable and for whom possession at any cost is now the only object of their sensual love, Nicolás would have remained firm of purpose, sustained by the señora's support—a major support for a daughter, regardless of how contrary she shows herself.

But Nicolás was a different sort of man. An Indian, humble by birth, and a laborer, he nevertheless was well aware of his dignity and his strengths. He knew that he was sufficiently worthy, as man and suitor, to be loved by Manuela. His stainless honor gave him a claim; his position, though middling but independent and earned by his own labor, ennobled him in his own eyes; his open-hearted, pure love, which aspired to a dignified marriage and not the passing pleasures of carnal desire, had caused him to value that love more and to esteem it, like a treasure that ought to be preserved intact.

In short, he loved tenderly, dutifully, but reverently, perhaps with passion, but with dignity, and to compromise that reverence and that dignity by some degrading action would have seemed for him to be degrading his character and dragging on the ground that sentiment he bore so high.

So, as soon as Manuela, in love as she was with another man, saw fit to remove the veil of dissimulation and began to show Nicolás a lack of favor that he instantly recognized and that increased day by day and that ultimately was transformed into a marked expression of repugnance, Nicolás began to feel deeply wounded in his pride as man and lover, and in the end he experienced the unbearable bitterness of humiliation. His love, now almost torn out by the roots by Manuela's previous slights, could not withstand this final test, and was quickly fading from his heart. Doña Antonia's affection, a glimmer of hope, and a certain acquired habit of visiting the girl every day still held feeble sway over him, as we have seen; but on learning that the woman he had thought indifferent to him, but honorable, had fled with that detestable bandit, whose name was the terror of that region, a pained surprise first, followed by a feeling of contempt, seized his soul.

Later, upon considering the perversion of Manuela's character, this contempt began to change into a feeling of another sort. It was abhorrence, but the abhorrence that inspires hideousness in a soul. And later still, a vital joy flooded his heart.

He, Nicolás, the poor Atlihuayán blacksmith, had escaped from that monster. He had been in love with a devil, thinking her an angel. Now that he saw himself free of the demon, his earlier blindness shamed him and he congratulated himself that heaven or his good fortune had saved him from the danger of having bound himself to that creature, or at least from the disgrace of continuing to love her, which would have been terrible for him, given his lofty, intensely passionate nature.

Far from that disgrace, and as a most gracious compensation, exactly when his spirit had swept away the last clouds in which that affection might have left him, when serenity had finally settled into his heart, a serenity insufficient to unsettle either the risk he had run or the indignation that had agitated him, he had seen a new image arise before his eyes, more beautiful and sweeter than the one that had disappeared, and he had felt, he had understood that, yes, this image was indeed the good angel of his existence. It could be nothing less: Pilar's love had been revealed at a solemn, decisive moment, with no ulterior motive and without expectations, with every sign of abnegation, generous sacrifice, and heroic resolution that must be the qualities of an extraordinary love. How could he not be instantly enthralled by a love so powerful? Nicolás not only felt that radiant new love pierce his soul like a torrent of fire, he also felt something else, something like remorse, like shame, for not having opened his eyes earlier to this happiness, for not having fathomed the affection he was breathing in and that had surely dwelt concealed alongside him, protecting him, enveloping him in an atmosphere of sympathy and love. And he, how he must have made the modest, beautiful young woman suffer with his evident courting of Manuela! Perhaps he had hurt her at some point, perhaps he had been cruel, unintentionally, wounding the delicacy of that heart, tender and pliant as a sensitive plant!

In his own eyes, such thoughts made him look inferior to his present love, but not with such inferiority that humiliates; rather, with the inferiority of the believer before his God, a sentiment that quickens and increases love, because it entwines love with admiration and gratitude.

Such reflections occupied Nicolás's spirit on the road from Cuautla to Yautepec, along which he traveled on horseback, impatiently and at full gallop, crossing through the *catzahuate* forest and the haciendas of Cocoyoc, Calderón, and San Carlos bordering that picturesque plain. At last, he crossed the river, went down the narrow streets, his heart pounding, and dismounted in front of doña Antonia's house. What news awaited him?

An Angel

It was growing dark when Nicolás walked through the rooms
of doña Antonia's house. At the sound of his footsteps, a
woman came forward to greet him, and she had scarcely
recognized him in the dim twilight that still permitted objects
to be distinguished when she threw herself into his arms,
sobbing.

It was Pilar.

Nicolás, upon sensing against his chest that woman,
now intensely beloved, felt a sort of dizzying passion and
pleasure. This was the first time in his life that he knew
so great a happiness: he, who until then had been able
to savor only the bitter aftertaste of disillusion; he, who,
almost always considered himself unloved, who would have
considered himself happy with a glance, merely sympathetic,
was now receiving a shower, an explosion of love, all that
joy of which he had not previously dared even to dream.

And there she was, the very beautiful young woman
who had occupied his thoughts during those days in prison
and those nights of insomnia; and he felt her lovely virginal
arms wrap around his neck, felt her lover's heart pound
against the heart that now beat only for her and felt his hands
moistened by her tears, his face bathed by her breath as with
a sweet scent. Nicolás could not speak. He was prisoner of
an enslaving passion that paralyzed his faculties.

Finally, after having held the young woman tightly
with a loving rapture more meaningful than ten declarations
of love, he said to her while kissing her brow: "Pilar, my
love, now truly nothing and no one will separate us. The
only thing I regret is not having realized sooner where my
happiness lay. But, nevertheless, I bless even the dangers
I've gone through, because by means of them I've been able
to find you."

Pilar, like any woman, although brimming over with

love and happiness, could not dispel a vague sense of fear and apprehension. She was not yet sufficiently certain that every trace of that old love for Manuela had vanished from Nicolás's heart, perhaps even excited by everything he had recently gone through. That is why, fixing her eyes timidly on the blacksmith's, she dared to ask him, in a tone shot through with her fear of losing that supreme joy: "But, is it true, Nicolás? Do you love me as you did Manuela?"

"Manuela?" Nicolás interrupted vehemently. "Oh, Pilar! Don't ask me that question, which hurts me. How can you compare the love I now show you and feel for you with what I felt for that wretched girl? That was a feeling I'm ashamed of now. I don't know how I was able to deceive myself so miserably, nor can I manage to explain what was the matter with me. Perhaps her rebuffs, her coldness aroused me and provoked my stubbornness; but if I must tell you the truth about what I felt: when I was alone, far from here, I set myself to reflecting, examining the state of my heart, and I confess to you that that was not love; it was not this pure, impassioned love that you make me feel now, but something different, unwholesome, like a sickness I wanted to get over, like a whim in which I invested my self-esteem, but not my happiness. But still, I want to tell you, even if you don't believe it now: over these past days, that whim was no longer there, that feeling had disappeared; Manuela no longer made the same impression on me as she did at the start, and if it hadn't been for doña Antonia's trying to convince her that she should marry me and having led me to understand that I'd succeed in the end, that I shouldn't lose hope and that I could count on her support, frankly, maybe I would have ended up detesting Manuela or, at least, forgetting her, and would have stopped coming to this house."

"But, and my godmother? And me? Didn't you think of us?" asked Pilar reproachfully.

"Oh, yes!" Nicolás replied, "doña Antonia, the poor
señora, was worthy of all my affection . . . And as for you,
Pilar, should I say it? I didn't even dare dream of being loved
by you. I'd already recognized how happy the man you
loved would be, I'd already lifted up to you my eyes full of
hope but had lowered them sadly, thinking you'd never love
me, either. To me, you seemed more elevated than Manuela.
And then, thinking about you, saying anything to you, after
Manuela's rebuffs, suffered in your presence, that seemed
undignified to me. If I had guessed . . . So you see, that not
now, much earlier, that feeling for Manuela had come to an
end. Are you still in doubt? Do you think my love, which
has grown by years in so few days, can be compared to what
I once harbored for that unhappy creature—the feeling that
has now turned into a dreadful disdain?"

"I doubt no longer, Nicolás, I doubt no longer," the
young woman said, pressing the blacksmith's hands between
hers. "And even if I were to doubt," she added, sighing,
"my happiness consists of this love that I've felt for you
for a long time, that I've guarded in the depths of my heart,
without hope then, increasing each day from pain and from
jealousy, and that could only be revealed when you were in
danger and I was close to losing my mind. I never could have
hoped that you might love me. On the contrary, I was certain
that you loved Manuela more than ever, perhaps because
you had lost her forever. But I wasn't in control of myself, I
couldn't contain myself, I listened only to my heart."

"But, my girl," Nicolás remonstrated, "you
misjudged me, perhaps because you didn't know my
character well. To go on loving Manuela, despite what she'd
done, it would be necessary to have loved her truly in the
first place, and I just finished telling you that wasn't how it
was; and then, you'd need to be a vulgar man, and, although
I'm lowly, although I'm a worker, although I'm an Indian
with no education and with no exalted examples to follow, I

can assure you that I'm not a vulgar man, that I feel unable
to esteem an unworthy object, and that, for me, esteem is
absolutely the foundation of love. Ought I to have continued
loving a lost woman who let herself be abducted by a
murderer and a thief? Impossible, impossible. From parents
to children in my Indian family, we have handed down ideals
of lofty honor that hereabouts have so often been thrown in
my face as a defect and earned me some enemies. We have
been poor, very poor, but sometime I'll tell you how my
ancestors, in their wild mountains, in their extremely humble
cabins have always known how to preserve their character
unstained by humiliation or baseness. They have chosen
death over degrading themselves, and not out of vanity or
to preserve an honorable heritage but because such is our
nature. Our dignity is part of our very being. So then, just
imagine whether I could have felt for Manuela, after what
she has done, any feeling other than contemptuous pity. To
do anything else would have been a disgrace . . . Are you
convinced?"

"Yes, Nicolás," the young woman said quickly.
"Forgive me, but in spite of what I knew of your character,
my affection, my pitiful affection, born in the midst of
jealousy, made me blind and distrustful . . . Don't be angry
with me . . ."

"No, what I hold for you, my good and beautiful
girl, is a sacred, eternal love . . . Will you, then, be my wife,
and immediately?"

"Oh!" said Pilar, crying, "that would be my joy, but
we've talked so long, we've gone astray, we've forgotten the
world, Nicolás, and we're talking close to a dying woman . . .
my godmother…"

"Oh! Yes, the señora . . . "

"My godmother is dying . . .," Pilar exclaimed
gloomily. "For two days now she's eaten nothing, her
weakness is terrible, her fever high, and everyone says

there's no hope."

Nicolás, on hearing this news, hung his head, filled with grief.

Death Throes

In fact the two young people, in their amorous ecstasy, for a moment had forgotten poor doña Antonia, who lay dying in the next room.

We have said that since the day following her daughter's flight, affected by the terrible crisis she had gone through more than by the dampness she had been exposed to for many hours, the unfortunate old woman had been bedridden, stricken with brain fever.

The care and attention lavished on her by friends and the kindly people ministering to her, especially Pilar, who, like a loving daughter, had not left her side for a moment, had been futile. The skills of those good people, with no doctor at hand, as well as all their efforts had been dashed by the seriousness of the illness. The señora was dying, and Nicolás arrived just at the moment of her agony's death knell. Nicolás, deeply dismayed, walked into the sick woman's dimly lit room and was greeted affectionately by the few people there.

Pilar, who had preceded him, approached her godmother's bed and, calling to her several times, told her that Nicolás was nearby and that he wished to speak to her. The old woman, as if waking from a deep lethargy, attempting to gather what little strength she had left, raised her head, fixed her eyes on the blacksmith who held out his hands to her affectionately and, then, recognizing him, cried out weakly, took those hands between her own, kissed them over and over again, gasping, "Nicolás! Nicolás! My son!" and then fell back, collapsing, as if that supreme effort had exhausted her existence.

Nicolás bent over the edge of that deathbed, and there, that man of iron, whom neither adversity nor peril had been able to overwhelm, began weeping bitterly, afflicted by so great a misfortune and cursing fate for bringing about such injustices.

Doña Antonia lived on for a few more hours, but the agony had been too prolonged, her life had been crushed by the weight of so many miseries, and before the night was over, that good and unfortunate old woman breathed her last sigh in the arms of her goddaughter Pilar and beside the man she had loved like a son.

The poor girl's sorrow was immense. Accustomed since childhood to looking to doña Antonia as a second mother, whom she loved, moreover, for her generous nature and her noble, solid virtues, Pilar was sincerely attached to the widow; and reflecting now on the señora's abandonment by her own daughter, Pilar's devotion and love, with all the selflessness and abnegation that come naturally to generous, intelligent souls, had turned into a filial adoration.

That is why her attentions during the old woman's illness had been exquisite, and the vigils and worry she had endured were revealed on her beautiful face, so pale and careworn.

Her godmother's death, however expected it had been, caused Pilar indescribable dejection; and if the love Nicolás had already confessed to her so firmly and resolutely, and so fortunately for her, had not come to console her and give her strength, like a ray of sunshine, her good, sensitive soul would surely have viewed the world as a dark, fearful night. But Nicolás was there, her beloved, her future husband. Precisely at the height of her sorrows heaven had sent him to her, the unhappy orphan, with neither inheritance nor more protection than an elderly aunt and uncle, and in the midst of that situation so danger-filled for everyone.

Then she thought of Nicolás, not just as her heart's chosen one, but as her savior, her providence; and, moved powerfully by that sudden change in her fortune, by that unexpected godsend of a rescuer, as if to compensate for her afflictions and sorrows, Pilar ceased sobbing, fell to her knees, and prayed fervently, with a feeling in which suffering and gratitude were mixed simultaneously.

She was called back from her rapture by Nicolás's voice, which spoke to her tenderly and earnestly pious, as he extended one hand toward the old woman's body: "Pilar, I swear to you upon this dead body that I will be your husband, and that I will not wait beyond the time of mourning to keep my promise. You are an angel, and I do not deserve you."

Pilar threw herself into his arms, crying; the bystanders, moved by the scene, also tried to console the young woman, and Nicolás left at once to make the arrangements for doña Antonia's funeral.

Since the old woman had left some money matters unsettled, it was necessary to attend to them, given that she had not left a will and that her only child had abandoned her maternal home.

Of course, the local authorities wanted to order that the house and orchard be sold to meet the necessary expenses, but Nicolás was opposed to that, offering to take the expenses upon himself, as a tribute to the memory of his good friend. He also refused to take responsibility, as the authorities charged him, for the care and distribution of her few effects, citing easily understood reasons of delicacy, given his situation; so that modest estate was legally impounded, but without the honest blacksmith's being involved.

After the señora's burial, which was attended by all those who had respected her virtues, everything returned to normal life, which is to say, to that life filled with the anxieties and dangers that we have described. Nicolás left for his Atlihuayán smithy, more beloved than ever by his employers, thanks to his noble conduct; Pilar went back to her aunt and uncle's truly humble home, which had become a paradise for her, because her future husband, awaiting the specified date, visited her every evening, as he had, in other times, at Manuela's home.

And that young woman?

We shall see how she was faring.

Among Bandits

Manuela, devoted to el Zarco and, for that same reason, blind, had not fully anticipated the situation awaiting her, and if she had anticipated it, she had formed only a most conventional notion of it.

Her lovesick, inexperienced woman's fantasy conjured up the existence she was about to enter upon as a life of adventures, dangerous, to be sure, but diverting, romantic, unusual, and powerfully attractive to a temperament like hers, erratic, impetuous, ambitious.

For the period up until then, and ever since that new scourge of bandits had been loosed upon the Tierra Caliente at the end of the terrible civil war that laid waste to the republic over the course of three years and that history knows by the name of the War of Reform, it cannot be stated that there had been any methodical pursuit of such criminals; occupied as the government was in continuing to fight what remained of the pro-Church army, Manuela had never seen a gallows erected for one of her lover's companions.

On the contrary, she had seen many of them strolling with impunity through the towns and fields, with an air of triumph, feared, respected, and feted by the rich, by the authorities, and by all the people.

If any reprisal was undertaken, from time to time, such as that feigned by our acquaintance, the brutal major, it was more as a matter of form, to maintain appearances; but, basically, the authorities were powerless to combat such adversaries, and everyone seemed resigned to living under such a degrading yoke.

Manuela thus imagined that situation, however temporary it might be, as lasting for quite a while and the Plateados' control as growing stronger in the region. Moreover, she was too young to recall earlier, massive pursuits and massacres carried out by forces organized by the

State of Mexico and placed under the command of energetic, ferocious leaders, such as the renowned Oliveros.[23]

That had all happened in times now remote, despite not fifteen years having passed since such events took place. In any case, circumstances had been different. In that period it had been a question of pursuing bands of common highwaymen comprising ten, twenty, at the most forty bandits, who scattered at the smallest attack and who constantly resorted to fleeing. It was a time of relative peace, and troops organized from several states could join forces to attack a large party of bandits; the towns and wealthy *hacendados* could lend their assistance, scouts would constantly travel the roads, and men who knew all the hideouts acted as guides or served as the pursuers.

But now things were different. Now the federal government was too occupied with the war still being waged by the armies of Márquez, Zuloaga, Mejía,[24] as well as by other *caudillo* clerics, who still rallied around the large numbers of partisans; the foreign intervention posed a threat that was beginning to be translated into deeds, at the time precisely when the events we are relating were taking place, and, as was natural, the entire nation was stirred, expecting a foreign invasion that was going to provoke a very long and

---

(23) *Oliveros*: Ignacio Oliveros, Chief of Public Safety in Morelos or Cuautla around 1850 and famed in the State of Mexico. The Mariano Riva Palacio Archive at the University of Texas holds various of his papers, including letters and one document signed by him and dated Toluca, December 8, 1849, with the title "Conditions for establishing a commission to pursue the malefactors, Highwaymen on the Camino Real."—*Sol, 242*

(24) *Zuloaga*: Felix María Zuloaga (1813-1898) was a Conservative general who, during the Wars of Reform, served as president of Mexico for short intervals in 1858, 1859, and 1860. With the Republic's victory, he was outlawed for his part in the murder of Melchor Ocampo. *Tomás Mejía* (1820-1867), an Otomí Indian, was a Conservative general who fought in the battle of Angostura against the U.S. invaders. He recognized the Empire and was one of its best-known generals, but with the empire's decline he returned to Querétaro, where he was eventually shot, along with Maxmilian and Miguel Miramón. —*Sol, 243*.

bloody war, that in fact broke out one year later in 1862 and did not come to an end until 1867, with the triumph of the republic.

All these considerations could not occur to the young woman's mind so lucidly as they appeared to the eyes of sensible people, but she heard the talk of earnest people who visited doña Antonia, or her mother passed on the rumors going round, and if randomly, as the multitudes summarize public events, still very precisely, she extracted the consequences that mattered to her for her future life.

In all other respects, the state of things in the Tierra Caliente was all too plain for her to harbor great fears for el Zarco's life.

It was true that the Plateados controlled that region; that the federal government was unable to do anything about them; that the then disorganized government of the State of Mexico, whose rulers, military or not, neither remained in office long nor established anything lasting; that the rich *hacendados* had either to flee to Mexico City, shutting down their haciendas, or to submit to the harsh condition of paying tributes to the principal ringleader, on pain of seeing their fields burned, their mills destroyed, their cattle and crews killed.

It was true that now it was not a matter of combating small bands of fainthearted thieves, such as had been hunted down in earlier times, but veritable legions of 500, 1000, and 2000 men who could assemble at a moment's notice, who had the best horses and the best weapons in the land, who knew that countryside, in even its most secluded twists and turns, who could count on innumerable agents and messengers at the haciendas, villages, towns, recruited on the basis of self-interest or fear but serving them faithfully; and, finally, who had trained in the recently concluded war, in which many of them had served as much on one side as on the other and knew enough to put up real battles from which they frequently emerged victorious.

As a result, Manuela, whom el Zarco had also instructed in their frequent trysts about the bandits' advantages, finally laid her doubts to rest, understanding that her lover belonged to an army of brave, determined men who had all the elements for establishing a rule as powerful as it was enduring over that miserable land.

So, with the irresistible impulse of her passion on the one hand and convinced, on the other, by all the explanations her lover gave her and the terror of the people around her, she ended by boldly resolving to entrust herself to her destiny, certain that she was going to be as happy as she had conceived in her unwholesome dreams.

But, in short, Manuela, who had done nothing but think about the Plateados after falling in love with el Zarco, did not really know the lives those bandits led. She did not even know them personally, apart from her lover. She had seen them several times in Cuernavaca, parading by her window in squadron formation, but the processions' swiftness and the circumstance of her having fixed her attention only on el Zarco, who was the one to captivate her from then on by his gallantry and ostentation, meant that she could not recognize a single one of those other men.

Then, brought back to Yautepec and living secluded, precisely because of doña Antonia's fear that she might be seen by those outlaws, Manuela had never again seen one of them, since, when they used to come into town during the day, she had had to hide herself, now in the parish church, now in the darkest part of the orchards, where people had set up hiding places where they remained for whole days, until the danger passed.

Thus, she knew nothing of the bandits except for hearsay: now by way of the seductive tales el Zarco told her, nevertheless intermingled with allusions to passing dangers, which, far from frightening her, aroused throbbing emotions in her; and now by way of the terrifying accounts from Yautepec's peaceable residents, exaggerated even further by doña Antonia, whose imagination had become distorted.

From such contradictory information and with the quite natural partiality of someone who loved a bandit, Manuela had formed an image always favorable to him and advantageous for her.

She thought that people's terror overstated the Plateados' crimes; that with an eye to inspiring greater horror of them, their enemies painted them as truly abominable monsters who were human only in shape; that the constantly dissolute lives in which they were supposedly bemired, when not going around robbing and killing, were nothing but tales told by people terrified or filled with hatred; that the frightful tortures to which they condemned their victims were nothing more than exagerations aimed at instilling fear and wresting money more easily from the hostages' families.

She believed that el Zarco and his gang certainly were bandits, that is, men who had turned robbery into a peculiar profession. Nor did this seem so extraordinary in those times of rebellion when various leaders of the political parties waging war had resorted many times to that means of supporting themselves. Neither did kidnapping, the measure most practiced by the Plateados, seem monstrous to her, given that although not employed formerly and therefore new to our country, it had been introduced precisely by political factions and with political pretexts.

So, in her eyes, the Plateados were a breed of rebels at war with society, but for that very reason interesting: ruthless but valiant, wild in their ways, but that was natural, given that they lived amid dangers and needed violent outlets as compensation for their awful exploits.

Rationalizing this way, Manuela concluded by imagining the outlaws as a clan of bold warriors and by giving el Zarco the magnitude of a legendary hero.

That same hideout, Xochimancas, and those rocky mountain heights where the Plateados set up the center of their operations appeared in the wayward girl's imagination like those marvelous fortresses in old stories or at least like the Liberal or Conservative armies' picturesque encampments that had been seen to appear, not so long ago, in almost every region of the country.

Manuela had thought all this during her hours of loving and musing, and now she resolved to share el Zarco's lot.

That is why on the night of her flight, she was expecting to enter a familiar world. Perhaps the stormy night, the rain, the emotion following upon leaving her home and her poor mother, who had always touched her deeply, in spite of Manuela's passion and her perversity, and now seeing herself delivered, heart and soul, to el Zarco—all this hindered her comparing her situation with her previous dreams and looking closely at her lover's companions. On the other hand, there was still nothing extraordinary about those moments. She was escaping from her house with her heart's chosen one; this man, gentleman or bandit, had required some of his friends to accompany him and face the danger with him as well as to guard his back—that was all. She did not know them, but they sympathized with her now if only by the act of contributing to what she deemed her happiness.

When compelled by the storm, el Zarco and his companions as much as Manuela, sought shelter in the Atlihuayán field guard's cabin, all remaining silent and not turning down their scarves, so that, in the dark silence, Manuela could neither distinguish their features nor recognize their voices. A few whispered words exchanged with el Zarco were all that broke the silence called for in that place.

But when, at dawn's first light and with the rain

already slacked off, el Zarco gave the order to mount, Manuela was able to examine her lover's companions. Still wrapped up in their ponchos, always covered to the eyes with their scarves, they kept their faces hidden; but their fierce, murderous looks sent an involuntary shudder through the young woman, accustomed to the descriptions given of these criminal figures. That was when Manuela, on a piece of paper given her by el Zarco, penciled the letter addressed to doña Antonia in which she reported her flight.

Afterward, the fugitives traveled in the direction of Xochimancas, quickly ascending the mountain where we saw el Zarco for the first time.

The procession moved on in silence. From time to time, Manuela, who was riding at the head with el Zarco, heard a certain stifled laughter from the bandits, to which el Zarco responded by turning back and winking, in a nasty-minded way that displeased the girl.

Later the cavalcade began to enter upon a labyrinth of trails, some snaking through small valleys boxed between tall rocks and others following craggy, steep gorges, scarcely used by bandits and woodcutters.

Finally, a little before noon, through the opening created by two mountainous hills, they glimpsed the ruins of Xochimancas, at that time the lair of the Plateados.

From a prominence overlooking that ruined hacienda a shrill whistle was heard, to which el Zarco responded with another, and immediately a group of riders, each with a musket at the ready, set out from among the ruins and came at a full gallop to greet el Zarco's file of horses.

El Zarco advanced and, with an agile movement of the reins while sliding back on his mount, streaked ahead to speak to the group, who then returned to Xochimancas at a full gallop to make a report.

A few moments later, el Zarco affectionately said to Manuela: "Now we're in Xochimancas, my love, all the boys are here."

And in fact, from among the old, dilapidated walls of the ancient estate's mean huts in which the hacienda's crews had slept as well as from the tumbled-down, blackened doorways of the main building, Manuela saw numerous gallows-bird heads peering out, all wearing silver-trimmed sombreros, but quite a few with old straw sombreros. And those men, as a precaution, all had a pistol or musket in hand.

Several voices howled snidely as the string of horses passed by: "Look at el Zarco, damn him, look what the cat dragged in!"

"Where'd you find that nice piece, Zarco, you old so-and-so?" asked others, laughing.

"She's for me, nobody else," el Zarco replied, in the same tone.

"For you, nobody else? . . . We'll see about that later . . .," those bandits answered. "Good bye, *güerita*, you're really pretty for just one man!"

"If el Zarco's got others, why's he want so many?" shouted an ugly mulatto, his face bandaged.

El Zarco, annoyed at last, turned around, and said with a scowl: "You want to shut up now, big boys . . .!"

A chorus of belly laughs answered him. The train of riders hastened their pace, heading toward a ruined chapel where el Zarco lodged, and he said to Manuela, leaning toward her and putting his arm around her waist, "Don't pay any attention to them, they're really jokers. You'll soon see how good they are."

But Manuela felt deeply disillusioned. Vain as she was and even knowing that she was giving herself to a fugitive, she had been hoping that this fugitive, who occupied a position among his men similar to what a general occupies among his troops, enjoyed ranking privileges and regard. She believed that bandit leaders were something so fearful that they made their men tremble with merely a look or that they were so loved that they saw around them nothing but respectful faces and heard only enthusiastic acclaim. And that reception at the Plateados' headquarters had shocked her. What is more, she had felt wounded in her womanly pride and, one could say, in her virginal modesty when she heard those mocking outbursts, those nasty jokes that had greeted her arrival—she, who at the very least had anticipated respect, entering alongside one of the leaders of those men.

Because, in fact, she could not forget so quickly, no matter how morally corrupt she might be, how blinded she was by love and by avarice, that she was a maiden, the daughter of honorable parents, a young woman who, not long ago, was cloistered by the respect and regard of all the inhabitants of Yautepec. Never in her life had such disrespectful expressions reached her ears as those she had just heard; nor had the flatteries customarily directed at beautiful young ladies, which, on occasion, had been tossed after her, ever been of such a shamefully vile nature, so odiously insulting, as those they had just thrown in her face, and in the presence of the man who ought to protect her, of her lover.

Therefore she felt her face grow red with indignation; but when el Zarco turned back to her, smiling, to say: "Don't pay any attention to them," her lover seemed not only as disrespectful as his companions, but also cowardly and despicable. She said to herself, by way of a very natural comparison at that moment, that Nicolás, the dignified Indian blacksmith whose love she had disdained, would never have allowed his heart's beloved to be offended in that manner. As fleeting as that judgment had been, it was entirely unfavorable to el Zarco, who, had he been able to peer into the depths of Manuela's thoughts, would have trembled to see in that soul, overflowing with love for him, like a burgeoning flower, the worm of scorn being born.

The intense pallor that followed the red of
indignation on the young woman's face must have been
apparent, because el Zarco noticed it and, leaning toward her
once more, said in honeyed tones: "Don't be angry, my love,
about what those boys say. As I've already told you, their
ways are very different from yours. This much is clear: we're
really not monks or *catrines*. We have our own expressions,
but you'll have to grow accustomed, because you're going
to live with us, and you'll see that all those jokesters are
good fellows and are going to love you a lot. I told you,
Manuelita, I told you: don't be shocked, and you promised to
adapt to our way of life."

That *I told you* of el Zarco's resonated like a
whiplash in the shocked young woman's ears. Indeed,
she was already beginning to sense the rashness of her
promise as well as the straying and blindness of passion.
She bowed her head and did not answer el Zarco except
for an indescribable gesture that mixed repugnance with
repentance.

In the meantime, they had already reached the ruined
chapel that served as el Zarco's lodging, since the rooms of
the hacienda's old house were reserved for other leaders of
those bandits.

That formerly sacred place now found itself
converted into a jackals' den. By the door and in the shade
of some small trees that had taken root in the crack-filled
walls or between the loosened, grass-covered paving stones,
two groups of bandits were playing cards on a serape spread
out to serve as a small rug holding the bets, the cards, a few
bottles of sugarcane brandy and glasses. Some of the players
were squatting, others sat cross-legged, others were stretched
out on their stomachs; some were humming tavern songs
nasally and shrilly; all wore their sombreros and all were
armed to the teeth. Not far from them stood their unbridled
horses, tethered to other trees, the cinches of their saddles

loosened, feeding on a few handfuls of corn fodder, and, lastly, mounted atop a high wall, another bandit kept watch, ready to sound the alarm in case of anything unexpected.

That is how those villains, even as safe as they felt at that time, took every precaution to avoid being taken by surprise, and only in that way could they give themselves over to their depravations or to the satisfaction of their needs.

Manuela took in that whole sight with a single glance and, on observing those gallows-bird faces, those silver-encrusted suits, those guns, and those safeguards, she could not help shuddering.

"Who are those men?" she asked el Zarco curiously.

"Ah!" he replied, "these are my best friends, my companions, the leaders . . . Félix Palo Seco; Juan Linares, el Tigre, el Coyote, and that *güerito*, who's getting to his feet, he's the chief, that's Salomé."

"Salomé Plasencia?"

"The same."

It really was Salomé, the most notorious leader of those villains, a sort of Fra Diavolo of the Tierra Caliente,[25]

---

(25) *Fra Diavolo*: "Brother Devil," protagonist of the comic opera (1830) by the same name with lyrics by Eugène Scribe and Germain Delavigne and music by Daniel F.E. Auber (1782-1871). Fra Diavolo, who comes from the mountains in Italy, is the well-known head of a mounted band of highwaymen. At the opera's end he is captured and led off to be executed. A real-life figure, whose career finds echoes in Altamirano's novel, Michele Pezza (1771-1806) was born north of Naples and at one time had been a monk, or had wanted to enter the clergy as a young man and sometimes disguised himself as a monk, or, through his luck in always avoiding capture, was considered both monk and demon. A notorious murderer and thief, he later responded to the Bourbon King Ferdinand's appeal for outlaws' help in retaking the kingdom of Naples from the Neapolitan republic and its allied French forces. Knowing the country well, he was able to intercept communications between Rome and Naples, and as leader of ex-convicts and brigands who attacked isolated forces, he also murdered stragglers and courtiers, threw men, women, and children from a cliff, and shot parties of up to seventy people. He wore military uniform, held military rank, and eventually was created duke of Cassano. A savage fighter, at the head of large forces, ranging from 400 to 1500 men at different times, he again came to the aid of Naples in 1806 when Napoleon's army invaded. Having fought many attack-and-flee battles with the regular army in the mountains, his

This sickly, audacious bandit had managed, thanks to the situation we have described, to establish a sort of feudal domain throughout the district and to make even the haughtiest of the wealthy landholders bow their heads before his miserable person.

Salomé came forward to greet el Zarco and his retinue.

"Any news, Zarco?" he asked in a fluty voice, extending his hand. "*Caramba!*" he added, looking at Manuela. "What a pretty girl you've picked out!" and then, touching his sombrero and greeting Manuela, he said to her: "Good morning, *güerita*. Bless the mother who brought forth such a pretty . . .!"

The other bandits had also risen, and they gathered around the recent arrivals, greeting them and paying amorous compliments to the young woman.

El Zarco dismounted with a belly laugh and went over to help down Manuela, who found herself bewildered and not succeeding at smiling or responding to those men. She was unaccustomed to such company, and it was impossible for her to copy their manners and their brazen, crude way of talking.

"Come on, here's a drink!" said one of the group, bringing a glass of liquor, of that strong sugarcane liquor, biting and unpleasant, that the people call *chinguirito*.

"No," said el Zarco, pushing the glass away: "This girl doesn't drink *chinguirito*, she's not used to it; what we want is lunch, because we traveled almost all night and all morning, and we haven't had a bite to eat."

"All right, women!" he shouted to the people inside

---

outlaw party disbanded that autumn, and Fra Diavolo was finally captured, alone, malnourished, and ill. He was subsequently executed on orders of the appointed King Joseph of Naples, Napoleon's brother. Known in his native land for a sort of Robin Hood generosity and courage as well as his atrocities, he gained worldwide fame as the hero of Auber's opera.—*Eds./Sol, 254* the chapel, out of which poured, along with smoke from burning wood, the unmistakable odor of *campesino* stews. "Make us lunch, and take this," he added, holding out the suitcase that contained Manuela's few garments. She retained only her leather pouch, in which was stowed the jewelry that had never seemed in greater danger than in that place.

A group of slatterns, ragged and filthy, rushed out to take those things, and the new arrivals made their way into that pandemonium, heaped high with motley, strange objects and people of varying appearances.

Inside, by the door stood the smoke kitchen, that is, the wood stove where tortillas were cooked and beside which knelt the *molendera*,[26] grinding corn with her *metate*[27] and other implements. A little farther back was another stove, where stews were prepared in stewing pots and black casseroles. On the other side were saddles resting on crisscrossed poles, fiber ropes from which hung clothing, that is, *calzoneras*, jackets, serapes, and old woolen and cotton *túnicos*;[28] in one corner a feverish sick man tossed and turned, his head wrapped in a filthy, frayed cloak; beyond him, a group of disheveled women were mending underwear or making bandages; finally, at the back of the chapel, alongside the main altar, fallen into ruin and separated from the nave by a curtain made from sheets and palm-leaf sleeping mats, was el Zarco's alcove, which contained a campaign cot, mattresses spread on the floor, some wooden benches and some wooden trunks covered in leather. Such were the furnishings that swain was going to offer the young

---

(26) *molendera*: woman who grinds corn.—*Eds*.

(27) *metate*: flat stone, often a piece of lava rock, on which corn is ground.—*Eds*.

(28) *túnicos*: a single garment composed of petticoat, shirtwaist, and sleeves.—*Sol, 257*.

lady he had just carried off from her peaceful home.

"Manuelita," he told her, leading her into that corner, "this, as you see, is terrible; but for now you'll have to adjust, soon you'll have something better. Now I'm going to bring you lunch."

The young woman seated herself on one of those benches, and there, screened behind that curtain, feeling herself alone, she let her head drop between her hands, deflated, overcome; and hearing the drunken bandits' bursts of laughter, their blasphemies, the women's shrill voices while inhaling that oppressive air, foul as that of a prison, she could only tear at her hair hopelessly, and shedding two tears that scorched her cheeks like fiery drops, she murmured hoarsely: "Oh, my Jesus . . .! What have I gone and done!"

Xochimancas

We have introduced the reader into one of the famous Plateados' dens, which, from that fateful period, running from the closing months of 1861 to the end of 1862, served as headquarters for the dreadful, fearsome bandits who were the curse and disgrace of our country.

Xochimancas was, and still is, an old, ruined hacienda, that is, a country estate, with good land suitable for cultivating sugarcane or corn, with abundant water, a fiery climate and, in sum, all the necessary elements for tropical agriculture, productive as well as fruitful. Cotton, coffee, indigo, sugarcane can be propagated there—just as in the Cañada de Cuernavaca or the districts of Tetecala, Yautepec, Morelos, or Jonacatepec— yielding the grower a return of a hundred to one.

Why, in that period, in that small and torrid valley, were no beautiful fields and bountiful sugar mills to be seen, as in the other regions we have mentioned?

We do not know precisely. Xochimancas was already a ruin by that time, but it still gave evidence that in times past, certainly from the period of colonial domination, it had been cultivated by the Spaniards as a fine country property, yielding substantial harvests. From when did its decay and ruin date? We have not ascertained, although that would not have been difficult, nor does that date much matter for the narration of these events.

But it is indeed evident that the place is suitable for farming and that only apathy, negligence, or very exceptional and fleeting circumstances could have turned it into a nest of malefactors instead of rendering it a pleasant, alluring place for work and industriousness. Because the Nahuatl origin of the name Xochimancas itself indicates that since the period prior to the Spanish conquest this site was fertile and agreeable, and perhaps a village of gardeners had its settlement there.

The learned young scholar, Vicente Reyes, in his valuable, unpublished work "Geographical Onomatology of Morelos," explains the hieroglyphics corresponding to Xochimancas:

> *Xochimancas.* Hacienda of the Tlaltizapán Municipality, in the district of Cuernavaca. Etymology: *Xochimanca*, place of caretakers and producers of flowers; from *Xochimanqui*, the caretaker and producer of flowers, plus *ca*. We form the pictorial name from the group in the Ramírez collection[29] that is used to decipher the word "*Xochimancas*," *Xochimanque*.

And then, quoting the venerable chronicler Sahagún, he adds:

> At the festival celebrated during the third month, Tozostontli,[30] the first flowers to bloom that year were offered in the *cu*,[31] known as Iopico, and prior to their offering, no one dared smell any of these flowers.
>
> The flower workers, known as Xochimanqui, celebrated their goddess named Coatlicue[32] also known by another name, Cuatlaton.

And the diligent, erudite antiquarian Cecilio A. Robelo, in

---

(29) *Ramírez collection*: José Fernando Ramírez (1804-1871), lawyer, politician, historian, and archeologist, deciphered countless hieroglyphs, including those of the Aztec calendar, which permitted the interpretation of innumerable codices. He wrote works on Mexico's pre-history and on the history of the conquest.—*Sol, 261.*

(30) *Tozostontli*: The Aztec calendar's third month, which began on March 14 and ended on April 2.—*Sol, 261*

his *Mexican Geographic Names of the State of Morelos*, a much-esteemed work, cites another ancient chronicler, Torquemada:

> *Xochimancas.* (*Xochiman?*) *Place where flowers offered to the gods were raised and cared for.* Among Aztec divinities, Cohuatlicue or Cohuatlantona, the resplendent serpent, goddess of flowers, received offerings of floral bouquets arranged with exquisite skill during the month of Tezozontli. The workers in charge of growing those flowers and arranging the bouquets were called *Xochimanqui.* The place in the state that bears the name Xochimancas perhaps could have been set aside as the goddess's garden or as the residence of the Xochimanqui, and perhaps from there it took the name, whose suffix, as a place name, we have not been able to discover.

Thus it seems that in Aztec antiquity this place, now abandoned and uncultivated, was a garden, surely a vast garden, perhaps a city full of orchards and flowers, a pleasing, delightful place devoted to the cultivation of the Aztec goddess Flora, at whose feet the intelligent, brave *Tlahuica,* inhabitants of this region and noted floriculturalists, paid lavishly aromatic and colorful homage with the most beautiful products of their land, beloved of the sun, air, and clouds.

Although, as Orozco y Berra, our wise, leading historian notes:

---

(31) *cu*: an ancient Aztec temple, usually in the form of a mound.—*Sol, 262.*

(32) *Coatlicue*: Aztec deity whose name means "she of the serpent skirt" and who symbolized earth, life, and death. Her well-known, 8.43-foot statue stands today in Mexico City's Museum of Anthropology —*Sol, 262.*

As a general rule, it is not always
easy to indicate current towns
that correspond to those named
in the ancient chronicles because,
while many retain their primitive
although corrupted names, others
changed names upon becoming
haciendas or ranches, or they
disappeared entirely.

Xochimancas was most certainly transformed after the
Spanish conquest from a garden or city of gardens into a
hacienda with *encomenderos*[33] and slaves; then it fell into
ruin and became a den for reptiles and wild animals; and in
the end into a den of thieves and, what is worse, as we shall
see, a place of torture and murder.

A sad fate for a place dedicated by intelligent, sweet
Indians to the worship of beauty!

---

(33) *encomenderos* (*en* + *comendar*, entrust to, charge with): Spaniards granted
title to land, income from it, and Indian labor upon it. Columbus gave the name
encomeniendas to the allotments of Taino Indians he turned over in servitude to
his favored companions, whom he called *encomenderos* (1499). Abuses develop-
ing from this arrangement, which paralleled earlier European ones exercised upon
conquered Moors, eventually decimated the native population of the West Indies.
In theory, a reciprocal exchange of protection and instruction in Christianity for re-
stricted rights to property (including slaves) and forced or tributary labor and goods,
this essentially feudal system degenerated into a wholesale, catastrophic oppression
and exploitation of the Indians in the New World. Attempts were made at reform,
including the New Laws of 1542, but a social hierarchy had been established that
historians have categorized as the most damaging, long-lasting institution introduced by the Spaniards.—*Eds.*

The First Day

Manuela spent the first five days of her stay in Xochimancas preyed upon by a hundred different emotions, formidable and capable of breaking a spirit far stronger than hers.

The first day was horrible for her. The shock caused by the spectacle of that outlaw camp; the alienation naturally produced by those loathsome habits, which did not even have the novelty of life in the wild; the absence of those people she had loved, of her mother and Pilar as well as some friendly individuals; even the lack of those sensations one is accustomed to but which go unnoticed in normal life and, once gone, leave a terrible void; her everyday chores, the tolling of the bells, the sound of the domestic animals, the distant murmur of people in town, prayer at certain hours—all, all that system of simple, commonplace, scarcely varying life in a small town that nevertheless, it could be said, molds character and fashions the discipline of existence, all that had disappeared in a few hours.

No matter how resolved Manuela had been to accept this change, no matter how her imagination had anticipated this new life, it was impossible that the reality could have failed to make a deep impression on the inexperienced young woman's mind. She, in love as she was with the young bandit, had poeticized that life, those companions, those horrors. We have said that in her fantasy, rustic as it was, she had created, a special man, a hero out of a novel. A young woman in love, however ignorant she may be, although assumed to be uncouth, is always something of a poet. Chateaubriand's Atala is lifelike, Virginie[34] much more

(34) *Atala . . . Virginia*: Heroines of two touchstone French novels that influenced the 19th-century world's view of indigenous or primitive life at the expense of unwritten reality. Jacques-Henri Bernardin de Saint-Pierre (1737-1814) published *Paul et Virginie* in 1787, on the eve of the French Revolution, and led the way for Chateaubriand. A botanist as well as a writer, Saint-Pierre imagined Virginie as a child of nature, the antithesis of the period's upper-class French art and society but

so. Lovers portrayed in ancient Gothic poems are entirely
real. Was it so much, then, for Manuela, who had received
some education and had lived among cultured folk, who had
even read some romantic books, among those that seeped
into the villages and into the countryside, to have forged
an extraordinary ideal, costuming her bandit lover with the
trappings of an errant imagination?

But thinking as she did, Manuela was far removed
from the reality, and her dream was going to dissolve the
moment she encountered reality close at hand.

In the first place, never could she have imagined
that the nest where her mountain hawk was going to lead her
might be that corrupt hovel of jailbirds or beggars. She had
imagined that el Zarco was going to take her to some rustic
little cabin, hidden in the forests, or to some unobstructed
grotto amid the rocks, locations she used to glimpse from
afar among the sierra's saw-tooth peaks. Such a place, such
a hideaway was worthy of the mistress of a bandit, an enemy
of society. There they would be alone, there they would be
happy, there they would conceal their love—criminal but
unrestrained. There she would wait for him, preparing their
meal, her heart palpitating with passion and concern. There,
on a rustic couch or seated on the moss, she would stroke
that beloved brow that had just been exposed to the dangers
of combat, she would kiss those eyes wearied from staying

---

also a victim of its superficial, artificial sentimentality, which penetrated even to a
remote island. François-René Chateaubriand (1768-1848) published *Atala* in 1801.
The short novel summarizes a Europeanized, Romantic world of fabricated scenery
and behavior in its subtitle: "The Love and Constancy of Two Savages in the
Desert"—exactly what Altamirano's novel counters in *El Zarco* with its precision of
geographic and botanic terminology, rooted in Nahuatl, and Manuela's anti-Roman-
tic discovery of Xochimancas, the site of el Zarco's actual life. In a lush New World
setting (Louisiana) Atala falls in love with a Natchez Indian, Chactas, who has lived
in France and is now held captive by Atala's tribe. Atala is half Spanish and also
Christian. She cannot marry Chactas and commits suicide because she had given
her mother an oath of chastity. Both Chateaubriand and his novel were the subject
of major paintings by Girodot, while dramas and images from the book circulated
widely.—*Eds./Sol, 266*

awake to keep an eye out for an ambush or nighttime attack; or, reposing upon his chest, she would keep vigil over her lover while he slept. When the danger was formidable, when they needed to flee the approaching government troops, el Zarco would come looking for her there, place her on the rump of his horse and escape; or he would bid her to hide in the deepest part of the forest or ravines until he came back to look for her. There, too, she would have a special spot, known only to her, for hiding her valuable jewels. Such was the image that she had formed of the place she was going to have to live with her lover until they could move away from those parts and go to be married someplace where they were not known.

Instead of finding that secluded, pastoral retreat, el Zarco was taking her to a sort of prison or dungeon, in order to make her live side by side with drunken women in tatters, with audacious bandits who did not respect their companions' loves and who soon were going to address her disrespectfully with "tú," to insult her, perhaps rob her during one of el Zarco's absences.

And perhaps, and this was the most horrible of all, judging from those criminals' nasty cracks and el Zarco's passively tolerant attitude, tired of her love, he was going to leave her in the hands of one of those satyrs dressed in silver, perhaps even those of that frightful, gigantic mulatto demon who had greeted her with a sarcastic remark, whose tone had the effect of a stab into her heart.

All these reflections darkened Manuela's first day, which she had imagined as a bright, merry day, a nuptial day of rapture and joy.

With such an impression in her mind, even el Zarco's endearments, naturally redoubled in those hours when they were, at last, together, were insufficient to calm her and restore the lost illusion.

The truth is, and this phenomenon appears

frequently in the love-struck woman's spirit, that the
lover, who had always appeared so favorably during those
nocturnal trysts, had now lost much of that stature. Now she
was looking at him up close: vulgar, coarse, even cowardly,
given that he laughingly put up with his companion's
insulting gibes, which deeply wounded the woman he loved.
He was not, then, el Zarco, the ferocious man who instilled
fear and respect in his followers! She had supposed that even
among thieves, the leader's woman would be a sacred object,
something like the general's wife among soldiers. Far from
that, she was being treated like a slut, like a captive from
a raid, and she served to increase the number of miserable
creatures who made up that sort of nauseating harem, lodged,
like a band of gypsies, in the old chapel.

Perhaps the mulatto was referring to them when,
upon Manuela's arrival, he remarked: "When el Zarco's got
others! Why's he want so many?"

That was detestable.

Unquestionably, Manuela felt that she no longer
loved el Zarco, that she had deceived herself about the
feelings that had compelled her to run away from her home.

But then, reflecting more seriously, plumbing the
dark depths of her conscience, she came to understand,
with dread, that she had within another passion that had
sustained her in this unwholesome love, that had seduced her
as much as el Zarco's personal stature, and that this passion
was greed, an unbridled, irrational greed, truly absurd but
irresistible, and that had corrupted her character.

And provoked by this reflection, she rebelled against
herself, denied it, and with a great semblance of reason.
It could not be greed, could not be the extremely precious
jewels, which el Zarco brought her almost every night of
their meetings, that could have prevailed upon her to love
the bandit; neither could it be the hope of obtaining still
better ones from successive robberies; because, in short, this

treasure and whatever might be assembled afterward, that is, the wealth already possessed and what she was expecting, could vanish in a moment, with the bandit's death, with his defeat. Nothing was more uncertain than thieves' gold.

On the other hand, women love jewelry for the pleasure of showing it off in public, and she could not wear it in front of anyone, at least for the time being. Not in towns, because she was not allowed to go down into them, nor in front of those villains, because that might tempt them to snatch it from her. Moreover, had it been the desire for finery that had led her into loving el Zarco, she would have decided in favor of Nicolás; because the blacksmith already possessed a sizeable fortune, free and clear, and although he was frugal, like all upright men who earn their money by hard work, it is certain that, as enamored of her as he was, he would have given her whatever she wanted in order to see her happy.

So then, it was not avarice that had hurled her into the arms of that bandit lover. It was love, it was fascination, it was a kind of vertigo that had driven her wild and made her abandon everything—mother, home, honor, all that is respectable and sacred—to follow that man who, only two days ago, she could not live without.

And now!

But this was dreadful! Manuela felt as though she were waking from a terrible dream. A few hours had been sufficient for her to recognize the total hatefulness of her passion, and the total irreversibility of her misfortune. And, with her unsound illusion fading and thereby extinguishing the unchaste flame that had consumed her heart, the light of her conscience began to shine again, fumbling in cold reality's cortège of terrifying truths.

To this painful turnabout, which acted on her with greater and greater intensity, were added, as must be supposed, the piercing memories of the poor old woman, her sweet, tender mother, so honorable, so loving, whom she had deceived so vilely, whom she had forsaken in her greatest grief, whom she had murdered, because Manuela was certain that upon waking up and searching for her everywhere in vain, on learning from her note that she had fled, the poor señora's desperation must have been boundless . . . she had probably fallen ill and was going to die!

Manuela did not want to think about that and as a consequence, overwhelmed by so many emotions, tortured by so many regrets, she was seized by dejection, a loathing of life, and she felt that she was going to lose her reason.

The punishment of her offence had not been long in coming.

Meanwhile, el Zarco lavished a thousand attentions on her, heaping her with favors; he took pains, along with the other bandits and their women, to arrange the section of the chapel that was set aside for her, bringing in new mats, spreading out ponchos, hanging engravings of saints, and, above all else, showing her his trunks holding some sacks of pesos, a stray satchel of silver mixed in with horse trappings, trimmings from silk dresses, men's and women's undergarments, and a thousand other sundry objects. It might have been said that those coffers were veritable magpie nests, in which all the stolen goods were jumbled in confusion.

"All this is yours, Manuelita, yours alone; here are the keys, and I'll bring you more."

Manuela smiled sorrowfully.

Seeing her like that, el Zarco assumed that she was homesick because of the change in her life, but not for a moment could he suspect what had come over his lover, of whose passion he was increasingly certain.

So he admonished those women to entertain her, to distract her by praising the life they led there, the amusements they improvised, and, most of all, el Zarco's fortune from his robberies and hostages.

In the afternoon, el Zarco brought her two bandits to sing, who sang to their own accompaniment on their guitars, and he bid them sing their best songs. Manuela beheld them with horror. They sang a long series of songs, from among those tiresome, foolish, senseless songs that common people sing on sprees.

The bandits intoned their songs in that piercing, off-pitch voice of the Tierra Caliente *campesinos*, the eunuch's voice, shrill and disagreeable, like the cicada's song, which cannot be listened to for long without intense annoyance.

Manuela felt exasperated and the musicians, recognizing that and very disappointed at not having pleased the *catrina*, said good night to her and withdrew.

Night fell, the frightful, doleful night of that bandit's camp. Manuela went to peer out the chapel door, wanting to take a breath of fresh air and to get a good look at that place, which was beginning to seem very dangerous to her in spite of having el Zarco as her protector.

The night was dark and, like the previous night, threatened to storm. Lights shining through windows and fissures in those ruins gave them an even more frightening look.

Here and there, patrols on horseback crossed back and forth, going out on scouting parties or making their rounds. A sepulchral silence reigned. Criminals are favored by nighttime, when they lie in ambush or venture an attack, but it is also full of terrors and dangers if they lie at rest in their den. That is why their sleep is never peaceful and is disturbed by every rustling in the trees, by every gallop heard in the distance, by every whistling of the wind, by every unusual noise.

Even as secure as the Plateados were in Xochimancas, as we have already said, they neglected no precaution. That is why scouts, sentinels, and night patrols guarded their camp and, still, the leaders could only go to sleep with one eye open.

At the time, they had an additional reason to keep watch. Manuela's abduction would have caused a great uproar in Yautepec. The Atlihuayán blacksmith, a dangerous man for the Plateados and one who hated them to the death and was the girl's scorned suitor, would have aroused the townspeople and his friends at the hacienda. He was well versed in this territory and very daring as well as valiant. Moreover, that day the cavalry who had gone in pursuit of the Alpuyeca attackers had arrived in Yautepec, and although the Plateados knew how much to heed that troop's bravery, there would be nothing strange about its having determined to attack, urged on by the blacksmith's hatred and the townspeople's resolve.

We have already seen that the bandits' precautions were not unwarranted; and what they feared, Nicolás did attempt, although in vain, thanks to the major's cowardice.

That is why vigilance was redoubled at Xochimancas.

Salomé, the Plateados' chief leader, had said to el Zarco at nightfall: "God willing, Zarco, your *huera's* not going to bring any harm to us. We have to be careful; you go with her, stay very calm, and have a good time, all right?" he added—winking and laughing devilishly—"and I'll stay on watch. I've sent the boys on scouting parties along all the roads, and Félix has gone ahead toward the outskirts of Atlihuayán, in case something turns up. So then, get along with you, and sleep well."

He said other things, but they must have been such as he wanted to utter only in a low voice and in el Zarco's ear. The fact is, the two were laughing heartily as they parted. Salomé mounted his horse and, followed by some twenty riders, went off to make the rounds. El Zarco went back to the chapel, where everyone was sleeping now, except

Manuela, who was waiting for him, seated on a bench, frowning and tearful.

Orgy

And some days went by like that, seeming like centuries to Manuela, centuries of boredom and grief. Now there was no possibility of her adjusting to that existence among the bandits, because the more intimately el Zarco behaved with her, she being his sweetheart now, the greater aversion she felt toward him, aversion complicated by a kind of fear or horror of the man who had dragged her into that pit.

As a necessity of her new life, Manuela had needed to initiate relationships, if not of friendship at least of familiarity, with those women living in the chapel with her, and even with other bandits' mistresses, who lived elsewhere.

Among them she paid special attention to one woman, not because she was any less vile, but because she was very familiar with Yautepec, where she had lived for many years, and she was always talking about people who Manuela knew: doña Antonia, Pilar, and Nicolás, most especially Nicolás, with whom she was well acquainted.

"Oh, Manuelita!" this woman had said to her on the first day they struck up a conversation: "I'm so happy you're here with us, because you're so pretty and graceful, and because I like el Zarco and my man likes him too, but that won't stop me from telling you, you committed a big blunder in coming here with him. If he'd put you in a house in one of the towns or haciendas or ranches where we have friends, he would have done better and you'd be safer and happier. But here, my dear, you're going to suffer a lot. For those of us who've followed our men in all the wars, and gone with them from pillar to post, this life's not such a burden now, and, on the contrary, we like it, because, after all, we're used to it, and the things that happen to us are amusing sometimes, aside from getting our share from time to time, and good things come our way. True, we also get some good scares too, and there are days we don't eat and nights when we don't sleep, and our men beat us and mistreat us but, I've already said it, we're accustomed and nothing bothers us. But you, a girl who's always been so sheltered, so homebound, so coddled by her mamá, who has such fine features and a delicate little body not made for doing chores, the truth is, my dear, I'm very afraid you're going to get sick or that some harm may come your way. Now that you're already seeing it, you're very sad, it shows in your face that you're unhappy, isn't that so?"

Manuela responded only by shedding a flood of tears.

"Poor little thing!" that woman went on. "I saw you two years ago, back there in Yautepec. So beautiful! So respectable! So well dressed! You looked like a virgin, and the *gachupines* at the shop and all the town's good-looking boys liked you a lot, although I'll tell you frankly, not one of them measures up to don Nicolás, the blacksmith. Nicolás, poor thing, he's swarthy, he's ugly, he's graceless, like the Indian hand laborer that he is, but they says he's a hard worker, that he's already laid away his money, and they love him greatly. Here you can't speak highly of him, because they're afraid of him and he's the only one they haven't been able to strike at, because he's so brave and won't let them, and since he owns neither land nor cattle, nor anything else they can seize, but keeps his money who knows where, so they'd have to catch him and torture him so he'd hand it over, but they haven't been able to, because he's very suspicious and always goes around well armed and with other stout-hearted men. But that man, yes, he would have suited you, my girl, and he was in love with you for a long time and everybody knew it; what I'm telling you is only the truth, and God save me from el Zarco's overhearing me because he'd put out my eyes, but it's the truth. El Zarco is certainly good-looking and likeable and good in a fight, and he has a large fortune, but I tell you, he's got a nasty disposition, and if he keeps seeing you sulky, he's going to get angry, and he could . . ."

"What!" Manuela interrupted briskly, "he might hit me?"

"Well listen, Manuelita, that's not so unlikely. He loves you very much, but I'm telling you now, he has a very nasty disposition."

"Well, that's all I need," Manuela replied. And immediately she added bitterly: "No, he won't do that, and why should he? What reason do I give him?"

"Apparently none at all, and on the contrary he's very much in love with you, but, for just that reason, he's a beast, and if he sees you always sulking and sulking, he's going to think that maybe you don't love him, that you regret following him here, and he'd be capable of killing you, in a rage . . .

"My advice to you is, appear happier, pretend to be, make el Zarco think you're happy, that you get along with us women, that you put up with the cracks from the boys, who also have realized by now that you don't like them. Anyway, just try to adjust to our way of life because, when it comes down to it, my love, right now you're el Zarco's, and unless something unfortunate happens, such as, for example, he's killed, you always have to be with him, if you don't manage some way or other to have him take you elsewhere; but then that could be worse, because you'd have to contend with people who are suspicious of you, and what's more, with that jealousy of el Zarco's, with his being away from you, he will always have to feel distrustful and at the slightest gossip they tell him, there'll be fights and deaths, and then you'll regret having parted from him. All in all, it's better you do what I tell you: lots of pretending, and winning everyone's affection."

Manuela easily understood that the woman was right and that, although painful and unpleasant, she had portrayed to Manuela the life she must lead with genuine truth drawn from experience. There was no replying to the woman's arguments. Everything that had happened and was yet to happen to Manuela was nothing but the inevitable consequence of her confusion, her blindness, her foolishness. Having plunged headlong into the abyss, with no deviation possible, she must fall to the bottom. Thus, there was no escape: she was like a little bird trapped in the nets, a fly enmeshed in a monstrous spider's dismal web, and the more she struggled to free herself, the more enmeshed she became.

With this reflection, Manuela felt death's chill course through her body, and she was overcome by a strong desire to escape, to take flight, followed by an indescribable collapse and despondency.

Pretend! Dissemble! How horrible, and yet, no other path lay open to her. She proposed, therefore, to take it, to change her behavior entirely and to deceive el Zarco in order to inspire his trust, with the aim of taking advantage of the first chance to escape from his clutches.

That life was full of ups and downs, of chance events; they would not always be in that headquarters, they would not always be crossing that rugged terrain. It was possible that at some time they would have to pass near some city; then she would take refuge there, appeal to the authorities, summon their help; perhaps she would encounter Nicolás, would arouse his compassion, and he would save her: Nicolás, who the bandits feared so, Nicolás, who was so brave, so honorable, and so generous!

Because, as is to be imagined, with the shift in thinking that had taken hold of Manuela's will, the more that el Zarco's figure dimmed in the shadows of fear, dread, and perhaps hatred, the young blacksmith's figure was being bathed in a rosy, new light.

Even to that woman who did no more than speak the truth, Nicolás was worth more than el Zarco, than all those bandits who feared him. He was not blessed with good looks but, on the other hand, how beautiful his soul was! Manuela had already learned, in so few days, to judge the value of outward show when compared to depths of spirit. El Zarco, young, good looking, formerly pleasing to her, now inspired her dread.

Nicolás, the unpolished worker, the sooty Indian with coarse, blackened hands, wearing a leather apron while brandishing his hammer at the anvil, illuminated by the forge's ruddy blaze, and earning his livelihood by the most honorable labor, now seemed beautiful to her, full of distinction, kindly in comparison to those sluggards, riddled with vice, covered in silver they had wrenched away by means of murder and theft, outcasts from society, always living anxiously, with one eye on the gallows, sleeping by starts, seeking in drunkenness and gambling oblivion from their regrets or their sole pleasures in that despicable life

How beautiful and how sweet life would have been in that worker's home, surrounded by the respect of honest people! Such a peaceful home, all the more so for being humble! Such happy days, dedicated from dawn to simple household duties! Such blissful nights, after the toils of the day, spent in quiet conversations and ease untroubled by a single bitter memory! And then, a delicious, well-prepared supper at the poor but spotless table, the children's caresses, the old mother's advice, plans for the future, hopes rooted in economy, industry, and goodness . . . a whole world of happiness and light . . . All vanished! All impossible now!

And in the midst of this picture arose, quickly but sharp and clear, an image that caused Manuela to tremble. It was the image of Pilar, of her sweet, good cousin, who seemed to love Nicolás secretly and whom she had regularly teased by saying so, as though to humiliate her! And now . . . this fleeting apparition, in that receding dream of happiness, produced a bitter, piercing emotion in Manuela. It was envy! It was jealousy!

Pilar deserved that happiness, which she, the fool,

had disdained; but still and all Manuela felt an indescribable uneasiness at the mere suspicion of it, and she could calm herself only by thinking that such a union was impossible, since Nicolás could not love the orphan, passionately in love as he was with her, with Manuela, and how inflamed that passion must be, as a result of her flight.

With everything else, these thoughts had scarcely arisen in Manuela's mind, after her conversation with the woman she had chosen as confidante, when they began to evolve doggedly and relentlessly. Pilar's image was now Manuela's constant nightmare, and her suspicions took on the quality of realities, as always happens with lively imaginations. And the fact is that Manuela now loved Nicolás, and loved him with a desperate, violent passion struggling against the impossible.

That is why, although she had intended to follow the advice she had received and take the path of dissimulation, she was not able to and enclosed herself within a silence and sadness still more obdurate than that of the previous days.

El Zarco finally let his anger show, and he rebuked her: "If you stay sad, you're going to make me do something drastic," he told her.

Manuela shrugged.

But one afternoon el Zarco arrived on horseback and very pleased. During the day he had made an expedition along with several of his cohorts. He jumped off his horse at the chapel door and ran in to see Manuela, who, as almost always, was to be found shut away in a sort of bedroom that she had improvised.

"Take this," the bandit said to her, "so you aren't sad any more."

And he placed in her hands a money-bag of doubloons.

"What's this?" asked Manuela uneasily.

"Look what it is," el Zarco replied, pouring the

doubloons onto the bed. "One hundred gold pieces," he added, "that they just brought me and tomorrow they'll bring me another hundred or I'll slit that Frenchman's gullet."

"What Frenchman?" Manuela asked horrified.

"Just some Frenchman the boys went to get me from near Chalco, almost all the way to Mexico City. Just imagine! He's rich, and he'll loosen his purse strings or die! His family already sent one hundred gold coins, but if they don't send five hundred, he's going to suffer! I've got him here eating one tortilla every twelve hours."

"My God!" Manuela exclaimed, appalled.

"What? You're appalled, you faker? Get out of here, what a show you put on! Instead of being happy, because with that money we're going to be rich. I'll give something to my pals, but we'll take the biggest share, and then we'll start clearing out of here, little by little, because we can't go right away. We'll leave here for Morelos or Zacatecas or the devil knows where, some place they don't know who I am, and I'll set up a tavern or we'll buy a ranch, because, the way you are, you don't look as though you want to lead this life—the way you promised me!"

Manuela, without showing that she had understood his reproach and after having glanced indifferently at the gold, answered him: "Listen, Zarco, even if you don't bring me any more money, I beg you to set that man free. You say he's eating one tortilla every twenty-four hours?"[35]

"Yes," Zarco replied, taken aback.

"Well then," Manuela went on, "I beg you to feed him well, and then set him free, even if he doesn't give you more money."

"What are you talking about?" el Zarco asked, his hoarse voice shot through with the most brutal rage. "Are

---

(35) *twenty-four hours:* Previously el Zarco told Manuela that he was restricting the Frenchman to one tortilla every twelve hours.—*Eds.*

you crazy, Manuela, saying this to me? Don't you know that every moneybags who falls into our hands has to purchase his life, with his weight in gold? Don't you realize that only for you, for you alone, you ingrate, I risked the boys' setting out to bring me that rich man, so he'd give us money, stuff us with gold pieces, for you to buy jewelry, silk dresses, everything you want, and now you come out with this compassion and these pleas? Then you certainly haven't learned yet who I am and what I'm capable of. You're a good girl, Manuelita, and you were brought up among very strict, devout people, but you knew who I was, and if you didn't think you could adapt to my way of life, what made you leave home? You already knew what I am, you already knew where the jewelry I gave you came from. What are you frightened of now? Did you come here to preach us sermons? Then you're wasting your time and wearing me down, because, really, I'm not standing for your grimaces and your scorn for my men, your weepiness and your humbug. For some days now Salomé and Félix and el Coyote have been telling me that I made a mistake bringing you here with us, and that you're going to cause some kind of trouble, and me, only because of my affection for you, I've been putting up with their innuendos and, thinking to please you, I put the lives of my best comrades in danger, to have them bring me some rich man so I could fleece him and give you money, lots of money, and what, only for you to come out with this foolishness . . . really, Manuelita, I don't have to put up with it. If your way of thinking was so different, why didn't you marry that Indian from Atlihuaya? That man's no thief! But with me, drink it up or spit it out . . . either you accept the life I lead, or you die, Manuela," el Zarco said, moving closer to the young woman, glaring, deadening his tone of voice, and placing his hand on the butt of his pistol.

Manuela shuddered at this outburst of rage.

"But I wanted you," she said timidly, "for my sake, not to go killing that foreigner . . . It was for you, only for you! Because I'm afraid of your committing murder . . . "

"Murder!" el Zarco echoed nasally, livid with anger . . . though already somewhat calmer. "Murder! Listen to the fool! You think this is the first cat I've skinned? Go to hell with your scruples! This Frenchman's going where the others went, even if it weren't to give the money to you. Don't you realize, you babe in the woods, that a rich man who falls into our hands belongs to all of us? Even if I wanted to set the Frenchman free, do you think the rest of them would let me? What, then, about their share?"

"All right, let's not talk about it anymore," Manuela said, frightened. "Do whatever you want, Zarco, I won't say another word to you."

"Well, that's good," the bandit replied. "and you'll be doing right. Now what we have to do is take advantage of the situation. Put these doubloons away without more fuss and don't talk or bother me with tears and complaints."

El Zarco had scarcely finished speaking than a clamor of voices was heard, blending with the strumming of large and small guitars, and into the chapel came Salomé Plasencia, Palo Seco, el Tigre, Linares and some twenty bandits . . . apparently celebrating and certainly drunk.

"Zarco!" they shouted, "you're rich now, brother, and we're going to have a dance to cheer up the little angel you've brought from Yautepec who's dying from grumpiness."

"Come on, bring her out, boy, bring her out so she comes and dances with us, the waltz and the polka and the schottische."

"Come, Manuela, and take care not to offend my friends," said el Zarco, taking the hand of the girl, who let herself be led like a lamb to the slaughter and tried to feign a smile.

"Here I am, brothers, and here's my little angel

ready to go dancing."

"*Huërita*," announced Salomé, who was carrying
a bottle in his hand, "you're coming with us to the dance
we're going to have, to celebrate the exploits of your darling,
el Zarco. Day before yesterday he tortured that Frenchman
with a sugar-cane whipping until he spit out the little gold
pieces you must have stashed away, you good girl you, and
we're going to drink and enjoy ourselves . . . Come on over
here and stop being sad over there, like the Virgin on Good
Friday."

"All right, all right," said el Zarco. "Let's go get
ready for the dance and set out the liquors, but I'll come back
and fetch Manuela. Get dressed, my love, and deck yourself
out for the dance, until I come back for you."

"Zarco, you're jealous," said Salomé, patting him on
the shoulder and teasing. "You're jealous, and you know that
doesn't go among us. For now we'll grant you this bluffing, but
don't keep it up for long, brother, because it's not right . . . "

Manuela trembled. Everything was turning into
new perils for her. Once she was by herself, she called her
confidante to come help her get dressed but really to speak
with her.

"Who is this Frenchman they're holding prisoner?"
she asked. "Do you know anything?"

"Of course!" the woman replied, "and I'm very
surprised you don't. The Frenchman's down there in the
cellar of the main house, and they torture him every day so
his family in Mexico City forks over their money. They say
they've already handed over a sackful and el Zarco's got
it. El Amarillo (that is what her man was called) is the one
who's attending to him now, just like the rest of them."

"Then, there are others?" Manuela asked attentively.

"Obviously there are others," the woman replied.
"There's a *gachupín*, there's another shopkeeper, another
real miser, an old man who complains all day long, and some

others who are sore pinched but can give up their hundred or two hundred pesos. After all, it's something!"

"And could I see them?"

"Why not! If el Zarco wants to take you, that's the easiest. But as you're so sensitive, it's going to disturb you."

"I won't be disturbed," Manuela responded determinedly. "I'm changed now, I'm going to follow your advice now."

"Oh, I'm so glad!" the woman exclaimed. "Then you'll really enjoy yourself. You'll see!"

As el Zarco was just coming in at that moment, Manuela begged him to take her where the hostages were.

El Zarco looked at her in surprise: "You?" he asked her. "You want to see the prisoners? But what's happened?"

"What's happened," Manuela answered, "is that I'm going to show you that I'm neither sad nor unhappy with this life, that I'm not afraid of anything, and that when I decided to leave my house and family for you, it was because I was determined to follow you everywhere and to share your lot."

"Good girl, that's what I like! I was really displeased with you, but since you were just making a show and you're just what I thought, now I'm really happy. I'll take you down where those godforsaken are, and don't go taking pity on them, because they've got money and don't risk their lives like us."

Dressed and primped now for the dance, and very pretty despite being pale and haggard, Manuela allowed the bandit to lead her down to the *pugares*, now used as a prison for the outlaws' unfortunate victims. [36]

_____

(36) *purgares*: Purification chambers on the hacienda where the final stage of refining sugar was accomplished by pouring the sugar into inverted conical molds and then sealing the mold's top with a layer of moist earth or clay, allowing the seal's moisture to seep through the mass below over a period of some forty days, thereby washing away the molasses and leaving the relatively clean crystals behind. While large, if not necessarily "vast, vaulted chambers," the *purgares* were usually separate structures built to accommodate the many workers needed in the process and

At the only door still working stood a guard of some twenty bandits, armed with muskets, pistols, machetes, and knives. They remained silent, their faces covered by kerchiefs.

Those vast, vaulted chambers, used for storing sugar loaves in earlier days and known on the haciendas as *purgares*, would have been completely dark if up in the quoins there had not been a small oil lamp shining into the corners close to where four men lay on filthy mats, their hands and feet tied, eyes blindfolded, and who would have been taken for corpses if from time to time their pained movements and faint sobs had not revealed that they were living bodies.

"Look at the Frenchman," el Zarco said to Manuela, leading her to one of the corners and pointing to an old gray-haired man, tightly bound and showing scarcely any signs of life.

Beside him were some crossed beams, ropes, lances, and some other instruments of torture, a pitcher of water and a bottle of cane liquor.

"Day before yesterday, we caned this damned *gavacho*[37] and that's why he's yielded the gold pieces, but if he doesn't let loose of any more money, we'll do something worse to him. He still doesn't know what it's like to have his neck throttled or his toenails and fingernails pulled out. He'll know soon."

At these last words, uttered in a loud voice, the miserable Frenchman, who had heard them, tried to sit up,

to protect the product from weather and theft; therefore, *purgares* tended to be dark, with a few windows placed high in the walls and, as a result, also came to serve as holding places and prisons.—*Eds./Sol, 127*

(37) *gavacho*, originally *gabacho* from Provençal *gavach*, a person who speaks badly (alternately from *gave*, a brook or stream in the Pyrenees): a colloquial, disrespectful term originating in the Spanish middle ages for an immigrant from the French Basque country or the foothills of the Pyrenees and thus, by extension, for a foreigner; also for speech that is full of Gallicisms. In current usage *gavacho* refers insultingly to Anglo-Americans, white men.—*Eds.*

and in a weak, plaintive voice, he said: "Listen, señor, for the love of God, kill me, I can't take anymore, kill me!"

"No, not yet, you old skinflint. Order them to send another four hundred gold pieces; if not, you'll see what happens to you."

"I don't have any more gold pieces," the wretch responded. "I'm poor, I have a family, I have little children, there's no one who will lend me . . . I don't have anymore! I don't have anymore! Kill me . . ."

"Go on," said Manuela, near to fainting, "if he has no money, let them kill him . . ."

"No," Zarco retorted, scoffing with a sinister, frightening laugh. "They all say that, they get desperate, they want to die, but since life only comes around once, they end up loosening their purse strings. Tomorrow, this one will give us what we're asking him for. His family's already been warned, and he's already written to say what's happening to him."

"All right," said Manuela, trembling all over, "but won't the government send troops to hunt you people down and free these men? Their families won't tell?"

"Oh, no! That doesn't serve any purpose for them, because they'll be afraid we'll kill the hostages. Besides, the government can't send forces against us, and even if it sent them, they wouldn't do anything to us. They wouldn't find us here. In case you're not aware, Manuelita, we're strong, we're safe, and, for the time being, no one threatens us! But, let's go to the dance, they're waiting for us now! You must dance with everybody and be cheerful: they're not going to tell me I'm jealous and we start having a brawl.

Manuela left the *purgar* in haste, pale, shaking violently, her eyes popping out of their sockets, crazed with horror and fear. However dreadful that dance might be, it could not cause her the fear, the immense aversion that the sight of those hostages had just produced in her.

Since the dance was taking place in the less run-down rooms of the hacienda's old main house not far from the *purgar's* vaults, the couple climbed the crumbling stairs and soon entered the large hall, lit with tallow candles and filled with smoke, where the bandits had gathered to have a good time.

A few oversize mandolins, regular guitars as well as the little ones called *jaranas* resonated there in the hall, playing polkas and waltzes; because, it is worth noting, the bandits were not partial to popular Mexican dances such as the *jarabe*,[38] and then danced them only as a kind of embellishment or on a whim. The Plateados had pretensions, they danced well enough, but for that same reason, their dances had all the repugnant appearance of parody or the grotesqueness of caricature.

Upon Manuela's entering with el Zarco, a frightful clamor arose. Vivas, flirtatious compliments, oaths, blasphemies all poured from a hundred mouths twisted by drunkenness and debauchery. Every famous bandit was there, covered in silver, and still armed, some singing obscene songs, others embracing the downfallen women keeping them company. Manuela shuddered. Scarcely had she let go of Zarco's arm, when the colossal, horrifying mulatto, who filled her with great repugnance, came over to her. He was still wearing the bandage that covered part of his face but revealed his enormous mouth, armed with sharp, white teeth, among which protruded two upper canines that seemed to pierce his lower lip. He was literally sheathed in silver, as if he had wanted to outdo the rest of his companions in ornamentation.

"Now you're going to dance with me, *güerita*," he

---

(38) *jarabe*: A popular dance typical of various American peoples and characterized by heel tapping or shuffling steps and with movements, tapping, turns, and variations particular to each locale; overall, the *jarabe* resembles the Spanish *jota.—Sol, 290.*

said to Manuela, one of his filthy paws grasping the girl's delicate, white arm.

With an uncontrollable movement, Manuela pulled back, frightened, and attempted to follow el Zarco in order to take cover behind him. But the mulatto followed her, laughing, wrapping his sinewy arm around her waist and saying to el Zarco: "Look, Zarco, your angel's running away from me and doesn't want to dance. Force her."

"Woman, what is this now, Manuela? Why don't you want to dance with my friend el Tigre? I told you before, you have to dance with everyone. That's why you've come."

Manuela resigned herself and, feigning a rueful smile, allowed herself to be led away by that monstrosity of hideousness and rudeness.

"Ah!" he cried, pushing back his enormous sombrero while he went on clasping and fitfully squeezing Manuela's waist. "I was right saying I'd have the pleasure of hugging you as much as I wanted! Right now, you're with a real man, and we're going to have a good time dancing this schottische."

Manuela almost closed her eyes, and allowed herself to be led by that sort of Cyclops, who devoured her with the one eye he had uncovered while bathing her with his panting, like a mist of liquor.

Watching them go by—he frightful, like a rabid beast, and she slight and bent back, like his prey—the other bandits shouted at him: "Hey, Tigre, don't gobble up that little doe!"

After having taken a few turns around that foul hall, bumping into and shoving fifty drunken couples of bandits and their women, el Tigre stopped dancing; but, bending down to his partner, he told her, in a voice strangled by desire . . . while brutally squeezing her arm: "My little angel, ever since I saw you arrive with el Zarco, I liked what I saw, and I spoke to la Zorra, el Amarillo's woman, about telling you, not so you'd respond to me right away but so you'd know once and for all, I don't know if she might have spoken to you?"

Manuela did not answer.

"Well in case she hasn't told you, I'm telling you now, frankly: you've got to grow to love me . . ."

"Me?" exclaimed the girl, scared to death.

"You!" el Tigre replied. "You'll soon see! El Zarco isn't steady, and he'll pay you back bad, like he's paid them all back . . . but I'm here, my lovely, so when he sets you straight, you keep me in mind, and then you'll see who el Tigre is. You don't know me, and you don't know el Zarco yet. Don't get scared seeing me with my face bandaged up like this, because I'm this way right now on account of you."

"On account of me?" Manuela asked, her curiosity mixed with fear.

"Yes, on account of you, and I'm going to explain it to you. I was wounded by the *gringos* we killed in Alpuyeca. I killed them, you better believe me! I was the one who kept up the fight, while el Zarco robbed the trunks. A *gringo* put a bullet in me with his pistol, almost put out my eye; but in the end he died, and everyone with him died, all the men. But el Zarco hardly gave us a hand during the thick of the fighting, and after all of them were already down and dying, that's when he came up and he killed them when they'd already been beaten, and he killed the women and children. Yes, señor, that's how it was. El Zarco's a worm and a chicken, but that man, oh yes, he took all the jewelry to bring to you, and he didn't leave us anything but worthless clothes, because, why would we want those things? Frock coats, jackets, old dresses, *catrines'* rags! And el Zarco snatched the best, after our victory! That's all right, eagles don't squawk. But once I saw you, I said, 'Now's the time, I'm pairing off! Let Zarco take the jewelry, but let him leave us the *güerita*, and we're square.'"

Manuela seemed to be imprisoned in a nightmare and she felt faint. Those revelations about el Zarco, his murders of the women, the dying, and the children, those threats of el Tigre—all that surpassed her might and her resolve to face such a life. She had fallen into hell. She had thought those men were simply bandits, and in reality they were fiends vomited out of the bottomless pit. Oh! If she had been able to escape at that moment! If at least she had been able to die! She was left paralyzed and speechless. El Tigre's hoarse, rasping voice tore her from that state, asking: "What's the matter, beautiful? Frightened by what I'm telling you? Didn't el Zarco tell you about all his feats and brave exploits? I bet not. Well, get familiar with them, and start accepting what I'm telling you: you have to come and stay under my protection."

"But do you think el Zarco's going to allow that?" Manuela finally exclaimed, choked with anger and disgust.

"What's it matter to me if he allows it or not, angel? So what? You think I'm afraid of that yellow-belly? If you accept my affections, give me the word right now and I'll kill el Zarco. That way you'll be free, once and for all . . . If not, I'll wait, and you'll soon see what happens."

"Then, I'm going to tell el Zarco about it, so he's on guard!"

"So you tell him, beautiful, you tell him," el Tigre responded with a scornful, evil laugh that revealed his terrible resolve. "El Zarco knows me already," he added, "and you'll see if what I said is true: the el Zarco you fell in love with, because you thought he was a man, he's nothing but a worm. So there, you tell him, and so that it's soon, I'm going to sit down right here and stay waiting."

Manuela went to sit down, terrified. Surely a catastrophe was in the offing. El Tigre wanted to provoke one at any cost, so he could kill el Zarco, and she was destined to be the victor's spoils. What a dreadful situation!

She felt tortured.

But when she anxiously looked for her lover, who, in spite of the horror he now filled her with, she still considered her only defense, she saw him coming toward her, frowning, cold, livid with anger. Manuela imagined that he was jealous of el Tigre, and she guessed that the moment had come for the fight she feared.

El Zarco, smiling sarcastically, hoarse with anger, said to her: "So now I know what's the reason for your sulking and your boredom these days! They've told me, and you're not going to play me false again, you wretch!"

"But, what is it? What is it? What have they told you, Zarco?" Manuela asked, as shocked as she was terrified at hearing those words.

"Yes, la Zorra's already told me what it's about: you regret having coming away with me, you've realized you didn't love me . . . truly . . ., the only man you loved was the Indian, Nicolás, you regret leaving him behind, your life with the Plateados doesn't suit you, and the first chance you get, you've going to run away from me."

"But I haven't said . . . ," Manuela interrupted herself, trembling.

El Zarco did not let her finish: "Yes, you did say that, you liar and cheat, don't try to deny it! I'm to blame for trusting a *catrina*, a plaster saint like you, who cares for nothing but jewelry and money. But, look," he added, taking hold of her arm and squeezing it brutally, "so far as what's mine, don't trifle with me, understand? You ran away with me, and now you're seeing what you were born for. As for that Indian blacksmith, I'll have the pleasure of bringing you his head so you can eat it, roasted with chilies, and after that you're going to die, but you're not going to keep laughing at me."

Manuela was scarcely able to say to el Zarco, with an imploring gesture: "Zarco, please, take me away from here, I'm ill . . .!'"

"I'm not taking you away—die!" the bandit
answered, in a fit of rage.

He had hardly finished saying these words when
there was a lot of noise at the door to the hall and several
bandits, covered in dust, and with their clothing disheveled
from a long journey, burst in dazed and asking for Salomé
Plasencia, for el Zarco, el Tigre, and the rest of the leaders.

Salomé and the others went over to meet them.
"What is it?" he asked, as all the Plateados gathered in a
circle around them and the music, as one would imagine, as
well as the dance's gaiety ceased.

"News," replied one of the recent arrivals, out of
breath: "We've raced ten leagues to warn you . . . Martín
Sánchez Chagollán,[39] the man from Acapixtla, with a squad
of forty men, has taken Juan the Gachupín and twenty of his
men by surprise, and left them hanging in the *catzahuate*
forest at Casano."

"When was that?" the terrified bandits asked all at
once.

"Last night, he surprised them around ten o'clock.
They were lying in ambush in the forest, waiting for a
shipment that was to go by, when Martín Sánchez fell upon
them, surrounded them, and only five or six were able to
escape and came looking for us, but they were wounded and
couldn't come all the way here."

"But . . . what? Didn't those boys put up a fight?"
asked Salomé.

"Yes, they fought back, but there were more of the
others and they were carrying really good weapons."

---

(39) *Martín Sánchez Chagollán*: Like many characters in *El Zarco*, Sánchez Chagollán is an historical figure. He lived in the town of Tlayacapan and later moved to
Yecapixtla, also known as Ayacapixtla. Altamirano must have heard stories about
his exploits—or perhaps he knew him personally—during his stays at the Santa Inés
hacienda, a property belonging to the Rovalo family.—*Sol, 297.*

"And . . . so? Didn't they have any warning?"

"That's what seemed strange to us, but I think people are starting to help Martín Sánchez and not keeping their promises to us."

"Then we have to avenge our men and put fear into the people so they don't turn away from us entirely. Tomorrow, at dawn, we'll all leave from here and meet up with the others scattered around, and we'll go looking for Martín Sánchez and see if he's as good against five hundred men as he is against thirty. So get ready for tomorrow."

"And what do we do with the prisoners?" asked one man.

"Well, those men, let them die," Salomé said. "What do we want with nuisances? . . . You, Tigre, go kill them right now."

"Look, Salomé," el Tigre said, stepping forward, "you better give that job to el Zarco: he really knows how to kill the dead," he added contemptuously.

"Kill the dead, you say, Tigre?"

"Yes, kill the dead," el Tigre repeated. "Remember Alpuyeca."

"Well, now you're going to find out if I know how to kill the living, too!" el Zarco replied, livid with anger.

"All right, all right," Salomé said, stepping between them, "we don't want any fighting, anybody's good for dispatching the prisoners. The thing is for them not to see tomorrow's dawn; carry the order to el Amarillo, and hurry up. The dance is over."

"Oh, and another piece of news!" added one of the new arrivals. "This morning, in Yautepec, they buried the mother of the girl el Zarco brought here."

Then they heard a shrill scream that made all those men turn their heads.

"My mother!" Manuela cried and dropped to the ground in a faint.

"Poor thing," the women said, coming back to themselves after being dazed by the deluge of bad news.

"Pick her up, Zarco, and carry her, and she'd better resign herself, because if not, she's going to be in our way."

El Zarco, helped by some of the women, raised Manuela up, hefted her, and bore her to the chapel, where he laid her down on her bed. The girl was nearly dead. So many emotions one after the other, so many dangers, so many threats, so many horrors had overwhelmed that delicate being and were extinguishing that spirit. Manuela was like a natural fool and did nothing but cry silently.

El Zarco, also worried by a thousand different thoughts, furious at el Tigre, jealous of Nicolás, more in love with Manuela than ever, but deeply vexed by the recent news and by the need to go into action, did not know what to do. He paced back and forth like a caged beast; he called on the women to assist his beloved, gave orders for the bandits to obey and serve him, packed valises, inspected the trunks, from time to time sat on the edge of the bed where Manuela was lying, and watched her with looks in which it was difficult to distinguish love, hatred, or the temptations of a disastrous decision and, at other times, he broke into pacing the length of the chapel, swearing.

Finally, he approached the girl and said and in a cold, dry voice: "There's nothing to do about it now, stop crying and get ready for our leaving here tomorrow, and help me pack the valises. Store your jewelry away safely; that's what matters. Just between you and me," he added, seeing that Manuela was sobbing more violently, "it's not our custom to lament so much or to show so much grief when someone dies. We were born to die. Besides, your mother was already old, and the good woman hated me; pray for the rest of her soul, and amen. Don't think about her again. Your Indian must have buried her, and he'll take charge of the orchard and pay the bills. Afterward you'll bury him, don't concern yourself, and you'll have the satisfaction of weeping over his grave."

So then, that bandit, that el Zarco, whom Manuela had thought at least a man, at least compassionate, was no less than a heartless fiend who delighted in increasing her suffering, in insulting her at the time of her greatest sorrow, and in maligning the generous man who certainly, and without ulterior motives of any kind, had helped the poor, old woman in her last moments.

Manuela had already pictured it. Pilar and Nicolás had kept vigil beside the unfortunate señora's deathbed, and they had buried her. Nicolás and Pilar! Once again, that couple, who never ceased appearing in her imagination! Now, how lofty and how noble those two young people loomed! But, such a disgrace that they did not appear like that to her but, instead, caused her the horrible torment of jealousy and the indescribable shame of recognizing herself as a contemptible, ungrateful monster in comparison with them!

And yet, tormented and degraded, and despicable as she was, the mere thought of Nicolás seemed a glimpse of solace in the midst of that frightful night surrounding her on every side with its utter darkness, its horrors, and its dangers, still unknown but terrifying.

Finally, she stood up and, swallowing her tears, set to packing the valises, feeling death in her soul.

Martín Sánchez Chagollán

Now then: who was the fearless man who had dared to string up twenty Plateados in the very places they controlled and thus cause that commotion at the bandits' headquarters?

Martín Sánchez Chagollán's name was not entirely unknown at Xochimancas, so it did not stir any surprise there, but learning what he had done, that truly stirred surprise and in no small degree.

Stringing up twenty Plateados on Tetelcingo's *catzahuates*, that is, in the very heart of that satrapy where only crime and terror reigned!

But, who was this man? Was he a government leader, backed by the law and counting on every element of public power, with public funds and the aid of the authorities and the people?

Not at all. Martín Sánchez Chagollán, a strictly historical figure, like Salomé Plasencia, el Zarco, and the bandits we have presented in this narrative, was a private citizen, a *campesino* without military forebears of any sort; far from it, he had been an absolutely peaceful man, who always refused to involve himself in the civil strife that beset the country many years ago and, thus, aloof, almost timid, he lived by devoting himself exclusively to rural labors on a small ranch that he owned a short distance from Ayacapixtla, near Cuautla in Morelos.

By all accounts he was a good man, one of those zealots for honor who prefer dying to committing an action that might tarnish their name or make them less respectable in the eyes of their family or friends.

With such principles and in those times of upheaval and corruption, when many simple men from the country saw themselves obliged to become involved in revolutions or the crimes committed in their shadow, Martín Sánchez had to suffer greatly in order to avoid commitments and entanglements. But by dint of skill and firmness he remained untouched, and although viewed with suspicion or misgivings by those on all sides, he managed to remain peaceful, living out of the way and hidden on his little ranch, attending to his small concerns and assisted by his children, already grown up.

Because Martín Sánchez was a man already well on in years. He would have been over fifty, but his was one of those vigorous, robust constitutions only to be found in the country and the mountains, fortified by clean air, wholesome food, hard work, and simple ways. That is why, although in his fifties, he seemed a man at the height of virile strength.

Of short stature, with a round head that appeared to be set directly atop his shoulders because of a squat neck, Sánchez's broad shoulders, herculean arms, and sinewy bowlegs revealed him as a tireless worker and accomplished rider.

His tiny eyes, sparkling and greenish, his aquiline nose, his dark, well-tanned face, his thin, pursed lips, his always clean-shaven chin, along with his low brow and brush-cut, almost spiky hair gave him a certain feline appearance. He vaguely resembled a leopard.

Such was the man who during that period exercised a major hold on the Tierra Caliente and whose actions principally terminated that frightful plague of bandits that had ravaged those rich, fertile territories for years on end.

Martín Sánchez was living, then, a quiet life dedicated to his labors, as we have stated, when once being absent with his wife, a large band of Plateados descended on his ranch.

Martín's elderly father and his children defended themselves heroically, but they were overcome by the horde, which killed the old man, as well as one of the sons, sacked the house and then burned it down, destroying everything that constituted the honest rancher's patrimony.

When Martín Sánchez returned from Mexico City,

where he had gone, he found only the ashes of his house and among them the bodies of his father and son who had not been buried yet because the other children, wounded and hiding on the mountain, had not been able to come down to the ranch.

That, in short, was the horror and the desolation.

Martín's wife lost her mind for a time from grief and fear.

Martín Sánchez said nothing. He went up to the mountain to find his children. Together they buried the corpses of his father and son, and bidding farewell to his poor ranch, turned into a pile of rubble and burnt fields, he took his wife and family to the town of Ayacapixtla, where he hoped to find greater security.

Then he sold what little he had left and with the money he had raised bought weapons and horses to fit out a party of twenty men.

Afterward, his sons having now regained their health, he armed them, spoke with some of his relatives and convinced them to join him, paying them with his own money, and once this small squad was ready, he went to speak to the prefect of Morelos, and told him of his resolve to embark on a pursuit of the Plateados.

The prefect, commending his proposal, nevertheless made him see the terrible dangers he was going to be exposed to in the thick of that situation. But since Martín Sánchez responded that he had fully made up his mind to perish in his undertaking, the prefect, fulfilling his duty, offered him what assistance he had at his command and authorized him to pursue thieves, in the capacity of a chief of the Civil Guard.

and on condition that he hand over the criminals he might apprehend to the appropriate court.

Thus authorized, Martín Sánchez set out with his small squad. But, understanding clearly that with such a feeble force he could never form a front against the vast hordes of Plateados marauding the districts of Morelos, Yautepec, and Jonacatepec, he limited himself to a purely strategic campaign, trying to do battle with small parties, with the aim of availing himself of their arms and horses in order to augment his own strength.

And that was how, fleeing and riding by night, and paying spies, and making fabled one-day marches, little by little, he went along defeating some parties of bandits and providing himself with arms, munitions, and horses.

He fought against the general despondency, against the fear of the Plateados, with the complicity of many people, with the hostility of some authorities, pusillanimous or complicit in those crimes; he fought, finally, even against the low spirits of his own soldiers, who, having no other incentive than a small salary, were risking their lives and risking them against the Plateados, who meted out to their prisoners and hostages a death always accompanied by horrific tortures.

So that is how Martín Sánchez had to overcome, day-by-day, tremendous difficulties. But his thirst for vengeance gave him superior fortitude. That thirst was his resource.

Motivated by a personal feeling, little by little the wide-spread rancor gathered in him as in a common breast; each avenging of a Plateado crime found an echo in his spirit; each murder they committed was inscribed in the imposing book of his memory; each widow's, orphan's, parent's tear was stored in his heart as in an iron urn. From an avenger of his family, he had been transformed into an avenger of society.

He was the representative of the honest and forsaken, a sort of Judge Lynch, uncouth and ferocious

---

(40) *Judge Lynch:* In 1780, Captain William Lynch and some of his neighbors in Pittsylvania County, Virginia drew up a compact whose "subscribers, being determined to put a stop to the iniquitous practices . . . of a set of lawless men . . . that . . . have hitherto escaped the civil power with impunity . . ., we will forthwith . . . repair

besides, and implacable.[40]

In his soul he had abolished fear, he had embraced his cause with faith, hoping to die for it, and he was resolved. But among his feelings he had also abolished pity for the bandits.

An eye for an eye and a tooth for a tooth. That was his punitive law. Were the Plateados cruel? He proposed to be so as well.

Did the Plateados provoke horror? He had proposed to provoke horror.

The fight was going to be fearsome, without respite, without compassion. Who would win? Who knows! But Martín Sánchez threw himself into it with his eyes closed and his sword drawn and his breast ironclad by his thirst for vengeance and for justice.

The bandits ought to have trembled. The exterminating angel had finally arrived!

Against such obscene birds of prey, there was only the mountain eagle, with beak and talons of steel.

Martín Sánchez was society's indignation incarnate.

---

immediately to the person or persons suspected . . . and if they will not desist from their evil practices, we will inflict such corporeal punishment on him or them, as to us shall seem adequate to the crime committed or the damage sustained . . . ." This vigilante practice became known as "lynch law." "Lynching" originally referred to a range of punishments, including flogging, tar-and-feathering, and riding-out-of-town, but it came to designate death by hanging at the hands of a mob. During the Reconstruction period after the U.S. Civil war, and especially from 1868 to 1871, the period shortly after the established time of Altamirano's novel and close to the date of the Ku Klux Klan's founding (1866), lynching reached a horrendous peak, principally in Mississippi, Georgia, Alabama, Texas, and Louisiana, first for political and then for more strictly racial reasons. Judge Lynch, innocent of such abuses, had died in 1820; his tombstone reads, in part: "he followed virtue as his truest guide."

In Martín Sánchez Chagollán's stringing up Plateados on *cazahuate* trees, as described earlier in this chapter, Altamirano has anticipated his invocation here of Judge Lynch and his "law."—*Eds./Sol, 308.*

The Attack

La Calavera was an inn on the old wagon road between
Mexico City and Cuautla de Morelos, less famous as a stop
for mule trains, stagecoaches, and foot travelers than as a
place for robberies.

In fact, not inside the inn itself but, indeed, a little
before or a little after, there was always an attack in those
times. And that is because in those parts the road's curves, its
mountainous location, the nearby dense forests and ravines
all offered thieves a great many places in which to hide,
ambush, or escape.

For that reason, stagecoach passengers and
muleteers never approached La Calavera without crossing
themselves and trembling with fear. The name itself is
doleful.[41] Probably, in olden times, at this place there had
been nailed among the trees along the road a skull that had
belonged to some famous bandit who had been executed
by the functionaries of the Acordada court[42] in the colonial
period; or perhaps there had been many thieves' skulls, and
the people, as is customary in Mexico, had singularized the
name, to shorten it.

The fact is that the place is extraordinarily sinister,
and in the past no one caught sight of the rambling old
building, dark, dilapidated, and gloomy, without feeling

---

(41) *doleful*: "calavera" means skull, death's-head.—*Eds*.

(42) *Acordada court*: Tribunal of Common Consent established in Mexico in 1710
to pursue and put to judgment thieves and murderers along the Camino Real.
The prisoners were judged summarily and immediately executed, attended by the
captain of the court, his deputies, a clerk to testify to the execution, a chaplain to
attend the captured man, and an executioner to hang him from a tree at the edge of
the Camino Real where he had committed his misdeed. This court had prisons in
Cuernavaca, Cuautla, and Huautla, and it functioned without interruption from 1785
until 1812, when it was abolished on account of its inhumanity. While being historically accurate, Altamirano is also glancing at the previously invoked lynch law and
Martín Sánchez Chagollán's hanging of the twenty Plateados.—*Eds./Sol, 310.*

uneasy and afraid.

It was there, then, on an autumn afternoon with the sun already setting, three months after the events we have just recounted had taken place, that there happened to be standing in front of the inn a cavalry unit made up of some forty men.

These men wore singular uniforms: black jackets with steel buttons painted black; black trousers, and high, sturdy, yellow leather boots with steel spurs; narrow-brimmed black sombreros with no adornment except for a white band with the lettering: *Civil Guard*. And as for their weapons: a musket slung diagonally over the back, a sword with a heavy, black hilt and a steel scabbard. Around his waist each man wore a cartridge belt packed full. Magnificent horses, almost all dark in color, with saddles and all equipment extremely plain and unornamented. Black ponchos tied to the horse's rump.

Nearly all these soldiers looked young, very hardy, and had a proud, martial bearing; but their uniforms and equipment gave them a doleful look, and that inspired fear. They seemed like ghosts, and at that La Calavera Inn, at that time of day when objects began to lengthen gigantically, near those desolate mountains, such a column of silent, grim horsemen looked less like a troop than like a sepulchral apparition.

One man, undoubtedly their leader, stood on the ground, holding his horse by the bridle and seemed to be quizzing the horizon, where the road disappeared, surely expecting someone.

He was dressed the same as his soldiers, except that instead of boots he wore yellow kidskin chaps and was cloaked in a kind of dark tippet.

In a few moments, an individual, advanced in years and well dressed, came out of the inn and, addressing this leader, asked, "No sign of them yet, don Martín?"

"Nothing, not a trace!" the other responded.

That leader, then, was Martín Sánchez Chagollán, and those were his troops, uniformed in black and without a single ornament, in accord with their leader's design, arising from hatred of the Plateados. Also from hatred of them, he had determined that his soldiers' sombreros have narrow, not wide brims and no hatband at all.

Martín Sánchez took a very dim view of everyone who wore a sombrero adorned with silver and, as his distrust grew more frightening, simple dark hats were becoming popular in those parts, since they offered a sort of safe-conduct.

Nevertheless, at that time Martín Sánchez was still very far from becoming the terror of the bandits and their accomplices. He still took a thousand precautions with his campaigns and expeditions, fearful of being defeated; he was still taking his "first steps," as he said. He had already strung up a good number of Plateados, but he had often been blamed for committing these violations for which he was not authorized, since, as we have said, he was empowered only to apprehend the criminals and turn them over to their judges. But Martín Sánchez had responded that he strung up only those who died fighting, and then only to set an example. In this matter it is quite possible that he was concealing something and that in truth he shot every bandit he caught; but he evidently had not been able to deploy all his energy nor did he have the resources necessary to do so, since he could rely only on those forty men and his own resolve.

The individual who had just addressed him and who appeared to be a wealthy *hacendado* or merchant, seeing that the people they expected were not coming, said: "Well, don Martín, assuming that these men are not showing up, if you have nothing else to propose, let's continue our journey, because it's getting late and we won't reach Morelos until late. Besides, the shipment has gotten far ahead now and some accident could happen to it."

"I think," Martín responded, "that there's nothing to worry about around here. They know I'm here and they don't dare. But this don Nicolás, I'm truly concerned about him. Something must have happened to him, since he's not showing up. He wrote me that he'd leave Chalco at dawn. He would have had lunch in Tenango, and it's already past the time for him to be with us. It's true he's traveling with a good escort and, besides, he's a brave man; but these damned outlaws are capable of having laid an ambush for him between Tenango and here, though I have no word that any party showed up yesterday or the day before. But you know the ones from Ozumba make deals with the others and that's how they form their associations. I'd really be sorry if something happened to such a good friend. I ought to have gone ahead to Juchi or Tenango, but he let me know that here's where he needed me to join him, because he'd been warned from here that his enemies, who've sworn to finish him off, and me too, would be waiting. And just think, the poor man's getting married soon and went to Mexico City with a good bit of money to buy the gifts for his bride, so besides killing him, those devils would get their hands on a lot of jewelry. Anyway, I'll leave some boys here in case he comes and we'll go on ahead, because the shipment must have gone a long way by now."

Then Martín Sánchez mounted his horse and rode on with his troop, accompanied by that merchant and his boys, leaving about ten men behind with the order to escort Nicolás, our acquaintance, who was coming from Mexico City.

They had been riding for scarcely half an hour when they heard shots and a mule driver came racing to meet them, shouting that the Plateados were stealing the shipment. Martín, at the head of his force, charged full tilt ahead and moments later fell upon the bandits, who greeted him with a shower of bullets and a surly roar, telling him that it was his last day.

The riders in black performed feats of valor, as did their leader, who hurled himself into the thick of the battle. But there was a multitude of Plateados, commanded by their top leaders; Martín's troop was literally besieged, six or eight of those brave soldiers had already fallen and others were beginning to pull back; they had taken to fighting with swords and knives, and Martín, surrounded by enemies and wounded, was desperately defending himself and trying to sell his life dearly when unexpected help arrived to save him. It was Nicolás, who with the ten soldiers Martín had left at La Calavera and another ten he had brought with him, having heard shooting, raced ahead and arrived at the height of Martín Sánchez's difficulties. That valiant Nicolás and those reinforcements produced a momentary confusion among the Plateados; even so, the bandits were far superior in number and continued fighting.

But Nicolás, riding a magnificent horse and bearing excellent weapons, was a man of overpowering boldness, so that on seeing Martín Sánchez surrounded, he threw himself upon the group, dealing out slashes and blows. And it was just in time, because the brave leader's sword was broken and he was wounded. El Zarco and el Tigre were among those surrounding Martín, but on seeing Nicolás they pulled back and tried to flee. Recognizing el Zarco, the blacksmith could not contain a cry of hatred and of triumph. Finally, he had him face to face!

He lashed out at him like a bolt of lightning; the bandit, at a loss from terror, fled the battle and headed toward a grove, where were hidden some of the outlaws' women on horseback.

Nicolás overtook el Zarco, precisely as he got near this group of women, and there, simultaneous with

the bandit's firing his musket at him, Nicolás split open
el Zarco's head with a single stroke of his sword and left
him stretched out on the ground, after which he returned to
the scene of battle, but not without shouting: "Now doña
Antonia is avenged!"

Furious as he was, he did not even hear the cry from
Manuela, who was one of the women on horseback and had
recognized him at the precise moment when he wounded el
Zarco.

After that, the battle lasted only a short time, because
the bandits fled in fear, releasing the shipment.

The sun had already sunk below the horizon. The
shadows were lengthening, and in the twilight Martín
Sánchez collected his dead and wounded as well as those of
the Plateados —an operation that took him several hours,
until night had fallen completely.

Then, fearing that the Plateados might regroup
and attack him once more, with all the advantages granted
them by their number and the night, he determined that
someone should quickly go ahead to Morelos and ask the
authorities for help and the needed stretchers. The mission
was very dangerous; the bandits had to be close by, and an
ambush along the road was to be feared. Only one man could
undertake the mission, and in that anguish Martín Sánchez
did not hesitate to ask such a sacrifice of Nicolás.

"Señor don Nicolás," he said, "only you are capable
of taking this risk, but finish your work. You already saved
us a little while ago. Now, save us for once and for all. You
know the roads, you've got a good horse, and you're a man
like no other. I beg you . . ."

Nicolás set off immediately. When Martín saw him
disappear among the shadows: "Never have I seen," he said,
"a man so valiant as that one."

"But just one slip and they'll kill him out there," said
the merchant.

"God willing, they won't," replied Martín Sánchez. "But, what do you want us to do in order to get out of here? There's no other way. Nothing's going to happen to him, now you'll see! Don Nicolás has good luck. And he's so strong . . . better they should kill me than him!"

Meanwhile, soldiers who had been searching in the vicinity of that place, to see if there were still more wounded, came back saying that nearby, in some scrubland, a woman was crying over a dead man.

Martín went himself to identify the woman, who was none other than Manuela, and, unlike the others, had refused to flee, not for love of el Zarco, whom she at first believed to be dead, but for fear of el Tigre, who would have taken her for his own.

Martín, examining the body, determined that el Zarco was still breathing. The wound he had received was terrible but not fatal. The bandit was bathed in blood, and it was difficult to recognize him, but Manuela made known that it was el Zarco.

Martín Sánchez shuddered with joy. That terrible, notorious bandit had fallen into his hands.

He was going to string him up, as soon as day broke. Unfortunately, the authorities from Morelos arrived in the early hours with reinforcements and stretchers. Martín turned over the bandit prisoners and the wounded, along with the woman. Nicolás scarcely noticed them, and Manuela, for her part, did not want to show her shameful face and covered her head completely with her shawl.

And that is how they left for Morelos, Martín to heal his wounds, which were serious, like those of his soldiers, and Nicolás continuing on to Yautepec to prepare for his wedding.

Manuela, as was only natural, a prisoner along with her lover, remained in jail, incommunicado and imagining the figure of Nicolás growing ever more handsome.

President Juárez

Martín Sánchez was indignant. The bandit party was still
very strong and could call upon powerful influences in both
Mexico City and the Tierra Caliente. The country's chaos
at the time lay behind its finding itself in such a scandalous
situation.

The Plateados depended on friends everywhere,
and if a good man, as we have seen with Nicolás, was hard
pressed to find backing, a bandit relied on a thousand means
he could bring to bear as soon as he ran any risk. And, since
they were powerful and held in their hands the lives and
interests of everyone who owned anything, people feared
them, enlisted them, and procured their benevolence or their
friendship at any price.

While the brave leader who had risked his life
in so unequal a fight was recovering from his wounds, el
Zarco, already recovered, had managed, by means of his
patrons, to have himself transferred and submitted to trial in
Cuernavaca, under pretext of having committed crimes there.
Trying and transferring him was the salvation of his life. He
would be able to find advocates and perhaps he could go
free. The same thing had been accomplished for the other
bandits who had fallen wounded or been taken prisoner in
the battle near La Calavera. The people of Morelos were
outraged, but since events of this kind were, regrettably, only
too frequent, nothing further happened.

Martín Sánchez then realized that as long as he did
not undertake all-out war on them, the bandits, with their
joint interests at stake, would always be countenanced; that
while he and other leading pursuers, lacked the resources
that men such as the famous Oliveros had had in other times,
all persecution must be futile, because when the bandits were
submitted to the state court, they resorted to expedients,
connections, and money to avoid punishment; and that as

long as the people did not see open battle without quarter between the authorities and the evildoers, there was no reason for them to make up their mind in favor of the former.

Being of this opinion, he thought to take a decisive step in order find out where he stood. And he resolved to go to Mexico City, to appear in person before President Juárez, to report accurately the state of affairs in the Tierra Caliente, to convince him of the good cause and to request resources, arms, and support.

His resolve became even more pressing when Martín Sánchez learned that while el Zarco, his sweetheart, and his companions were being conveyed to Cuernavaca, escorted by a small, weak force, the Plateados had laid an ambush at the narrow, craggy pass known as Las Tetillas and attacked the escort, routing it and freeing the prisoners. And so, el Zarco had returned with his old companions, once again ready to sow terror in the region with his crimes.

Martín Sánchez went to Mexico City and, despite having neither influence nor reputation in his favor, provided only with some letters from some of Juárez's friends, he appeared before the president as soon as he was able.

Juárez was not then the magistrate of unimpeachable and accepted authority, before whose person everyone bowed, as he became at a much later date.

At that time, although he had just triumphed in the famous War of Reform, he was still struggling with a thousand problems, a thousand adversaries, and a thousand perils, from which only his energy and good fortune could rescue him beforehand.

The clerical forces commanded by Márquez, Zuloaga, and others were still engaged in bitter, bloody battle and diverted the government troops, which were occupied in hunting them down. In the Liberal party, powerful rivalries for the presidency arose, although, if the truth be told, they did not constitute the major threat. The country's treasury was bankrupt and, to make matters worse, the foreign invasion had already desecrated the land, and the adversaries of the Liberal government, that is, the reactionary and clerical faction, had gone over to the invaders.

Juárez thus found himself in the period of greatest conflict. We have already said that, owing to these circumstances, the bandits were tyrannizing the Tierra Caliente.

Martín Sánchez expected to find in the president a man who was grim, perhaps predisposed against him. And he found in him a man who was cold, impassive, but attentive.

The *campesino* leader approached him resolutely and presented the letters he had brought. The president read them and, fixing a deep and scrutinizing gaze on Martín Sánchez, said: "Some of my friends write here that you are an upright man and the best suited to pursue those villains infesting southern Mexico whom the government, owing to its other affairs, has not been able to crush. Report to me about this."

Martín Sánchez gave him a detailed report, which the president heard with his customary calm but which he interrupted at times with signs of indignation. When Sánchez finished, Juárez exclaimed: "That is an outrage, and we must put a stop to it. What do you need in order to help the government?"

Encouraged at that point by those words from the president, Martín Sánchez, laconic in his usual way but firm and resolute, told him: "First, señor, I need the government to grant me the authority to string up all the bandits I capture, and I swear to you, upon my word of honor, that I will kill only those who deserve it. I know all the villains, I know who they are and I have sentenced them already, but after having deliberated at length in my conscience. My conscience, señor, is a very fair judge. It is not like those judges who release criminals for money or from fear. I do not want money and I am not afraid. Second, señor, I need you not to lend an ear to certain people who go around arguing on behalf of the Plateados and presenting them as meritorious individuals who have lent their services. Don't trust these defenders, señor Presidente, because they receive a share of the stolen property and are getting rich from it. Around here, there's a señor who wears a blond wig, who takes powders from a gold case, and who receives high pay each month from the bandits. This man gives licenses to the *hacendados* so their shipments of sugar and cane liquor go through without event, after their paying a big fee, of course. This man, with the same Plateado money, buys favors and appoints authorities in the Tierra Caliente and frees prisoners, as just the other day he freed el Zarco, a thief and murderer who deserves to be hanged. Ultimately, this man is the real captain of the kidnappers, and he lives off their thievery without risking anything, and this man, if I found him in my part of the country, even if it cost me my life afterward, I'd tie by the neck to the branch of a tree,"

"Who is this individual?" Juárez asked impatiently.[43]

Martín Sánchez held out a few of the letters, and said to him: "Here you have his name disguised, but you will know him from the initials."

"All right," Juárez replied, after reading the letters and immediately putting them away. "Don't worry about him, he will not be freeing anyone else. What more do you require?"

"Guns, nothing more, guns, because I have only a few. I don't need many, because I'll confiscate them from the bandits, but to start with I'll need about a hundred."

"Depend on them. Tomorrow, come to the Ministry

---

(43) *"Who is this individual?"*: According to Pedro Robles's *Los Plateados de Tierra Caliente* (Mexico City, Premià, 1982, p. 153) the individual was Marcos Reza, a political leader of Jonacatepec, whose activities coincide precisely with those described by Altamirano.—*Sol, 324*

of War and you will receive everything. But clean those
bandits out of there for me."

"Señor, I shall do it."

"Good, and you will be doing a patriotic service,
because now the government must not be distracted, so as
to concentrate exclusively on the foreign invasion and on
saving our nation's independence."

"Trust me, señor Presidente."

"And be very scrupulous, señor Sánchez. You have
been granted extraordinary powers, but only on the condition
that you act justly—justice before all else. Necessity alone
can oblige us to use these powers, which occasion such great
responsibility, but I know who I am giving them to. Do not
make me regret it."

"Order my execution if I don't act justly," Martín
said.

Juárez stood up and held out his hand to the
fearsome bringer of justice.

Seeing those two short men stand, one facing the
other, one in a black frock coat, as Juárez often wore then,
and the other in a jacket, also black; one dark and with the
appearance of a pure Indian, the other a sallow mixture of
campesino and *mestizo* features; both serious, both grave,
anyone who could read a little into the future would have
shuddered.[44] It was the law of public welfare, arming honor
with the thunderbolt of death.

---

(44) *anyone who could read a little into the future*: Altamirano's enigmatic words
have troubled more than one reader of *El Zarco*. Evodio Escalante asked: "Do these
words point toward what will happen later in the novel or to a reality outside the
text?" I am inclined to think Altamirano points toward a parallel, extra-textual reality in which, only a few months later, the congress would grant "omnimodous powers" to President Juárez as the country faced the French Intervention. Who, then, at
that time, would have thought that Juárez would later exercise these "extraordinary
powers" in order to hold on to the presidency despite the discontent generated by
his government?—*Sol, 325-26.*

Ambush at Dawn

A few days after this interview, one December morning, mild and sweet in the Tierra Caliente as a spring morning, the town of Yautepec awoke joyous and jubilant, as if for a celebration.

And in fact, it was looking forward to a celebration, not a religious or public holiday, but a family celebration, an intimate celebration but with all the people taking part.

Nicolás, the especially high-principled blacksmith from Atlihuayán, was marrying the beautiful and pure Pilar, the pearl of Yautepec on account of her character, her beauty, and her virtues.

And as we know, these two young people were very dear to their fellow citizens. Which is why their union was being celebrated with all the prescribed formalities. From very early, after dawn's first light had spread its pearly, pastel mantle in the cloudless sky and over the mountains, the orchards, and the houses, rapid pealing from the parish bell tower had awakened the neighbors; town musicians were playing joyful sonatas, and firecrackers and the ritual cannons had already announced the nuptial mass.

Nicolás was a modest man and had not wanted such an uproar, but the authorities, the priest, the townspeople had all chosen that way to demonstrate their love for the respected worker and his beautiful wife. The church, the altars, and especially the high altar where the marriage was to be performed, were teeming with floral decorations and bouquets. Every orange and lemon tree in Yautepec, and they number in the hundreds of thousands, had made its contribution of blossoms. Without exaggeration it could be said that no other bride in the world had ever viewed decorations in which the symbolic blossom showed forth so gorgeously and lavishly as did Pilar on the road from her house to the church, inside the church, and in the little house made ready for her at Atlihuayán. It was a deluge of snow and of fragrance that surrounded the couple on every side. At seven in the morning, the bride appeared, radiant, in the doorway of her house and went to the church, accompanied by her aunt and uncle and a numerous train of followers.

On the previous night the civil ceremony, being something of a novelty, had already been celebrated, before the recently appointed judge, because the Reform Law had just been introduced in Yautepec, as in every town in the republic. Nicolás, a good citizen, had respectfully complied first and foremost with the new law.

But still in those days, just as today, the wedding celebration was reserved for the religious ceremony. The bride and groom, then, came before the altar.

Nicolás, dressed carefully but without ostentation, exhibited a pure joy on his face, a feeling of outright happiness all the more genuine for being offset by a sweet, grave aspect. Pilar was charming. Her natural beauty was now heightened by her elegant white gown, and by the silken black hair of her coiffeur embellished with the bridal wreath, that garland she had always taken such pleasure in stringing, still not knowing, as she used to say, if it would serve for her bride's headdress or for the headdress of her virgin corpse.

She was now finding that it served for the first of these events and that a kindly guardian spirit had always foretold her happy destiny. She could scarcely believe it: there shone in her most sweet and languid eyes something like the reflection of a heavenly vision that gave her a saintly appearance, an angelical look.

The natural blush occasioned by that moment and by being the object of every eye, her timidity, her love, that assembly, that altar full of candles and flowers, the organ music, the murmur of prayers, the incense filling the nave— all this had produced so many and such varied feelings in her that she seemed to have been carried off to a strange world, a world of dreams and joy.

With all that and despite the light-headedness that had come upon her, that kind young woman had a thought for the poor old woman she had loved as a mother, for the unhappy martyr for whom the mourning had just ended and whose blessings protected her. An affectionate tear rolled down her cheeks as she recalled her and recalled as well the unhappy Manuela, for whom she prayed at that moment when she herself was so happy.

Finally Mass ended and the newlyweds, after receiving congratulations from their friends and the rest of the village, prepared to leave for the Hacienda de Atlihuayán, where they had their house to which they had invited many people whom they regarded highly to join them for a modest banquet.

To that end, a mounted procession was to escort the four-wheeled *guayín*[45] carrying the newlyweds, the priest, and other friends.

And at eight in the morning they departed and began traveling along the road that leads to the hacienda.

But shortly before reaching the place with the towering *amate* tree from which the owl always hooted at el Zarco on those nights when he went to his meetings with Manuela, the group stopped, thunderstruck.

At the foot of the thick tree stood a formation of cavalry, dressed in black and with their weapons at the ready.

No one was expecting to see there that squadron,

---

(45) *guayín*: a light, four-wheeled carriage with seating for several passengers, enclosed by leather curtains. The characteristic vehicle of the Colonial period and even for years after Independence, these carriages were to be seen at the time of *El Zarco* in Mexico City where some, bearing the words "way in" painted on their door, had been imported from the United States. The "g" is silent in Spanish, and their name derives from a hispanization of that English phrase. Although the word *guayín* does not appear in the Royal Academy's *Diccionario de la Lengua Española*, it is still very much in use in Mexico. For example, on the Internet one can read ads for the sale of a Guayín-Volkswagen or a Bonita Datsun Guayín '69.—*Eds./Sol, 330*

which just arose, as though come up out of the ground: what could it be?

It was Martín Sánchez Chagollán's troops, around one hundred men, with that doleful, terrifying look that we recognize.

Perceiving the wedding procession, rejoicing and accompanied by musicians, the commander, that is, Martín Sánchez, rode ahead to where the newlyweds' carriage was approaching and, respectfully removing his sombrero, said to Nicolás: "Good morning, don Nicolás, my friend. You weren't expecting to see me here, nor was I expecting to have the pleasure of greeting you and wishing you every happiness and the same to your wife, who is an angel. I will soon explain to you the reason for my presence here. Now my troops will present arms, as a sign of respect and affection, and I beg you then to proceed without stopping until you reach the hacienda. I'll be going there afterward."

Martín Sánchez's look was so calm and so open that Nicolás suspected nothing ominous. So he contented himself with shaking his friend's hand and introducing his wife and the other people in the *guayín*.

But while he was doing that, a woman, a young woman whom everyone later recognized as Manuela, made her way through the column of horsemen and came running, groveling, disheveled, shattered, trembling, scarcely able to speak and, desperately clutching at the carriage doors, she called out hoarsely, her words choked: "Nicolás! Nicolás! Pilar, sister . . .! Help me! Have mercy! Take pity on me! Forgive me! Forgive me!"

Nicolás and Pilar were left in a state of frozen dismay.

"But, what is it? What's the matter?" Pilar cried out.

"It's . . ." Manuela said, "it's . . . right now they're going to shoot him . . . el Zarco! He's tied up over there, hidden behind the horses . . . They're going to kill him right in front of me! Forgive me! Forgive me, don Martín! Forgive me, Nicolás . . .! Oh, I'm losing my mind!"

As a matter of fact, the column of black-dressed riders did conceal a narrow strip in the center of which el Zarco and el Tigre, seated on a rock and tightly bound, pale and enfeebled, were nearing execution. Seeing the approach of the procession and foreseeing that it could be Nicolás's wedding procession, Martín Sánchez had tried to hide the bandits in order to spare the newlyweds this sight.

"If I'd known you were coming this way, at this time, believe me, don Nicolás, I'd have taken these devils somewhere else. But I didn't know. What I did know, though, and which is why you find me here, is that these villains and their people were lying in wait for you, and that you've had a narrow escape. I found out in time, and rode sixteen leagues and surprised them at dawn not far from here . . . I've killed almost all of them, but I've come to string up the captains on this road: el Zarco right here, and el Tigre I'm going to string up at Xochimancas."

"But, don Martín, I beg you, considering the man you are . . . if you can, pardon this man, if only for this poor woman's sake."

"Don Nicolás," the commander responded, frowning, "you're my master, you give me the orders, I'd give my life for you; ask me, and it's yours, but don't ask me to pardon any bandit, and least of all these two . . . señor, you know who they are . . . there aren't two murderers and kidnappers like these in the whole country . . . If they don't pay with their life…! And they were going to kill you . . .! They swore it! And they were going carry off the señora, your wife! That was the plan. And so, you tell me if it's possible for me to let them live. Señor don Nicolás, you and your friends continue on your way with all these other people, and leave me to do justice."

Pilar was trembling. As for Manuela, in a fit of

madness, she had run to el Zarco's side and embraced him, and she went on shouting incoherent words.

"At least we'll take Manuela with us," Pilar said.

"If you like, you may take her, but that girl's a wicked creature: I just seized a pouch from her in which she had the jewelry of the English family they killed in Alpuyeca . . . valuable jewelry. She deserves no compassion!"

Nevertheless, on orders of Martín Sánchez, one of the soldiers tried to drag the girl away from el Zarco, whom she clasped tightly, but it was futile. El Zarco told her: "Don't leave me Manuelita, don't leave me!"

"No," Manuela responded, "I'll die with you . . . I'd prefer death to seeing Pilar, with her crown of orange blossoms, alongside Nicolás, the Indian blacksmith who I gave up for you . . . "

"Let's be on our way," said the priest along with the other terrified villagers. "There's nothing to do about this."

Pilar began sobbing bitterly; Nicolás bid Martín Sánchez farewell.

"Father, you can stay behind," he said to the priest. "These men may want to make their confession."

"Yes, I'll stay," said the priest. "It's my duty."

And the wedding procession, previously so joyous, departed like a funeral cortège, and in haste . . .

When they had disappeared into the distance, and no stragglers remained on the road, Martín Sánchez asked el Zarco and el Tigre if they wished to make their confessions.

El Zarco said yes, and the priest promptly heard his confession and absolved him.

But el Tigre asked Martín, "But me, am I going to die too, don Martín?"

"You too," he replied, with terrible calmness.

"Me?" el Tigre persisted, "me, the one who gave you the signal to come and gave you landmarks for which road we were taking and let you know I'd be wearing a red scarf on my sombrero so you could recognize me?"

"I have nothing to do with that," Martín responded.
"I promised you nothing, all the worse for you if you
betrayed your own people. Come on, boys, shoot el Zarco
and then string him up from that branch . . . blindfolding him
first . . ."

El Zarco could hardly stand up. Terror had overcome
him. Still and all, he raised his face and seeing from which
branch the soldiers were hanging a rope, he murmured: "The
branch where the owl was hooting . . . I was sure of it . . .!
Goodbye, Manuelita!"

Manuela covered her face with her hands.

The soldiers propped el Zarco against the tree trunk
and fired five shots and the coup de grâce into him. His
clothes smoked a little, his brains were dashed out, and el
Zarco's body rolled on the ground in slight convulsions.
Then he was hung from the branch and left swinging.

Manuela seemed to awaken from a dream. She stood
up and, without seeing her lover's corpse hanging there, she
began shouting, as if the married couple's *guayín* were still
there before her: "Yes, you keep that crown on, Pilar, you
want to get married . . . to the Indian blacksmith, but I'm
the one who has the crown of roses . . . I don't want to get
married, I want to be el Zarco's mistress, the mistress of a
thief!"

At that, Manuela lifted up her head, saw the body
hanging . . . and next observed the soldiers, who were
watching her with pity, then don Martín, then el Tigre,
slumped over and silent, and at last she raised her hands
to her heart and let out a piercing scream, and fell to the
ground.

"Poor woman," said don Martín, "she's lost her
mind. Pick her up and we'll carry her to Yautepec."

Two soldiers went to raise her up, but seeing that
blood was pouring from her mouth and that she was stiff,

and that she was growing cold, they told their leader: "Don Martín, she's already dead!"

"Then, bury her," Martín said gloomily, "and let's go finish our work."

And on rode the terrible, doleful troop.

Glossary

Recurring terms, chiefly Mexicanisms derived from Nahuatl, are defined here. If a term occurs only once in *El Zarco*, a footnote gives its meaning.

Apantle: irrigation ditch; any exposed irrigation pipe or channel. *Apantle* derives from the Nahuatl *apantli*, ditch or channel, formed from *atl*, water + *pantli*, line, thread, strip.

Calzonera (used in both the singular and the plural): suede pants, split along the outer seams and with eye-holes and buttons or studs with small chains for closing them, partly or all the way, as the wearer requires. *Calzonera* were worn especially for horseback riding. The word derives from *calza* from the Latin *calcëus*, shoe; formerly, pants of regional and torreros' outfits.

Catrín, catrina (plural *catrines*): dandy, fop, swell, priss, vain person. (According to the *Diccionario Breve de Mexicanisms* (2001) *catrín* perhaps derives from the French name catherine (pronounced kat-rín) for unmarried girls celebrating St. Catherine's day (Santa Catalina, 25 November) upon reaching twenty-five, the age at which the legendary figure was martyred for refusing to marry on command. Celebrants dress up, wear elaborate head and hair pieces, and special foods are prepared.) Although José Guadelupe Posada's best-known print, "Calavera de la Catrina" (Catrina Skeleton), dates from 1913, and so after the publication of *El Zarco*, the figure's outlandish hat suits the traditional *catrina* as well as the upper-class female dandy that Posada caricatured (perhaps as a servant over-dressed in her employer's regalia) from the *porfirato* (1876-1911) when Porfirio Díaz was in power.

Catzahuate: the morning glory tree or arborescent morning glory (*Ipomea arborescens*) found in the area's dense thorn forests. This treelike shrub grows anywhere from ten to thirty feet high, with a spread of up to twenty-seven feet, and in the dry season, when nothing else is in bloom, displays cream-colored, two-inch flowers. *Catzahuate* is also known as *palo santo* (holy wood) or *trompillo* (little trumpet, referring to its flowers); but for its name *palo del muerto* or dead man's wood, the tree serves Altamirano beyond geographical accuracy: later, in the chapter "Orgy," Martín Sánchez Chagollán is reported to have left some twenty outlaws hanging from the *catzahuate* trees in Casasano. The tree evokes a further bad association since legend has it that if one drinks water in the tree's vicinity, he will go mad.

Charro: Mexican horseman dressed in iconic, festive regalia, consisting of a short jacket, white shirt, small bow or butterfly soft tie formed from a square piece of cloth, close-fitting trousers with splits or broad pleats along the outer sides, ankle-high boots, and a broad-brimmed hat with a tall crown whose four indentations protect the head in case of falls—all embroidered and garnished with ornamentation. The word *charro* appears to derive from the Basque *txar*, meaning bad, defective and in its Spanish form denotes a country person whose poor taste finds expression in garish mixes of colors and excesses of ornamentation; apparently the Spaniards scoffed at these Mexican outfits, so different from their own more somber riding clothes, saying that the Mexican riders dressed "charramente." Thus, in origin, the term is disparaging.

Gachupín: (pejorative) a Spaniard recently arrived and not yet established in Mexico. Originally neutral in tone and used by the Spanish themselves, the word is the equivalent of *cachupín* and may derive from the Portuguese *cachopo*, child; however, by the time of the Mexican Wars of Independence, it figured negatively in the popular, abbreviated version of Father Hidalgo's battle cry, the Grito de Dolores, at the start of the insurrection against Spain: "Viva Nuestra Señora de Guadalupe y mueran los gachupines!" (Long live the Virgin of Guadalupe and death to the Spaniards!)

Güero, **a** (also *huero*): blond and/or fair skinned. Sol (175) quotes
Francisco J. Santamaría, *Diccionario de mejicanismos* (Mexico:
Porrúa, 1992): the word is used, "almost without exception, in
place of rubio [blond]," and "also is often used as an expression
of affection." This latter sense may explain why the black-haired
Manuela is addressed as "güerita," but more likely refers to her fair
complexion.

Hacendado: landowner, farmer, owner of a hacienda or ranch.

Huero, **a**: see *Güero*

CUERNAVACA
Jiutepec
Cuentepec
Laguna de Coatetelco
Coatlan
Mazatepec
Xochitepec
Telecala
Tetelpa
Ixtlan
Xoxutla
Picazo
Rio Amacuzac
DE GUERRERO